BURIED SECRETS
CAN BE
MURDER

Connie Shelton

BURIED SECRETS

CAN BE

MURDER

Charlie Parker Mysteries, Book #14

Connie Shelton

Secret Staircase Books

Buried Secrets Can Be Murder
Published by Secret Staircase Books, an imprint of
Columbine Publishing Group
PO Box 416, Angel Fire, NM 87710

Book layout and design by Secret Staircase Books
Cover image © Ateliersommerland,
Cover silhouettes © Majivecka

Publisher's Cataloging-in-Publication Data

Shelton, Connie
Buried secrets can be murder / by Connie Shelton.
p. cm.

ISBN 978-1945422140 (paperback)

1. Parker, Charlie (Fictitious character)--Fiction. 2. Women
private investigators--New Mexico--Fiction. 3. Albuquerque, New
Mexico--Fiction. 4. Christmas stories—Fiction. 5. Women dog
owners—Fiction. 6. Missing persons—Fiction. I. Title
BISAC : FICTION / Mystery & Detective.

Charlie Parker Mystery Series : Book #14.
Shelton, Connie, Charlie Parker mysteries.

PS3569.H393637 B88 2013

813/.54   2014434546

As always, this one is for Dan, my best friend and constant inspiration through all the years.

And special thanks go out to Susan Slater, Shirley Shaw and Kim Clark for spotting my errors and helping me to make this book as good as it can be.

Chapter 1

How well do we really ever know someone? How can we know the secrets that lie buried in one's past, often for years at a time, things hidden so deeply that they aren't likely to ever see the light of day—unless someone asks too many questions? I would ponder it all later, but I was not to know the darkest of those secrets yet.

For now, all my secrets pertained to Christmas, which was coming up in a few days, and the gifts for friends and family that I'd stashed in obscure little places.

For instance, knowing that my brother Ron frequently violates the sanctity of my desk in his search for some random office item—such as a paperclip—which he can never locate in the perpetual mess of his own office across the hall, I'd hidden his gift where he would never look—under the kitchen cabinet where the dishwashing liquid resides. Sally Bertrand, our part-time receptionist, would find her own gift in two seconds flat in the kitchen, so the handmade quilt for her soon-to-be-born baby was securely hidden away somewhere else on the premises. I just had to remember where.

My thoughts were flitting through all the possibilities when my phone rang.

"What time does your party start, hon?" Drake, my hubby. I felt lucky that he remembered our office open house today, and that he would be in town to attend. His helicopter business kept him pretty busy, between winter wildlife counts for the government and a few photo shoots for local businesses.

I told him to come any time and hinted that it would be nice if he arrived wearing something other than his flight suit, which permanently smelled like jet fuel. Don't misunderstand me—he *really* cleans up nicely. I'd begun to clean up a little better, myself, since Ron's fiancée Victoria came into our lives. We girls had shopped for holiday outfits and I felt ready to dazzle the guests in a pair of sleek black slacks and a fitted long-sleeved top that I would have called red, but Victoria assured me was cabernet. All I knew was that Drake would like the extra cleavage on display and I loved the way the draped front concealed all the extra fudge I'd consumed in the past week. I stood up a little straighter and smoothed the slacks.

"Charlie? I took the quiches out of the oven and put those little chicken things in. What's next?" Sally stood in the doorway to my office, looking as if she had a basketball stuffed under her shirt.

A glance in her direction reminded me that I'd stashed her gift on top of my bookcase, right behind where she now stood. Luckily, it was already wrapped.

"That's great," I said. "Why don't you just go down and get off your feet. You look tired."

I might be the boss, but I felt heartless asking her to help with the party preparations at the eight-and-a-half-months stage of the game. "Do you know where Ron is?" I asked.

"Went to pick up more ice. He should be back pretty soon. And Victoria . . . that lady's a dynamo."

My watch said that the guests could begin arriving any minute. "Why don't you find a comfy seat up front and just be ready to greet the people. I'll finish up the food and hopefully this whole thing will come together without a hitch."

I watched Sally waddle down the hall and carefully descend the stairs. She was right about Victoria. Two weeks ago she decorated the Christmas tree we'd set up in the conference room. This morning she brought scads of fresh flowers and turned our big table into the backdrop for a feast, then proceeded to fill the fridge in the kitchen with trays and boxes of premade goodies. An hour ago she'd presented Sally and me with The Schedule—a complicated chart that would allow us to heat the hot hors d'oeuvres at the proper oven temperature for each, transfer them to serving dishes, bring out the cold foods and get everything to the table at exactly the correct time. Leaving us with that little task, she'd gone to pick up Ron's three sons, promising that they would be well-dressed and behaving as gentlemen. I've seen those kids in action enough to cringe at the idea of their presence, and I would be ready to bestow sainthood on Victoria if she could pull it off.

Down in the kitchen the oven timer pinged and I turned toward the stairs, working to avoid a twisted ankle as I negotiated them in high heels. For a girl who is seldom seen in anything but jeans, t-shirt and sneakers this dress-up version was taking a little time to get used to. I grabbed oven mitts and retrieved the chicken skewers, consulting the chart to see what was supposed to happen next.

Luckily, it looked as if we'd reached the end of our tasks because everything seemed to happen at once. Two vehicles pulled into the parking lot behind our Victorian office building—Drake in his pickup truck, quickly followed by Victoria's blue PT Cruiser. At the same moment I heard the front door chime, Sally's cheery greeting and at least three other voices I couldn't readily identify.

Showtime.

I met Drake at the back door with a kiss, a tray full of treats, and instructions to carry them to the table in the conference room. "Don't take any," I warned with a slap toward his hand, "at least not until you've set them down."

Outside, Victoria stepped from the car with the grace of Princess Diana, while strange boys in dark suits—with white shirts and ties!—emerged from each of the other doors. I'd not seen my nephews in several months, not since before my trip to England last fall, and I nearly didn't recognize Justin when he stood up. He'd sprouted up and now stood a couple inches taller than Victoria. Wow.

She guided the boys toward the door—none of them broke into a run—and they greeted me with a simultaneous "Hello, Aunt Charlie." Double wow. I think my mouth hung open until I remembered to reciprocate with a polite welcome.

"Boys, go check in with your dad," Victoria said.

"He's up in his office . . ." I said, watching them walk single file toward the hall. I turned to Victoria. "What did you *do* to them?"

She looked a little worried.

"No, it's a miracle. A *wonderful* miracle," I quickly added.

"They just needed some guidelines," she said.

It was true. Between Ron's fear of reprisal and his ex's complete lack of discipline with the kids, they'd run pretty wild the last few years. Add manners and they were basically good kids.

"Did I ever mention how great it's going to be, having you in this family?"

She gave me a hug then stepped back. "You look gorgeous in that outfit."

"Did I ever mention how *really* great—" We both laughed.

Drake came in, eyed the front of my new blouse, sent an eyebrow-wiggle my direction, and asked if we needed anything else carried to the other room. Victoria checked the chart and took a quick peek into the fridge.

"Looks like we're ready to party," she said.

I put on my best hostess smile and walked toward the crush of people who'd begun to fill our offices. Drake pulled me aside just before we stepped into the reception room.

"I invited somebody, the client I just finished flying on that TV commercial," he said. "I hope you don't mind."

"Absolutely not. We've got a ton of food here and eighty percent of these people come from the law firms we usually work for. They'll all get phone calls and go dashing out before they have a chance to eat much. Unless we get a huge crowd, you and I will be taking a bunch of this stuff home."

He smiled and nodded toward the food table. "Looks like that won't be a problem."

Ron's boys were loading plates as though they'd just

arrived home from a famine-struck nation. I caught my brother's eye and gave a slight head-jerk. He called a little huddle and I could tell that he was taking charge.

"At least if there is anything left, we know who to send it home with," I mumbled.

Scanning the reception area and conference room, I was pleased to see that someone had remembered to plug in the lights on the ten-foot tree in the corner. The candles on the table glowed warmly and sprigs of evergreen gave the table a festive feel. Victoria's fresh garland and holly wreath on the front door had replaced my old fake ones, giving the whole place a lot more finesse than my half-hearted measures ever did. A dozen people were circling the food table, chatting amiably and scooping into the guacamole.

Brett Hascomb, an attorney we'd recently worked for, stepped in the front door, abruptly patted his pocket and pulled out a cell phone. With an apologetic little grimace he turned back to the porch to take the call. Kent Taylor, Ron's best contact within APD, edged past the lawyer and stepped inside. Kent sort of tolerates me. I've gotten more involved than he would like in a couple of his cases but, except when I need something, I really do try to stay out of his way. Officially, my position in our little private investigation firm is that of business manager and financial whiz. It's not my fault that people tend to glom onto me and beg me to solve their problems.

Kent sent a friendly smile my direction, which told me he was off duty for the day. When Ron offered him a Scotch and he accepted it, I knew that to be the case. The two of them chatted as the homicide detective filled a bowl with posole, that favorite holiday stew of hominy and pork marinated in savory red chile broth.

At her desk, Sally leaned back in her swivel chair with one fist bunched in the small of her back.

"You feeling okay?" I asked.

"Tired. Achy back. Nothing unusual these days."

"Go home. You don't have to stick around for this."

She blessed me with one of her warm smiles. "Really, what would I do? Sit in a chair and rub my aching back at home too. Nah, I'll just sit for a minute and then mingle. It helps to alternate sitting and standing."

"If you're sure."

Never having done the pregnancy and childbirth thing myself, I'm usually somewhat at a loss for what's needed. Sally hadn't seemed this tired with her first one, from what I recalled, but what do I know? I offered to bring her a cup of hot cider or tea but she stood up and said she'd manage it herself.

I scanned the room for a sign of Drake and saw him talking to a guy who looked really familiar. He caught my eye and I edged through the crowd to where they stood near the stairs.

"Hon, this is Jerry Brewster," Drake said. "Remember, I told you I'd just flown a job for his business?"

My brain didn't immediately click into gear. Jerry flashed me a grin. "Brewster Acura, Brewster Mercedes . . ."

"Ah yes, all the car dealerships," I said.

No wonder he looked familiar. His face had been on local television since he was a little kid, mugging cute shots to draw folks into his father's Chevrolet dealership thirty years ago. When his generation inherited, they expanded and upgraded the family empire. He still did plenty of camera face time—I just didn't watch nearly as much TV as I used to.

"I understand we're nearly neighbors," Jerry was saying. "We're in the old Talavera place."

"Ah." Calling the Talavera Mansion a 'place' was like referring to the White House as 'you know, that big one with the columns.' And while we might technically be neighbors, the four blocks between our houses was at least seven figures in price level. We're all part of the old Albuquerque Country Club neighborhood, but our house and those in the surrounding blocks consist of decent-sized ranch homes on decent-sized city lots. Brewster's section of the community has stately edifices on actual acreage, housing the most successful business people or those willing to go into crazy debt.

Jerry and Drake were chatting on about their flight this afternoon as all this mansion-envy filled my thoughts.

"Say, Felina and I are doing a little thing at our house tomorrow night," Jerry said, turning to me again. "Cocktails with a few friends and neighbors. We'd love to have you guys come."

I glanced at Drake, who had visions of more flight time dancing through his head. And while I couldn't think of a single thing I might have in common with Brewster's crowd, I had to admit I'd spent a good part of my life wondering what the inside of the Talavera Mansion was like. We both said yes at once.

An hour later, our open house crowd had thinned as most everyone needed to get home or off to the holiday concert at the university. Outside, darkness had closed in and the streetlamps were on. I was consolidating the remains of the party food, trying to make it fit onto smaller trays and hoping I could send it home with Ron, when the phone rang.

Sally had given in to her backache and gone home; Victoria must have taken the boys with her. I heard Ron pick it up before I had the chance to tell him that the machine would get it. His voice sounded businesslike and the conversation went on for about ten minutes before he appeared in the doorway to the conference room. I stretched plastic wrap over a plate of cookies and looked up at him.

"A new case," he said.

"Uh-oh . . . this week?" So much for our idea of a holiday break.

"A woman is dying. The family wants to locate her sister before it's too late."

I knew that we couldn't turn them down, but my holiday spirit took a dive.

Chapter 2

I trailed Ron upstairs to his office to get the details.

"Mel Flores was the man who called. It's his sister, Rosa, who is missing. She packed a bag and took off from San Diego about a year ago and they've heard nothing from her. Now their sister, Ivana, is critically ill. Likely only has a few weeks to live." He flopped down in the chair at his messy desk. "Their parents are gone, so the whole family consists of the three siblings. Ivana is asking about Rosa. Mel says it's heartbreaking to watch. And he has no idea how to find her."

"There has to be more to this. Of all the investigators in all the world, he happened to call us?"

"Apparently, Rosa left because of a man. Some guy that she called Chaco. Mel never knew his last name. Rosa's only twenty, the man was in his thirties and Mel didn't approve of that. When he forbade her seeing Chaco they ran off together. At least he assumes they did. She hasn't contacted them."

Where was he going with this?

"Mel said he's been wracking his brain and he remembered that Chaco came from Albuquerque. It's a sketchy connection but it's all he had. He found us in the Yellow Pages."

"Gosh, Ron . . . a year ago? They could have traveled the world in that amount of time."

He didn't look very hopeful. "I know it. I tried to tell him that I wasn't too confident about this. I don't know, Charlie. You should have heard the desperation in his voice."

I could well imagine. Well, I really couldn't imagine. We weren't always the closest family but at least we touched base often enough that my two brothers and I always knew we could find each other. I blew out a breath.

"We can start working on it Monday, but you know Wednesday is Christmas. Offices won't be open, records won't be available."

"We don't have that long. He wants Rosa home by Christmas."

What? I stared at him. "You didn't promise that, did you? Ron . . ."

He held up one hand. "I didn't promise. I know better than that."

"But you told him—"

"I told him we would do our very best. I'll get on the phone first thing in the morning."

It was all we could do.

* * *

I woke up at seven the next morning in a mild panic. We had planned to close the RJP offices this week, using the time for a complete refinish of the hardwood floors downstairs. Business was always slow during the holidays and it would be a chance to get the work done when Sally wouldn't be there to breathe the dust and vapors. My plan was to supervise the crew and finish some final accounting entries for the year. And now Ron had dropped a new case into the mix.

The workers would arrive at nine and I still had furniture to move. I jabbed Drake in the ribs and he moaned his way out of a deep sleep. I threw on yesterday's jeans and sweatshirt and dashed through my morning routine, pulling my hair into a ponytail while I swished with mouthwash.

Freckles, our seven-month-old pup, bounded out of her crate and trailed me to the kitchen; I let her out to the back yard, keeping an eye on her to be sure she didn't head off through the break in the hedge to Elsa Higgins's house. Although my lifelong neighbor and surrogate grandmother loved the new baby of our family, the vigor of the little shepherd mix puppy sometimes threatened to take the ninety-year-old woman off her feet. I always felt as if I had to keep an eye on both of them at once.

This morning, the dog's desire for breakfast won out over her curiosity at getting through the hedge. She circled our yard in record time and zoomed toward me, hoping that her dish would be filled by the time she skidded across the kitchen floor. I gathered her close and ruffled her chilly brown and white fur for a moment before I let her at the food. Drake came into the kitchen, rubbing his eyes.

"It's Saturday," he complained.

"I know. I wish we'd been able to schedule the floor

guys for next week, but they were already booked right up to Christmas Eve." I rubbed my knuckles against the grizzly whiskers on his chin. "At least we're getting it done early in the day."

"And we have the Brewster's party tonight," he reminded as he bent over and nuzzled my neck.

I'd completely forgotten the hasty invitation for cocktails but I sure wasn't going to pass up a chance to see inside the Talavera Mansion. I had no idea what I would wear to this shindig and there would be no chance to fit a shopping trip into this crazy day.

"We'd better go," I said. "Those floor guys will be showing up soon."

Freckles had wolfed down her breakfast, and I grabbed a package of muffins I'd bought a couple days ago, promising Drake there would be coffee at the office.

Outside, the air was crisp and cold although the New Mexico sky was a clear, deep blue. No forecast of snow—not even a cloud to make it feel like winter. Freckles led me toward my Jeep, having picked up the word 'go' in our conversation. She wouldn't settle down until she was allowed into the backseat. We all piled in and headed east on Central.

A blue panel truck sat on the street outside the converted Victorian that houses RJP Investigations, and I could see a man standing at the front door, looking as if he'd just raised his hand to knock. He watched me pull into the driveway. Drake hopped out to speak with him, while I steered down the long drive to the back, leashed the dog and entered through the kitchen. Once I had the eager mutt settled in my upstairs office I joined Drake and the crew downstairs where they'd already begun moving furniture. The plan was to stash everything from the reception area and conference room in the kitchen and a storage room near it—stacked, piled, shuffled around in whatever way we could. I directed traffic for a couple of minutes but they seemed to have everything under control.

Upstairs, Freckles whined to join the action.

"Sorry, kid, that's not happening." I patted her fuzzy little head and stretched the collapsible baby gate across the stairway to let her have free run through the second floor. After five minutes or so she settled beside my chair.

Ron had left a sticky-note on my clean desk, advising that he was going to the city offices to see if he could get any information on a Saturday morning. Although I didn't hold out much hope for his success, I was glad to see that he was working the Flores case quickly.

The phone machine contained two messages, the first from a man who identified himself as Chester Flowers from Seattle and said he wanted to chat with Ron about working together on a cold case that had once been in the headlines. That sounded enticing. The second was a tearful female who thought her husband was cheating. I hate those cases. I jotted the names and numbers for Ron and erased the messages. I could feel for the lady but since my standard answer would be, "So leave the jerk," I'd learned to pass them along without comment to my brother. Let him follow the guy and snap the dirty pictures. I impaled the message slip onto the tip of his letter opener so he would realize it was a new note, not something that had languished on the messy desk for weeks.

Accompanied by the whir of machinery from below, I started up my computer and checked my email.

Ron arrived and peeked in once, told me he'd had

no luck downtown. While I sorted invoices and entered customer payments, I heard him pecking away at computer keys, most likely as he checked certain online records such as news stories or the police blotter for possible leads on Rosa Flores or the elusive Chaco.

At some point Drake came in with sandwiches, which we ate at my desk and shared with Freckles. I think he took her outside on the leash at some point—I'd lost track of time locked in my fascinating little world of debits and credits.

Ron ate a sandwich and went back to his office, where I heard parts of a series of phone calls which all seemed to last only a few seconds. Poor guy, nothing worse than having to call every number in the book in hopes of finding your quarry.

When calls of "Ma'am? Ma'am?" drifted up the stairwell, I snapped to and realized the sun was already low in the sky.

"We're finished down here," the guy called out. "Don't let anyone touch those floors for forty-eight hours. The polymer has to dry really well or you'll get smudges and tracks."

"Okay."

"We're letting ourselves out through the kitchen," he said, and I heard the door close firmly.

My phone rang. Drake. "Sorry to abandon you," he said, "but I'm on the way. Five minutes. Are you ready to leave? We're supposed to be at the Brewster's in thirty minutes."

I stared around the room, a little disoriented. I thanked him and didn't admit that I hadn't realized he and Freckles weren't there. How could anybody with even half a life get so wrapped up in tax codes and accounting entries?

I peered around the doorjamb into Ron's office, where

he was still on the phone. "No luck yet," he said as he ended the call. He held up a photo that Mel Flores had faxed over. The pretty young woman in it had billows of brown hair and large dark eyes. I stared at her for a full minute, hoping we would find her in time.

* * *

For the second time in a few days I slipped into the outfit I'd worn to our office party. I don't think I only imagined that the slacks fit a bit tighter. I briefly debated wearing the same thing to a second holiday party right away, but only two people were likely to have been at both events. Drake wouldn't dare say anything, and the other was Jerry Brewster. I decided that, A) men don't usually notice those things and B) they couldn't care less. Women are the ones obsessive about clothing.

The Talavera Mansion, as it's been known for about a hundred years, is a magnificent structure of stone and slate, towers and intricate stained glass windows. Originally built by a man who reputedly made his fortune in silver mines in the northern part of the state, the house had been occupied only a few years before he died and the estate became embroiled in a battle of the heirs. By the time they finished fighting it out in court, the four sons and widow were all penniless and the house had to be sold for past-due taxes. It stayed unoccupied until another self-made millionaire took it over, but his fortune was equally shaky and again the tax man came into possession. During the 1930s it became a care facility for all those people who were sent to the Southwest where the dry air would heal their various lung ailments, then it became a private residence again when the neighborhood association fought against its becoming a ward of the state and being turned into a tourist attraction. Supposedly, one family closed off most of it and lived in three rooms on the third floor, to save on the gas and electric bills while they kept up the brave pretense of a genteel lifestyle.

Enter the 1960s, when the Brewster family's line of car dealerships began to take off, and Jerry Brewster's father bought the then-empty old mansion. Rumor had it that he picked it up for a few thousand and a promise to restore it—at least the exterior—to its former glory. Or, if not exactly glory, at least keep it from becoming an eyesore. He did a lot better than that. During my childhood in this neighborhood, the grounds were trimmed and the house looked every bit the magnificent castle it was meant to be. I'd never been inside and actually didn't know anyone who had.

While the mansion looks pretty impressive all year, during the holiday season it becomes truly glorious. The normal outdoor lighting, which casts the brown sandstone structure in a reddish-gold glow at night, is switched off and every tree and shrub on the entire four-acre property is tastefully covered in red Christmas lights. Traditional New Mexican luminarias—which all the homes in the neighborhood use—line every walkway, driveway, roofline and balcony. In earlier times these were made the old way, from paper bags with a couple inches of sand in the bottom and a votive candle that would burn all night. The paper ones are still used along the sidewalks, lit only on Christmas Eve, but those that actually touch the houses, especially on rooflines, are now electric. We give up ambiance for safety and convenience nowadays.

Drake noticed a cluster of cars near the triple garage and a few bordering the circular drive, so we joined the gang. Someone else pulled in behind us and we said polite little hellos to each other and walked up to the front door together.

Jerry Brewster answered the door himself and ushered us into a foyer of deeply carved mahogany paneling and slate flooring. An elaborately carved staircase with sturdy balusters rose to the left. Jerry draped our wraps over a coat rack in the elegant entry hall. He wore dark wool slacks with a sweater, and he seemed a little preoccupied. But he brightened his expression for the newcomers and waved vaguely toward the living room where Christmas music played softly. The couple who'd arrived with us headed that direction.

"Drake! Glad you could make it. Come in. Charlie, great to see you again." He shook Drake's hand. "Now where did Felina go? I want you to meet my wife."

Felina must have heard her name. The model-slim woman came breezing into the foyer and latched onto Jerry's arm. She was *très élégant* in a floor-length casual hostess gown of some wispy fabric in emerald green. Her shoulder-length blond hair and her makeup were perfectly done. Beside Jerry's burgundy sweater they looked like a classy set of Christmas ornaments.

"Darling, I think everyone's here," she said. "And I can't seem to work that fancy wine opener. Can you come?"

"Drake is the pilot that I worked with on the new ad campaign," Jerry told Felina as he introduced us. "And Charlie is a private investigator."

Felina's eyes narrowed slightly.

"Well, an accountant, actually," I said. "I'm a partner in the firm."

"Hey, accounting is a solid profession," Jerry said. "It's how I got my start with the dealership. Dad was a consummate salesman but he wanted a family member handling the money."

"These days, Jerry is the fabulous face of the entire business," Felina said, sending adoration in waves toward her husband.

Jerry shrugged. "Fate. I just happen to look okay for the cameras. But I still read the balance sheets every single month."

"I've admired your home my whole life," I said to Felina. "We live over on San Feliz and I wandered the neighborhood all the time as a kid."

"Amazing that we never knew each other," Jerry piped up. "I guess I'm enough older that we wouldn't have been in the same class."

I had a hard time imagining the Brewster kids in public school, but he was probably right about the age difference too. He was closer to Drake's age, I guessed.

"Let me show you around," Felina offered.

I didn't have to be asked twice. We broke away from the men and she led the way up the curved staircase. At the first landing, candles and greenery topped a small table. Above it, a round leaded window, with about a million tiny pieces of glass, depicted birds and flowers. It would be stunning during the day.

"The window is original to the house," Felina said when she saw me staring at it.

We arrived at a wide hall, from which doors opened in

three directions. All three doors led to one massive room with fourteen-foot ceilings. Four impeccably trimmed Christmas trees, each with a different theme—birds, flowers, snowflakes and glass beads—along with garlands on the chandeliers and massive potted poinsettias, filled the room with holiday cheer and probably made some nursery salesperson ecstatic the day Felina showed up. At the moment, the lights were dimmed and the lavish room felt lonely.

"We'll have the New Year's Eve party here in the salon," she told me. "You and Draper must come. I'm afraid there will be enough food for a cruise ship full of people." Felina laughed at her own joke, a high trill. "We'll catch the third floor quickly and then go down to join the party."

I followed her upward to the next level, not bothering to correct her on Drake's name since she was already five stairs ahead of me. The elaborate wood paneling from the first two floors had given way to faux-finished walls. The traditional portraits that hung in the stairwells below were replaced here by modernism, paintings which seemed purchased to match the color scheme and not because anyone actually liked them.

Felina led me toward the door on the right, showing off a master suite that took up half the width of the house. It had probably originally been two or three rooms. She confirmed this when she told me they had knocked out a wall and combined the bedroom with the old study, and made a maid's room into a closet. The closet was nearly as large as my living room.

"The children are in this wing," Felina said, ushering me back to the hallway after I'd been sufficiently impressed by the master suite.

We headed down a corridor of ivory walls and burgundy carpeting, the kind that's wide enough for there to be an occasional table or chair or potted plant, without danger of everyone tripping over them. She passed two or three doors before stopping to open one. The room was furnished for a young child, with a rocking chair in one corner and a youth bed made up in puffy blue linens. A young woman sat in the rocker with a blond-haired child on her lap.

"My baby, Adam," Felina said with a little wave toward the pajama-clad boy.

I stepped forward to say hello but he buried his face in the bosom of the au pair. His slender arm had a tiny cast on it.

"Mrs. Brewster, he's fussy and complaining about the arm. Is it time yet for more of his pain medication?"

Felina glanced at a diamond watch on her wrist. "Yes, Julia, that's fine. Give it to him and put him to bed. He probably just needs sleep."

Adam's face was flushed and his blond curls seemed damp. He whimpered a little and buried his face against Julia's neck.

"Poor little guy," I said.

"He went down a couple of the stairs pretty hard. It was very frightening," Felina said. "So scary what can happen to kids when you turn your back for a minute."

Adam fussed again.

"Julia, it's past his bedtime, isn't it?" Felina gave a pointed look. "Soon. Please."

"Yes, ma'am. We've almost finished our story."

Felina continued to stare until the helper put down the book and started to rise. At the interruption to his story,

Adam began to cry.

Felina put on a bright smile. "All right, darling. You may have the rest of your story. But then it's time for beddy-bye."

Julia settled back into the chair, picked up the book and settled Adam back into his comfortable position. Felina turned quickly and I trailed behind her with a quick "nice to meet you" aimed at the nanny and baby before Felina closed the door behind us.

She rearranged her skirt a little and started back down the corridor when one of the closed doors flew open. Out stepped a teen female dressed in black tights, a short, flouncy black skirt, and oversized black jacket that hung lower than the hem of the skirt. Her hair was cut in ragged lengths and colored in hunks of hot pink, black, and platinum blond and a tattoo of some mythical creature showed at her wrist.

"Katie. What are you doing?" Felina looked a bit distressed.

"Just going to check on Adam," the girl said. She had a gentle voice that belied her intimidating ensemble.

"Julia's with him," Felina responded.

"I just want to say good night." Katie raised her blue eyes to meet Felina's dark ones. "Since you probably didn't."

"I just—" Felina caught herself and put her smile back on.

"That's nice, dear. Be quick about it." She started to turn away. "And get your rest."

The energy in the hallway began to feel charged. I stepped out of the crosscurrent of electricity that flew between the two of them.

"I'm going downstairs to say goodnight to Daddy too," Katie said.

Felina stepped into her path. "We have guests. I'll send him up here." She caught my eye.

"You two need a minute," I said. "I'll go look for Jerry, if you'd like." Then I escaped to the ground floor.

From a vantage point two steps above the foyer I spotted Jerry Brewster. I walked up to him and after I'd passed along the message that Katie wanted to say goodnight, I edged into the gathering.

The living room was elegant on a far smaller scale than the salon upstairs. Only one Christmas tree here, this one all done in blues and greens, down to the wrapping papers on the gifts. Just as in a magazine. I'd never actually seen a real person take a decorating scheme that far. Looking around I noticed that even the area rugs and pillows on the all-white sofa followed the theme.

I scanned the room for Drake. He stood in a corner near one end of a buffet table, a glass in hand, a group of men standing around and laughing at something one of them had said.

Two women I remembered from a charity event at the country club last year chatted nearby. They glittered with jewelry and had that same perfectly turned out appearance as Felina. I was *so* in over my head here. A high-profile businessman who did his own TV spots was laughing with another man, the two of them holding heavy crystal glasses with a couple fingers of amber liquid in them. I thought the man owned a big appliance store, but I wasn't sure.

To my left, just inside the door, a young man waited behind a bar. From the array of bottles and mixers, blender and glassware, it appeared he was ready for anything. I pointed to a wine bottle and he poured it into a delicate glass. I lifted it carefully, hoping like crazy that it wasn't as fragile as it looked.

An older woman was standing next to me as I turned from the bar. She introduced herself as Lila Snyder and said the man beside her was her husband Claude. They lived next door, she added. The man informed me that he was retired from investment banking. Men, it seemed, needed to define themselves in terms of their careers while women usually discussed their homes or what books they liked. I followed that line of chit-chat with Mrs. Snyder until a young woman came around with a tray of canapés which caused the three of us to have our mouths full at once. I used the moment to drift toward a wall hanging of holiday-themed ribbons and bells.

Jerry had come back downstairs and was making the rounds with a pat on a shoulder here and a handshake there. I wandered to Drake's side, wondering how long I had to handle cocktail party chit-chat before we could duck out. I didn't want to jeopardize his business chances with the Brewster empire but I can only do so much of this stuff. I took small sips of my wine and smiled gamely.

About the time I'd coasted over to look at the buffet, Felina appeared at the wide doorway near me. Her dark eyes were narrowed, the color in her cheeks high. Had there been an argument after I left?

"Everything okay with the kids?" I asked.

A bright smile zipped to her lips. "Of course. Katie just—" She didn't quite meet my gaze. "Typical stepdaughter, daddy's girl."

"Ah. That has to be tough. But then all girls her age are tough, right? I know I was." Trying to find some common ground here. "Maybe you already know that. Do you have any other children?"

She gave me an odd little stare. "No. Only Adam."

Someone called her name just then and Felina turned her dazzling smile toward a woman I recognized as the mayor's wife. I smiled and edged away.

"Hey you," a familiar voice said close to my right shoulder. "Your office party was nice, but I have to say that you need to upgrade your digs if you want to compete with this."

"Linda!" We shared a quick hug, a 'what's new' in which I mentioned our new assignment to locate Rosa Flores.

Linda Casper is one of my oldest friends, my personal physician, and a gal who has shared an adventure or two with me. She's also pretty well connected in this city so it shouldn't come as a big surprise that she snagged an invite to the Brewster's party.

"So, how about this place?" I said. "My first time inside the house and it's every bit as amazing as I thought it would be."

"First time I've seen it decked out for a party," she said. "It's definitely something."

"So, what . . . you've been invited before? A special guest?"

"Strictly professional. I've been the Brewster's family physician for a long time. Over the years I've even made a few home visits."

I told her about my brief tour with Felina. "Are the rest of the rooms sized for massive parties?"

Linda looked around. "Besides this room there's a fairly normal sized dining room, a study where old man Brewster's hunting trophies stare at you from all sides . . . And I suppose there has to be a kitchen somewhere. And then I was taken up to the master bedroom on the third floor. All very fancy, of course. I got the impression that Felina's big project when she married Jerry was to completely redecorate the place." She lowered her voice. "Maybe to erase traces of the first Mrs. B."

We had moved toward a quiet corner of the room and settled into a pair of wing chairs. Laughter from other conversations flowed around us.

"That would be Katie's mother? I met the girl upstairs."

"Jerry and Kathie Jo came to me for years. Poor Katie. Losing her mom was really hard on her. Well, Jerry too. They were high school sweethearts. Cancer. Very aggressive. She was gone four months after diagnosis. Jerry and Katie both were in shock."

"I can imagine." Actually, I couldn't imagine. If something happened to Drake— I found myself looking around the room for him.

"The poor man walked around like a tornado victim for a couple of years. I guess that's about when he met Felina."

"Well, she seems to be good for him," I said. Jerry had rejoined the party and Felina stood with him, her arm linked through his, smiling up at him in the way of a good politician's wife. Or a great businessman's wife.

I spotted Drake weaving his way through the crowd.

"You haven't been to the buffet yet?" he said, handing me a plate. "You ladies share this and I'll bring more if you'd like."

"Oh no, no, no," Linda said raising her palm. "I've been to way too many parties this week and I have to stay away from that stuff."

"You're sure?" Drake pressed.

She closed her eyes and shook her head. "Positive."

"You seemed to have a group enchanted with something

over there awhile ago," I said to my hubby. "Things going well in the prospective-client department?"

"Yeah, I think so. Look, I'll leave you gals to your chat. I'll work the room a little more, and I'll be ready to go whenever you say." He straightened up and planted a little peck on my head.

"You don't have to babysit me while I eat," I told Linda. "I mean, maybe this is a social networking thing for you too."

She shook her blond curls. "Nope. I'm good with just sitting here a minute. Besides, if I don't keep an eye on you, I know you'll be right over at the dessert end of that table."

I had to laugh. She was absolutely right.

Chapter 3

Sunday morning I woke feeling a bit blimp-like after the two nights of holiday food. Linda was right—I had indeed found my way to the desserts at the Brewster's house. I rolled over to discover that Drake's side of the bed was empty. The clock said it was already after nine.

Sounds from the other side of the bedroom door assured me that he hadn't gone somewhere, so I wrapped my thick terry robe around myself and ran my fingers through my hair before I went to search out my two sweethearts.

Freckles caught the click of the door latch and came bounding across the living room toward me. I had to laugh at the way her floppy ears flew outward, like big wings beside her wide doggy smile and lolling tongue. She tried to put on the brakes but went into a skid on the hardwood floor and plowed into my legs.

"Wow, girl, you're getting some muscle on you," I said, stooping to ruffle her fur and give the ears a rub.

Drake peeked through the kitchen doorway. Dazzled me with his smile and even more so with the mug of coffee that he held up. I managed not to trip over the dog as I made my way through the living room and joined him.

"Pancakes?" he asked after we'd exchanged a long hug and kiss.

"You're too good to me." I leaned against the doorjamb and sipped my coffee while he turned on the burner under the griddle.

"I know it." He poured milk into a mixing bowl and gave the whole mixture a stir. "But you're pretty good at rewarding me too."

I knew by his lusty grin that he was referring to the fact that we'd both been feeling pretty uninhibited after the party last night. A tingle went through me at the memory. I covered by checking the kitchen table to see what I could do to help with breakfast. He'd already set the table, complete with a bowl of fresh fruit and plenty of butter and syrup for the cakes. How did I get so lucky as to find this guy?

The batter hit the griddle with a sizzle and Freckles turned her complete attention to him. I topped my mug and looked out to the back yard, a mental list running through my head of the final preparations for Christmas Eve, just two days away now.

We'd planned on our usual stay-at-home evening. Since we live on the route for the city's extremely popular Holiday Lights tour, we either have to get out of the neighborhood by midafternoon and stay away until midnight, or just stay in and ignore the continual line of buses that trail through. There is no getting in and out of our own driveway, except on foot. The nice thing is that the tour route is barricaded at each intersection so, on the years when our street isn't included, we have an amazingly quiet and peaceful setting. Beautifully decorated homes and yards where we can stroll as if it's our private Disneyland. It's a time to see neighbors that we rarely run into.

Elsa had already informed me that she was making her traditional posole and I knew from a lifetime's experience what a treat that would be—far better than what we'd purchased for our office party.

"Don't let 'em get cold," Drake said.

I heard the hiss of more batter on the grill and looked over to see that a plate of perfectly browned hotcakes sat at my place. I didn't have to be told twice.

He joined me in a minute with his own plate in hand, and the dog sat nearby giving both of us the stare-down.

"I guess I better run by the office at some point and check that the floor finish dried all right. The whole place may need airing. What's your plan?"

He said he needed to clean the helicopter and see where he stood on the maintenance schedule. Keeping an aircraft up to the standards for government work meant certain inspections at certain times, and it seemed that an oil change or engine overhaul was nearly always coming due. He hinted that once he knew all was well with his business there could be a secret errand or two, and then he and Ron planned on whiling away the afternoon in front of a TV set filled with football.

He swabbed the last of the syrup from his plate and carried it to the sink. A maple-flavored kiss and he was out the door. Freckles and I finished the dishes and I gave a quick survey to the living room before heading to the shower.

Nearly everything was ready—seven-foot tree in the corner, fully decorated, and a nice little stash of gifts accumulating beneath it. I'd been forced to put nearly everything for the puppy up on the mantle, though. She'd already discovered a box of treats and chewed right into it. I supposed kids of every species are the same—can't understand why we want to wait until a certain day to open all those fun things. I remembered our big old red-brown Lab with a pang—he'd done the same thing, several times.

I stared out the front window. The bare limbs of our sycamore sketched dark lines across a brilliant blue sky. Lawns had gone brown weeks ago and I could still see frosty patches in the shady spots. But where the sun hit, it had melted to a dewy glimmer. The forecast showed temperatures in the high fifties and the only storms on the horizon should pass well to the north.

Drake had hung the outdoor lights a week ago and we'd begun turning them on in the evenings right away. I'd become lazy about making my own traditional luminarias, though. After nearly missing the Christmas Eve deadline a few years ago, I'd started buying them from the neighborhood Boy Scout troop. We purchased enough for Elsa's house too. The boys would deliver and set them up so all we had to do was to get all the candles lit without setting the paper bags on fire. If our clear weather held we would be in luck.

I saw Freckles sniffing around the gifts under the tree so I put her in her crate while I showered and dressed. Thirty minutes later we'd driven to the office, where I made her wait in the Jeep while I walked through and surveyed the newly finished floors. The job looked beautiful but I had to admit that I was as restless as the puppy and not especially wanting to hang around the office. With luck, maybe Drake would be free early and we could spend part of this lazy Sunday together. I locked up, went back to the Jeep and drove home. Drake's truck sat in the driveway.

"Hey babe," he said, emerging from the house with a duffle bag in hand. "Glad I caught you. There's a job."

"What's this?" The duffle meant he expected to stay away overnight.

"I was about to call you. Up near Trinidad, bunch of stranded cattle on one of the big ranches."

I eyed the bag, tamping down my disappointment.

"It's for just in case," he said. "Should be an hour up there, drop off a dozen hay bales or so, come back . . . but you know how things never go as fast as you think."

How well I knew.

"I'll call you when I take off and when I land." Our standard procedure. Someone had to officially follow the flight to be sure he didn't run into problems, and we'd found it easier to track it ourselves than to file every single flight plan with the FAA. "If I end up staying over, I'll let you know."

I grabbed his lapels and pulled him close. "You'd better."

He kissed me, then added two more. "Goal is to finish by this afternoon. See ya later." He touched Freckles's nose through the glass and then climbed into his truck.

I stood there and gave a sad little wave as he backed out.

By this time the dog's nose had generously smeared my side window. She wasn't getting any more patient. I gave a sigh and decided we both needed exercise. My grabbing her leash sent her into a frenzy of excitement and she danced around me in the driveway as I clipped it onto her collar.

"Park? You wanna go to the park?" I knew I was taunting her, but it was a fun kind of torment. She paid me back by practically dragging me the two blocks. We needed to get more serious about our leash training.

Our little private neighborhood park sits in an almost hidden spot, surrounded on three sides by the back walls of house lots. Two narrow alleys give gated access and one short side is open to a cul-de-sac. Once I had the dog safely within the confines of the walls, I unclipped her leash and sent her running with the throw of a tennis ball. I ambled along at a more leisurely pace, soaking up the abundant sunshine and marveling that this sunny day was what passed for winter here in New Mexico.

Freckles came racing back to me, proud to return the bright yellow ball. I tossed it again and caught a whiff of cigarette smoke. At the southeast corner of the park, in the sandy bed filled with playground equipment, sat a lone figure on one of the swings. Dressed in black jeans and a hooded sweatshirt, the person sat absolutely still. I couldn't get a look at the face and felt a momentary chill.

With one eye on my dog and the other on the stranger I motioned Freckles to return to me. She went down on her front forelegs, hind end in the air, bushy tail waving lazily as if to say, oh yeah, make me.

The person on the swing laughed and I realized it was a teenaged girl. I relaxed a bit.

Freckles stared at me, turned to look at the girl, back at me.

"Come on, baby!" I called in my best I-won't-really-beat-you voice.

The girl laughed again and the dog stood up and trotted toward her.

"Freckles!" This time I tried to put some authority in it, but the puppy was having none of it.

The girl dropped her cigarette and ground it out with her toe. She put out her hands and my baby ran straight to her. When her hood flopped back I caught sight of pink and platinum streaks and realized who it was.

"Hi Katie," I huffed as I trotted to catch up to my dog. "Sorry."

"She's pretty cute," Katie said, reaching down to pick up the ball that Freckles had dropped at her feet. From her seat on the swing, she tossed it and gave me a direct look for the first time. "You were, like, at my dad's party last night, weren't you?"

"Yeah. Charlie Parker."

In the light of day the girl was no less scary than she'd been last night. With the black hoodie and sloppy-big pants maybe a little more so. Silver rings pierced each eyebrow and I thought I'd glimpsed a ball sitting on her tongue when she spoke.

"Your mom was showing me around upstairs."

"Felina is *not* my mom." Her face went hard, the narrowed eyes glaring at me.

"Sorry. I knew that. Stepmom."

Katie stiffened her legs and walked the swing backward. "I don't need a stepmom. My dad and I, you know, we can do fine on our own."

I wasn't sure what to say. Clearly the girl had been devastated by the loss of her mother and not at all ready for another woman in the household. And now there was another child. I stayed quiet as she pushed off and the swing swooped by me. When she reached the back end of the arc she straightened her legs and jolted to a halt. Freckles had retrieved the ball once more and carried it to Katie. She made some baby-talk and tossed the ball again.

"I'd be out of there so fast," Katie said to me, "if it wasn't for my little brother."

"He's really cute. How old is he?"

"Three. I feel sorry for him." Katie jumped out of the swing and scuffed at the sand, making a little trench with her toe while she watched Freckles grab the ball.

"Why is that?"

"He's never going to survive this."

Survive what? I tried to come up with a response, but Katie threw the ball again for Freckles and then dashed away and disappeared through one of the narrow alleyways.

I grabbed the puppy's collar to keep her from following and watched as the black-clad wraith vanished behind a fence. Kids. Anything for shock value, I supposed, including dressing Punk and showing her sophistication by smoking. Hadn't Felina told me Katie was only twelve? Sheesh.

I picked up the half length of cigarette and dropped it in a nearby barrel. Clipped the dog's leash to her collar and together we headed home. I had more things to do this week than wonder how this rebellious pre-teen was going to turn out.

Chapter 4

With Drake away, I would be happier catching up on my office work than hanging around the empty house. I grabbed my purse and let the puppy back into the Jeep. When we arrived at the office, Ron's car was parked out back. The kitchen looked like a used furniture store and smelled like a fast-food breakfast sandwich.

"I'm not having much luck finding any info on Rosa Flores," Ron said peeking in at my office door. "I spoke to a lieutenant with San Diego PD. They never investigated because she was over eighteen and they were sure she left voluntarily. Her brother pretty much confirmed that when he told me about the guy Chaco. Now all I've really got to go on is her social security number."

"So, you better get right on it. You're running out of time before Christmas."

"Drake's gone. You're not all that busy, are you?"

I patted the stack of papers in front of me, but he didn't have a clue how many actual hours those entries entailed. The end of the tax year had a zillion deadlines.

"Okay, okay," he said. "I'll keep making calls. But if I need some extra hands . . ."

"Sure. Just give me something concrete to do. You know that I'm not very patient when it comes to wading through bureaucracies with phone calls."

He disappeared and I heard the reassuring musical beeps of his phone being dialed. I went back to my debits and credits.

By noon I was feeling the distinct desire for a burger so I informed Ron that I would bring one back for him too. We met in the cluttered kitchen for food and a pow-wow.

"Rosa Flores's name doesn't come up on any police blotters in New Mexico," he said. "But that only means *she* hasn't been in trouble with the law. As for Chaco, who knows? The number of men with that as part of their name or nickname . . ."

Tracking all of them would be impossible.

"I've got somebody in the Department of Labor checking to see if her social security number is active."

"That could be a long road to travel. Employers only have to report wages quarterly and then it's not uncommon for the figures not to be available until a year later." I tossed a French fry to Freckles, who was drooling on my shoe. "And we don't actually know that she came to New Mexico or whether she's worked here. Nothing like Mel Flores waiting until the trail is cold and the deadline is near."

Ron took a huge bite of his cheeseburger, without comment.

"So, what kind of work did she do back home?" I asked. Wherever they move, people tend to follow their professions and hobbies.

"Retail cashier," he said glumly. Hard to get retailers to answer the phones this time of year, much less take the time for questions. Not to mention that it would entail hundreds of calls. Albuquerque isn't a huge city but it's far too big to do this kind of search by legwork alone. We needed something to go on.

"Let me see her picture again."

He pushed the fax across the table at me. "There's a better one Mel sent in my email. I should print out a few copies."

Rosa was pretty, smiling, with large eyes and abundant dark curls that went to her shoulders. It would be nice if I had a flash of recognition and knew that I'd seen her somewhere, but I didn't.

Drake wasn't home yet when I got there—no surprise really. I'd put the kettle on for a cup of hot chocolate when I heard a tap at my back door. Freckles went into her automatic barking frenzy until she realized it was Elsa. I motioned my neighbor inside while I grabbed the dog's collar and led her to her crate in the living room. We couldn't afford a tragic accident between an exuberant puppy and an increasingly fragile ninety-year-old.

"Why is your tea kettle whistling, dear?" Elsa said. "We need to leave in five minutes."

Leave? My mind went blank until it hit me that I'd promised to take Elsa to the food bank, where a bunch of women were assembling boxes to distribute to the needy. In a rash of poor planning, I'd committed to drive her and stay to help with the meals myself. I was also supposed to be baking cookies with Victoria later this afternoon for the cookie swap. Something had to give.

"Can you turn off the burner?" I called out to Elsa. "I'll be right there."

I stepped into Drake's office and used his phone to call Victoria and explain why I had to beg out of the cookie job, although it was with a lot of reluctance. Sneaking bits of cookie dough is one of my favorite holiday traditions.

"All set," I said to Elsa when I walked back into the kitchen with my jacket in hand.

The downtown warehouse where the food bank was set up buzzed like a hive. Our assignments put Elsa at a table where she would stick address labels on the filled boxes and bags and tuck a few candy canes in at the top. Burly guys would carry them to waiting vehicles. I got to relieve a lady who'd been placing a frozen turkey into each box. She handed me a pair of gloves and gratefully headed toward the refreshment station for a cup of anything warm.

We had a little assembly line going, I discovered. A volunteer would pull an empty box from the mountain of them that seemed to be appearing from thin air at one end of the building. She put some reinforcing tape across the bottom and pushed the box toward me. A small bottomless pit of a freezer stood near me and I was to pick up a turkey and put it into the box, then push it to the next lady who added a few cans of various foods—yams here, green beans there. Along the way there was rice and cranberry sauce and other things. In the distance somebody added a shopping bag with dinner rolls. I didn't have much chance to really analyze the nutritional content. Just keeping up with the box-train had me hopping.

"Phoebe, take over for Carolyn, would you?" said the

same woman who'd given me the turkey assignment. The honchos seemed to have a good handle on who might be reaching their endurance limit, and the woman who'd been adding the green beans stepped aside for the newcomer.

"Hi," Phoebe said quickly. "Oh, you're Charlie Parker, aren't you? We met last night at the Brewster's."

Five sets of ears perked up. "I hear that's quite a house," someone else said.

"Oh, it is," Phoebe said.

A small blond woman in her fifties looked at me, as if for verification.

"It really is," I said.

"That poor man was devastated over losing Kathie Jo. We all were."

"Kathie Jo used to be here at the food bank every single year," Phoebe explained to me. "Working right here alongside all of us."

"That new one doesn't pitch in with anything. Just wrote a big check but she sure won't get her hands dirty."

"It was a *very big* check. And it came from the dealerships. Really generous of them."

"And we are truly thankful for that," said the blond woman who seemed to want a positive spin on everything.

There were nods all around.

"They have a very cute little boy," the redhead added.

"Well, all I know is that she's young and pretty."

"Some say a little younger each year," said the first woman, who had greeted Phoebe. "I'm just saying. Not a wrinkle in Felina's forehead, and that jawline is pretty tight. She's had a little work done."

There were a couple of titters nearby.

"She adores her husband and I wish them well," Phoebe

said, putting an end to the gossip.

I silently picked up icy turkeys for another thirty minutes, until the freezer bin was empty. When a man brought another one, the coordinator assigned a new person to my spot. As my predecessor had, I headed out to find a way to warm my hands.

Elsa met me at the coffee urn. I held out the foam cup I'd just drawn but she declined.

"I'd be awake until Friday if I had that," she said. "It's hard enough to sleep more than two hours at my age anyway."

I doctored the coffee with heaps of sugar and creamer and gave it a taste. She was probably right—the brew had sat far too long and become bitter and strong enough to lift a bin of frozen turkeys. Two sips into it I found a trash can for the rest.

"Well, it looks like things are winding down," I told Elsa. More people were standing idle and the supplies appeared to have been pretty well distributed. "Do you have any other errands to do before we go home?"

Although Elsa claims she can still drive herself around town, I've noticed that she has started to accept transportation offers more frequently. About a month ago she commented that she couldn't believe the rudeness of other drivers, honking their horns and speeding like crazy. While that's true enough in this city, I suspect she has slowed down to the point where she's becoming a bit of a hazard. Ron and I have tried to start checking in with her often enough that she's not tempted to get out in her own car. One day soon, we would need to have "the talk" and try to convince her to quit. I didn't relish it.

She mentioned a few grocery items, while I helped tuck

her scarf around her neck. Buckled into my Jeep, we headed out.

"That group you were working with seemed to be in a pretty lively conversation," Elsa said as I steered toward Lomas Boulevard.

"A couple of us were at a party at Jerry Brewster's home last night. His house was the subject of the conversation."

"He's that car guy, isn't he? Always had his family with him in the TV ads. His wife and the little girl always made me think of you and your mama with your long brown hair."

"Well, he's got a different wife now. The mother of the little girl died a few years ago. The new wife is a blond. Felina's her name. They have a son."

"Oh, that's right." Elsa's eyebrows pulled together as she made the connections.

I spotted our turn for the market. The place looked packed. Elsa pulled out her shopping list and I yanked a stubborn cart from the batch of them just inside the store. She began reciting items such as milk and lettuce, so I gave the cart over to Elsa the second my phone rang.

"I'm here," Drake said, "and I can already tell that I won't be home tonight. Nothing's organized and we'll probably be lucky to start dropping hay in the morning."

Picturing a herd of cattle, huddled and bawling out in the snow, I felt for the critters but I would miss Drake. He hung up with a promise to call later if he got the chance. I looked up to discover that Elsa had vanished so I started the grocery aisle trek, hoping she was nearly done with her list. I had just passed the tortilla chips when a cart nearly rammed me.

"Oh! Sorry." The woman's blond hair was arranged to stick every which direction out of the clip that held it up.

"Charlie?"

It was Felina Brewster. Again, her makeup was perfect. I caught myself looking at her jawline. She wore skin-tight jeans, a silky shirt and leather jacket with a furry scarf wound expertly across her shoulders.

I complimented her again on the party and thanked her for inviting us.

Her cart was filled with pre-made frozen snack foods and several large bunches of flowers. She caught me noticing.

"Ah. Things for another little gathering. Decorate once, entertain a lot, I say. Works great around the holidays."

I nodded. Not being much of a hostess I was still recovering from the preparations we'd made for our office open house. And Victoria and Sally had done most of the work for that.

A few notes of rock music blasted and her slender fingers plucked a phone from her purse. I turned to see Elsa at the opposite end of the store, near the bakery.

"Well, tell her to get home *now*," Felina was saying as I walked away. "Darling, can't you just . . ."

I met Elsa at the checkout stand and resisted tossing a candy bar into her basket, as I'd done so very many times during my teen years when she most certainly met her life's challenge in raising me to adulthood. She smiled up at me— when had she gotten so much shorter?—and plucked one of my favorite Milky Way bars from the display and added it to her order.

The evening and next morning dragged by. Without Drake at home the Christmas tree just seemed like so much colorful noise in the corner of the living room. I walked the dog and took her with me to the office, where I finished billing our hours for the past two weeks and printed out invoices for the clients. Merry Christmas.

Ron came in and he and I got all the conference room furniture back in place and I checked the answering machine to discover that there were actually a few messages. Two of them mentioned new cases and I wrote down the info and passed it along, reminding him that one was from the Seattle man who'd left a message over the weekend and that this time he sounded more urgent.

Ten minutes later Ron was standing in my doorway. I looked up from the journal entries I'd been trying to make.

"I got a hit on Rosa Flores's social security number," he said.

"That's great!"

"Only semi-great. She was employed here in Albuquerque as of the last calendar quarter that has been entered into the records."

"September?"

"No, last March."

"So the information is basically nine months old. Where did she work? Maybe she's still there."

"D.O.L. wouldn't give me that information. I had a hell of a time getting them to tell me as much as they did."

"So, how can you get that information? Would they release it to her brother?"

"I doubt it. He's out of state. Even if he were to show up here and fill out a few reams of forms, it would probably take weeks to get answers."

I raised my eyebrows. "So . . . what next? Do you want me to sneak down there and break into their offices or something?" Not that I wouldn't actually do it, but he declined the offer and slumped back to his office.

Chapter 5

My cell phone buzzed insistently and the readout told me it was Drake. I pushed my door closed for a little privacy in my office.

"Hey hon, how are the cows?" I asked.

"Better. Their little white faces sure looked happy to see that hay. But there's bad news. A new storm is moving in this afternoon. By the time we finish dropping another batch of feed, it may be too late for me to get out of here tonight."

"So, then you'll be back tomorrow?"

"Well, that's the thing. Depends on how much snow this new storm dumps. If it's a lot, I'll have to stay and keep these cattle fed for at least another day."

I felt my spirits lag.

"I'll do my best, hon."

I knew he would. And how long could the storm last anyway? They usually blew through in a day. He would be back by Tuesday afternoon, in plenty of time to light the luminarias and snuggle in for a romantic Christmas Eve. I put some holiday cheer in my voice and told him to stay safe.

Across the hall I could hear that Ron was talking again on the phone, so I left him to it while I filed some paperwork and organized my own to-do list. I was trying to remember all the ingredients for mulled wine when he appeared at my door.

"Here's what Mel Flores emailed me." He held out a color photo on letter-sized paper. It was a different shot from the one used for the Missing Person poster we'd first received by fax. This was one of those department store ones where mothers take the kids for pictures but the photographer makes mom jump in and get included. I sent a puzzled glance his way.

"I thought she didn't have kids."

"The boys are Mel's. "He said it was one of Rosa's favorites because she adored his kids."

That much was evident. Rosa cuddled with her two nephews, ages probably seven and ten-ish. They all had wide smiles. The little one, in particular, had a devilish little grin and I could so easily remember myself at that age.

"Keep it," Ron said. "I printed a few copies. Maybe you'll be out somewhere and see her."

Yeah, right. Just accidentally. I stared at the face anyway, trying to memorize it.

* * *

The house felt hollow without Drake there. I let Freckles have the run of the back yard for a few minutes while I changed from office clothes to sweats and brewed myself a cup of tea. The photo of Rosa Flores lay on the dining table. I picked it up while the dog gobbled her dinner. What was this woman's story? Even if she'd left home voluntarily why wouldn't she touch base with her family at Christmas? Most likely Mel had glossed over the bitterness of their parting words.

For a minute, I frankly didn't care. I sank into a corner of the sofa, giving myself over to pure selfish pity, fuming over the fact that it was nearly Christmas and Drake wasn't home. Freckles sensed my mood and came over to nudge my leg with her nose. The spotted muzzle resting against my thigh, the huge brown eyes staring up at me . . . I couldn't help smiling. Pet therapy is the best kind.

I ruffled her fuzzy neck and gave her a kiss on top of the head. She ran across the room and picked up a squeaky toy so I indulged her in a little tug of war until I felt all better. By eight-thirty I'd grown bored with the sitcoms on TV so I took a book with me to bed. At some point my eyes drifted shut and so did the book so I turned out the light.

In the dream I was in the mall, madly rushing around because I'd forgotten all about buying gifts this year. I flipped through some kids T-shirts on a rack but they all had the same logo; I couldn't buy the same shirt for all three of Ron's boys and I was getting frantic because something was telling me that I still had twenty-three more gifts to choose. The shirts scooted along the metal bar and I felt myself breaking out in a sweat. When I woke up it was only 12:36. I felt as if I'd just run two miles. I got up and put on a robe. Something about a cup of hot chocolate sounded like the answer.

I tiptoed past Freckles' crate but she heard me and her ears perked up. She'd had four hours sleep and obviously felt ready to start a new day.

"Not so fast, you." I handed her half of a biscuit and rummaged for the hot chocolate mix.

While the water heated I paced. Maybe I could count it as exercise and convince myself that I was tired enough to go back to sleep soon. I passed the dining table and stopped, electrified.

The photo of Rosa. One of the nephews was wearing the very same T-shirt from my dream. The logo was so distinctive that I couldn't believe I hadn't clicked to it sooner. I knew where this shirt came from because I'd bought an identical one for Ron's middle son. It came from a small boutique chain of kid's shops, The Yurtle Turtle. And their things weren't cheap. If Rosa liked to shop there, it was possible that she might apply for a job with the local store when she'd come to Albuquerque.

It was a long shot. I looked at the clock again and debated calling Ron. He could be something of a night owl, but since Victoria had come into the picture I had a feeling they wouldn't appreciate a call from little sis at one in the morning.

As it turned out he didn't much appreciate it at eight either when I phoned from the office.

"Don't you ever take a day off?" he grumbled. Clearly I'd interrupted a little morning delight. I thought of Drake and felt a stab of envy.

I told him about my T-shirt theory and that I'd like to follow up with the Yurtle Turtle chain.

"Fine, whatever," he said. The line went dead.

"Okay. Fine. Whatever," I muttered to my phone. Freckles raised her head from her comfy spot on my Oriental rug.

I looked up Yurtle Turtle online and found that they did, indeed, have branches all over the southwest. And although there was a store here in town, the website didn't include any employee information. For that I decided to rely on good old-fashioned trickery.

I waited until the local store opened at nine and dialed the number. "Hi, is Rosa Flores in today?"

"No, she's in Dallas all week," said a female who sounded about twelve.

It was half the answer I wanted. Rosa obviously did work for the chain.

"Ooh, I really need to talk with her."

"If it's about something you bought here, any of us can help you."

"No, it's more of a personal matter. I've got a message from her brother in California."

"I'm sorry, I can't give out any employee information. You would need to call the Dallas branch on Preston Road."

At least she was willing to share that phone number with me. I jotted it down and debated how to handle this. If Rosa was truly avoiding her family, saying that her brother was looking for her wouldn't get me anywhere. And it seemed pretty brutal to deliver the news by phone that her sister was dying. I was still sitting at the desk, tapping my pen against the notepad when Ron walked in.

"Sorry I disturbed you guys this morning," I said.

He growled and then softened it with a grin. "It's okay."

I told him what I'd found so far about Rosa and handed him my note with her work numbers on it.

"I seriously doubt that calling her and suggesting she ought to contact her family because of the holidays will carry any weight with her. If Rosa wanted to be home she would just go. As for her reasons for staying away so long, she'll have to take that up with them," he said.

"So, we tell Mel where she is, he can go out there and have that little heart-to-heart, right?"

"He won't leave Ivana's bedside. I already know that. Rosa has to come to her and it has to be soon."

"Shouldn't they call Rosa and let her know this? Give her a little preparation?"

"He wants me to do that. I need to see Rosa face to face, break the bad news and get her home." He didn't sound really thrilled about it.

"Looks like you're going to Dallas." Notice I didn't volunteer for that task.

"Looks like." He shuffled across the hall to his office. Twenty minutes later he was back in my doorway. "I've got a flight this afternoon. And I played hell getting two seats out tomorrow. You can't believe how full the planes are this week."

Well, *yeah*. That's what holidays are all about. People travel.

"Good thing Mel agreed to cover all expenses. This can't be cheap."

He rolled his eyes. The last thing in the world he likes to do is get on a plane for a quick trip somewhere. But he'd accepted the job and there was no way I was doing it. I had plenty to do at home and legally I was still responsible for tracking Drake's flight back home later today. I hadn't heard from him yet and that was making me a little uneasy.

I handed Ron all the information I'd gathered on Rosa

Flores and her workplace. He dashed out, telling me to call him if I learned anything new. I had no intention of devoting any more time to this case today, but I didn't tell him that. I switched on the answering machine and escaped.

I had promised Victoria that I would meet her at the mall for a couple of last-minute gifts. She still hadn't figured out a gift for Joey, Ron's youngest, and in exchange for lunch out, I'd agreed to help her. And, we would hit the boutique stores and load up on designer stocking stuffers. I can't quite describe how minute was my desire to be in the mall two days before Christmas, but I went along with the plan, swinging over to Menaul Boulevard and driving east and then spending fifteen minutes cruising until a parking slot opened up. I spotted Victoria in the bookstore, right in the kids book section, as planned.

We browsed awhile, until I spotted the newest title in Joey's favorite vampire series. Victoria decided to get him the e-book reader and electronic version of the book. I knew he would love it.

Out in the mall, we pushed through the cluster of kids and parents waiting to see Santa, on our way to The Dog and Pony Pub. As with every space within a mile, the place was packed. We put our name on the list for a table and when I looked up from the hostess, someone's waving arm caught my attention. Lisa Miscotti, a friend I'd known since our school days, was sitting alone at a table and she pointed to the empty chairs beside her and raised her brows in a "want to join me?" gesture. Since the hostess had informed us it would be a forty-five minute wait for a table, Lisa didn't have to ask twice. We wound our way through the maze of shopping bags and chattering diners.

At the table I made quick introductions as Victoria and

I took chairs.

"Pretty crazy, huh?" Lisa asked as we settled in.

"I normally wouldn't be in the mall on a bet," I said.

"She's right," Victoria added. "My fault. I begged."

We laughed that off and quickly ordered sandwiches before our server could get very far away and forget about us.

"I would have been done with the shopping by ten this morning," Lisa said, "but I got snagged into a mess at a neighbor's house. Somebody called Child Protective Services on them because their kid showed up at a play date with a couple of bruises."

"Oh my god, what happened?" Victoria asked.

"Well, I was there when they showed up at Annie's door and she begged me to stay. They wanted to see all the children and they asked her a bunch of questions. She said little Robbie fell off a swing in the back yard. He had bandages on both knees. Really, I can't think of a better, more diligent mom than Annie. It's amazing how much trouble one phone call can cause."

My parents were extremely lucky that there'd been little government oversight when I was a kid. I'd fallen out of every tree in the yard, poked myself in the eye more than once, and it was a wonder I'd never sliced off a finger with my little Girl Scout pocket knife.

"So, they went upstairs, then checked out the play equipment outside, and got the same version of it from the two little kids and I guess they finally believed Annie." She dipped a shred of bread into the shallow bowl of olive oil that had appeared in front of us, popped it into her mouth, and chased it with a long swig of white wine.

"Who reported it in the first place?" I asked.

"They don't tell you that. Annie guessed that the older daughter might have called them. She wasn't even home when the accident happened. It's a stepdaughter and at fifteen she's in that hormonal stage that means nothing but trouble." Lisa stopped with another hunk of bread in mid-dip. "You don't have kids yet, do you Charlie?"

"No. No plans to." That was beginning to look like a really good decision.

Lisa drained her wine and picked up her water glass. "Annie tries so hard with her but that girl is having a hard time adapting to the idea of a stepmother in the house. Her mom took off a few years ago and now there are two others to share the parents' attention."

Luckily, the arrival of our sandwiches ended that line of conversation.

Victoria stayed pretty quiet during the meal, I noticed. We found ourselves eating quickly so we could pay the check and free up the table for one of the dozens of people waiting to get in.

"So, do you think that's what I'm in for?" she asked as we walked toward The Bath Shoppe. "It could get really intense if all three boys gang up on me."

I brushed off the worry. "Totally different situation," I said. "First off, their mother is still around. In Annie's situation the girl is hurting because her own mom left. Plus, boys tend to take out their aggressions on other males, usually behind the school gym. Girls can't help but being nasty to the nearest female authority figure. You'll do fine with Ron's boys."

She seemed pensive but by the time we'd spent a few minutes breathing in the scents of lotions and soaps she gave over completely to the sensory fun.

"I just wish Ron hadn't had to go to Dallas right now," she finally said after we'd made our choices and checked out.

"I know. But he's got a ticket that will get him home by tomorrow afternoon. So Christmas Eve is still safe."

Almost as if the cosmos could hear our conversation, both of our cell phones began to chime about two seconds later. Hers was Ron, mine was Drake. We broke out in giggles as we stepped out of the mall-traffic flow to answer.

"So, are you about to head for home?" I asked by way of greeting to my husband.

"Well, I hate to say this . . ."

"What? No!"

"We're grounded. Ten inches new snow overnight and it's coming down like crazy."

I felt my mouth flap. How could that be? A few yards from where I stood was a set of doors to the parking lot. I peered out. The sky was white with high clouds, but nary a sign of moisture from them.

"It's still north of Albuquerque," he said. "The storm may not even dip that far south, but up here it's a mess."

"So, what's the forecast?"

He didn't say anything for a minute. I couldn't tell if he was checking data on some report or if he just didn't want to answer.

"I'll keep you posted," he said. "We may not know until morning."

Morning. Christmas Eve. We were supposed to light the candles and have dinner at Elsa's. Cuddle under big warm blankets and have drinks in front of the fire. Hot sex, exchange gifts, make a special breakfast on Christmas Day. I tamped down my disappointment. There was still hope that the front would blow through and he could get back in time for it all. I clicked off the call and wandered back to where Victoria was still talking.

She hung up and turned toward me with a sigh. "Ron says to tell you he got there just fine and is sitting in a rental car outside the shop where Rosa works."

I nodded.

"Does all investigative work feel kind of like stalking?"

"I guess it does. A little." At least Ron was accomplishing something toward a goal. My only goal at this point was to buy pies for the big dinner and then sit around and hope my husband was there to eat them.

Chapter 6

I arrived home from the mall venture to find that my street had been invaded by youngsters in blue. The Cub Scouts had arrived. They moved like ants on a hill, toting paper sacks filled with sand. Each kid set a bag down, straightened the turned-down cuff and paced off two steps before setting another. Following shortly behind the setters came another one with a box of votive candles. Quite the production line.

I pulled into my driveway and greeted the Scoutmaster who, like a coach with his team, blew on a whistle occasionally. The troops responded and I could see that they'd already lined the sidewalks to the curve in the road a block away.

Tucked against my front doorjamb was a flyer with instructions to the residents: Don't light the candles until tomorrow night, be sure to have all your candles lit by five p.m., don't worry about blowing them out because they will burn down and go out in the sand. If you'd paid for pickup service the Scouts would be back the day after Christmas. If not, you were on your own to empty out your sand and dispose of the bags. I'd been doing this since I was five; I pretty well knew the drill.

I went inside, gave Freckles some happy-talk and surveyed the living room. The stockings were hung from the chimney with care—well, actually the mantle—and enticing packages waited under the tree. I'd set aside a few that I planned to deliver and, since the foreseeable hours looked pretty empty, I made a plan to see to the Santa chores.

Collecting tins of cookies from the kitchen, I noticed my answering machine light blinking.

"I'm trying to reach Ron Parker and I've already left two messages at his office," said a semi-familiar male voice. "I hope I have the right number. Chester Flowers. Please give me a call."

Darn you, Ron. What was the point in my handing him those previous messages if he wasn't going to return the calls? Okay, granted, he'd been pretty tied up with this Rosa Flores thing. I lifted the kitchen phone from its hook.

"Mr. Flowers? Charlie Parker here. I'm sorry Ron hasn't returned your other calls." I went into a spiel about how busy we'd been.

"I wasn't sure whether Ron would remember me," Flowers said. "We worked a case together a few years ago. I've got a lead on something in your area and really need to talk to him about it."

His voice sounded urgent enough that I gave him Ron's cell number, explaining about the quick trip to Dallas and hoping this wasn't someone Ron was purposely trying to avoid. I hung up the phone and turned back to my cookie tins.

After making my list and checking it twice, I headed out to see a few friends, first getting to the ones that Drake didn't know quite as well. Hope held out that he would be back tomorrow and able to make a few visits along with me.

Heavy clouds obscured the late afternoon sun and I realized the entire western sky was getting pretty gray. Streaks of white were headed east toward the Sandia mountains too. I set the packages in the back seat of my Jeep and buttoned my jacket up to my neck. A phone call to Sally's house was answered by her five-year-old daughter, Chrissie, who went all shy when she heard my voice and turned the receiver over to her dad.

"Hey Ross," I said. "Just checking to see if you guys were home. How's Sally feeling?"

"Like a blimp, she says. But yeah, we're here."

I told him I would be there in fifteen minutes. Although I'd given her the quilt for the new baby, I knew Chrissie better get something of her own, so I'd chosen a cute little dress that Victoria assured me would be just right. And I'd made up little stockings for each of them with a few goodies.

Ross was right; Sally had a decidedly dirigible-like look about her. She was reclining on the couch with a knitted throw over her lap.

"My poor back could only handle so much this morning," she said, apologizing for not getting up.

"I won't stay long. Just wanted to play Santa real quick." I caught Chrissie staring at me. "Uh, I mean, I brought some things that Santa left at our house. He, um, left a note that they were for you."

I covered by holding out the fuzzy red stocking to her.

"Santa brought them for Mommy and Daddy too." I handed out stockings for Sally and Ross. "This," I said, showing the wrapped dress box, "is from me and Uncle Drake and it goes under the tree for Christmas morning."

Chrissie was busily delving into the stocking and already had a piece of candy stuffed into her mouth. Ross extracted the toys and tactfully set the rest of the candy aside for later.

"So, how's little mama doing?" I asked, perching myself on the edge of a chair near Sally.

"I went to the doctor this morning," she said. "It could be anytime now." She went into some of that pregnancy lingo with words such as effaced and dropped, which I halfway tuned out. The whole process sounds really messy to someone who's never done it. At least I had guessed correctly about the stocking stuffers. Sally oohed over the massage cream and fuzzy socks I'd put in hers.

When I saw her eyelids begin to droop a little I said a quick goodbye and headed toward my next stop—Linda Casper's place. Her house in the northeast heights seemed the lone holdout on lawn decorations. On either side of hers, neighbors had gone a little crazy with puffy inflatable snowmen, Santas and packages that looked good enough to open. Linda's house, with its red-brick façade, sported an evergreen wreath on the front door, nothing more. It was refreshingly low-key by comparison.

When she opened the door the scent of spices just about made my mouth water.

"I'm making mulled wine," she said. "I promised Alex's mother I would bring it for Christmas dinner at their place and I've never made it before. Thought I better do a trial run. You're just in time to be my guinea pig."

Well, I wasn't going to argue with that. And if it was a success I could ask for her recipe.

I handed her the little gift I'd brought—a scented candle which, at the moment, would greatly conflict with the spices from the wine. She set it beside her small tree and led the way to the kitchen. A pot simmering on the stove sent up tendrils of that heavenly clove and cinnamon smell. Linda pulled two cups from a shelf and ladled the mulled wine into them.

"I think I could OD just breathing this stuff," I said before taking my first sip. "This is wonderful."

"Taste. Then tell me that."

We raised our cups. I had to admit that the result was every bit as good as the promise. The only problem was that the cups were too small. Before I knew it she'd ladled out some more.

We retired to the living room where we nestled into opposite ends of her plushy couch with a bowl of popcorn.

"I just came from Sally's," I told her. "She looks really ready to have that baby."

"All pregnant women get impatient at the end. Constant heartburn, no sleep, and getting your guts kicked around day and night. They're always relieved to deliver, but then nothing much changes. You don't have as much heartburn but the sleep issues only multiply."

I nodded. "And then parents have to worry about all the mishaps that can possibly happen to a kid, like poor little Adam Brewster. Felina said you treated his arm."

"I did. It wasn't a bad break and seemed to fit how they said it happened. But we're under such rules these days. If there's even a suspicion we have to file a report."

"So it might not have been an accident?" The popcorn

kept going down as if I'd not eaten a thing all day.

"I don't know. Sometimes things are obvious, sometimes not. You get a feeling, based on the injury and on how the parents act. I didn't get that feeling around the Brewsters. I might not have reported it but as I said, rules are rules."

I took another sip from my wine.

She gave me the eye. "I've already said too much. And none of it leaves this room."

"Absolutely." I did a little cross-my-heart move.

We caught up on a few of our holiday plans while I drained my cup and stared at the empty snack bowl. Linda offered to make some dinner for both of us, but when I glanced out and saw that the late afternoon sky had turned completely white I decided I should get on home. I hugged Linda and walked out to my Jeep. I had gifts for Ron's boys in the car but the idea of facing his ex put a damper on my desire to deliver them. I would send the packages home with Ron when he got back from Dallas tomorrow morning.

I headed west on Lomas. The sun had set, fading into oblivion in the clouds rather than showing off its usual array of red and gold. I cranked up my heater another notch and threaded my way through the streets toward Old Town where I pulled into the tiny parking area at Pedro's Mexican Restaurant.

A twinge of guilt nudged at me. Drake and I talked about coming here for our favorite green chile chicken enchiladas as soon as he got home. But he was stuck up north and I was stuck here—hungry—and I selfishly went ahead without him.

"Where's that new baby?" Concha greeted as I walked into the place.

For a second I thought of Sally, but then realized that

she was referring to Freckles. Pedro and Concha had, for years, relaxed the rules on letting our big Lab come in and sit beside our table. Freckles had happily taken up the tradition. I explained that I'd left her at home while I did my errands. But realizing that the puppy had been home alone for awhile now I ordered my enchiladas to go. Concha added a jar of their fabulous salsa to take home and wished me a merry Christmas.

The sky had darkened by the time I reached my neighborhood and everyone's lights were on except mine. I plugged in the outdoor lights and carried my dinner inside. Freckles whimpered until I let her out of her crate, but her interest was in the enchiladas more than going outside or eating the yummy nuggets I scooped into her bowl for her.

Eating my favorite dinner from a Styrofoam container, without the freshly blended margarita that goes so well with it and without my hubby beside me, just wasn't the same. I know they tasted every bit as good but something was missing. Face it, everything was missing without Drake here. I ate half the meal and shoved the box into the fridge.

Freckles stared up at me as if I were crazy. Obviously, she'd never seen this behavior before.

"C'mon baby, let's take a little walk." I checked the readout on my phone for the tenth time and then jammed it into my pocket. I found my scarf, some gloves and my heavier coat, then clipped the leash on her collar. The change in routine didn't faze her a bit; she began pulling at the lead before we'd stepped off the porch.

We passed rows of unlit luminarias—amazing how dreary a line of plain paper sacks looks without the candles glowing inside. Freckles sniffed at the first few but came to realize they didn't contain food. We did a brisk walk to the corner. The temperature had dropped by ten degrees and a breeze bit at my face. She tugged, wanting to head for the park but I convinced her that one circle around the block would be plenty.

Bits of sleet began pelting me as we came to the final corner, a block from the house. Under a street light I saw a familiar figure walking toward us. She wore a flowing sweater coat and black tights with dainty flat shoes. She appeared to be hugging herself to ward off the cold.

"Katie? What are you doing out here?" Only when I came within a few feet of her did I realize that there were tears on her face.

"Hey, girl. You look like you're freezing."

She ducked her head, the wings of bright pink hair falling to hide her expression.

She was five blocks from home. "Look, it's getting colder by the minute. Come to my place. You can warm up there and I can drive you home."

A loud sniff escaped her as Freckles rubbed against her barely-clad legs.

"Katie, really. It's way too cold to be out here without a coat. At least let me loan you one if you want to keep walking." I stretched out my free arm and circled her shoulders. I couldn't tell if the trembling came mostly from the cold or from whatever had upset her.

"Come on, it's just a few more houses. We can call your folks from there if you'd rather ride home with them."

She jerked away from me. "No!"

"Katie . . ."

"I mean, I don't mind riding with you." She sniffed again.

I urged her to walk along with me but I didn't touch

her again. "I've got some truly excellent hot chocolate," I said, hoping I didn't sound too much like a stranger offering candy. The girl was spooked about something. I didn't say anything more until I'd unlocked my front door and let her inside.

She rubbed briskly at her arms and looked around the living room.

"Not nearly as fancy as your place," I said, taking off my jacket. "But have a seat if you want. I'll just get the cocoa going."

Her fingers trailed over the back of the sofa and she stood in front of the Christmas tree. Aside from the bright pink and platinum in her hair she reminded me of some sort of apparition—an adolescent ghost of Christmas future. She wiped the sleeve of her sweater across her eyes and stared blankly at the tree.

"I'll just—" I realized I'd already made that announcement so I left her alone while I went into the kitchen. What had happened to upset her so much?

When I walked back into the living room with two mugs that bristled marshmallows from the tops Freckles sat beside Katie, staring up at her. The girl's arms hung down at her sides and her expression remained empty.

"Here's the chocolate," I announced with a little perk in my voice.

Katie didn't move so I carried her mug over and nudged her arm. She didn't look at me. I set the cup on a nearby table.

"It's the worst. The holidays." Damp tracks started down her cheeks again. "I miss her so much."

So that's what it was about. Her mother.

"I know." I held my own mug with both hands, pulling warmth from it.

"*No one* knows," said Katie.

"My mother died too. And my dad. I think I do know."

For the first time her gaze slid toward me.

"Seriously?"

"Seriously. I was fifteen. They went down in a plane crash."

"Wow. How do you handle it?"

"It gets a little better with time. I was fortunate to have a grandmotherly woman who took me in."

"At least I have my dad."

"You're lucky with that," I said. "I—" All at once I couldn't say another word. The Christmas tree, sitting right where Mother always put it, faded to a blur of lights. My throat constricted. I felt something drip from my chin.

Katie's arms came around my waist and I felt her shoulders shake. Now I was the one sniffling like crazy. We stood there for a few moments, or maybe it was an hour. Finally, I set my cup on a side table and held her at arm's length.

"Hey. It's good to meet somebody who understands this," I said.

She nodded and the sheaf of pink hair draped across her face.

I wiped it aside with my finger and tucked it behind her ear. "Anytime you want to talk. I mean it."

She nodded again.

"Now drink your cocoa before it gets cold."

We picked up the mugs and sat on the sofa, each quiet with our own thoughts for awhile.

"My dad isn't the same," she finally said. "Since Felina came along."

Surely she was right. Beautiful young wife, another child, a man still in his prime, trying to forget the pain. Somehow he'd minimized the connection to his daughter and she was hurting for it. I decided I should talk with him when I drove her home.

Chapter 7

As it turned out I didn't get the chance to speak to Jerry Brewster. When I pulled up to the mansion Katie jumped out of my car, said a quick thanks, and dashed inside. Her mood had lightened considerably and I'd seen past the all-black attire and pierced eyebrows as she played on the floor with Freckles. Maybe the old-fashioned remedy, a good cry, had done both of us some good.

I was debating whether to follow her to the door and see if I could corner Jerry long enough for a little heart-to-heart when my phone rang down inside my pocket. Ron.

"I am not a happy camper," he said. "We're stuck here in Dallas. They're calling it the winter storm of the decade, and the last plane they allowed to take off was the one right before Rosa's."

The low pressure system over Colorado had apparently

circled southeast, catching northern New Mexico in its edges, sending the heavy center of the storm into Texas.

"Soonest they can even *think* about getting planes off the ground here is sometime tomorrow," Ron was saying. "But it could even go longer than that. There are thousands of people in the terminals and I gather only a lucky few were able to get cabs to take them to hotels. The roads are a mess."

"Oh great. How's Rosa taking all this?"

"She's nearly frantic. Feeling guilty as hell because she didn't stay in better touch with her sister. She did *not* take that news well at all. I thought we were going to have a security issue when she found out that her plane wasn't leaving after all. She wanted to dash out the door and try for a bus or rental car to get back to California. It was a job to convince her that waiting for the planes would still be the quickest way. A couple of airport officials had to help me calm her down. A female guard just took her into the ladies room to fix her makeup and get herself together."

"What was her story? Why didn't she contact her family in the past year?"

He sighed. "I get the feeling she really butted heads with her brother and then it became a matter of pride that she was not going to back down before Mel did. She broke up with that Chaco guy almost right after they left San Diego together, but she was too embarrassed to tell Ivana. She got her job with that kids' clothing store in Albuquerque and has actually been pretty happy there. I got the idea that she wanted to get a little money saved so she could visit California with her head held high, show Mel that she hadn't completely messed up her life by leaving."

I had pulled out of the Brewsters' driveway and was

driving toward my house. "So, what now?" I asked.

"I guess we're staying the night in the airport. Not much choice. I'll get Rosa to call her sister—hopefully, that won't upset her even further. Mainly, I guess I'll have to keep an eye on her to make sure she doesn't do something crazy."

I wished him luck and we disconnected before it crossed my mind that I should have asked whether he'd heard from Chester Flowers.

Already, little sleety things were flurrying through the air. A white Christmas happened so rarely here that I would have loved one—but only with all my family safely tucked in at home. It was the last thing I wanted with Drake away on a job and now Ron having to sleep in an airport.

I called Drake as soon as I got into the house. His situation was the same—weather too bleak to drop bales of hay to cattle, much less try to fly cross-country to get back home. I put Katie's and my cocoa mugs into the dishwasher and went to bed early.

Christmas Eve morning dawned gray and frigid but so far we had no snow on the ground. I switched on The Weather Channel while I loaded the coffee maker. The forecast only served to confirm what I already knew—heavy snow in Colorado and the storm system was moving eastward at a slow pace. A good part of the southwest would be under its influence for awhile, possibly days.

I called Victoria to see if she'd heard from Ron. The news was mostly what I already knew, with the additional information that he'd had an extremely uncomfortable night attempting to sleep in one of those molded plastic seats in the airport terminal and was pretty sure he was catching a cold from some little kid who had sneezed on him.

"Looks like it's not going to be the holiday any of us

had envisioned," I told her.

A sigh came from the other end of the line. "Well, let's see if we can make the best of it," she said. "Elsa was going to have everyone over for dinner tonight. We girls should just bundle in at one of our houses and make it a girl's Christmas Eve. What do you think?"

I pushed past my earlier Grinchy mood and agreed with her. "My place, four o'clock? If you wait until dark you'll never get into the neighborhood because of the light show tours. Bring your jammies and plan to stay for the duration."

"Oh, excellent plan! I'll bring fudge and cookies. I've been baking for a week and without Ron here, the kids will stay at their mother's place, so we might as well break into the good stuff for ourselves."

She almost made it sound more fun than the original plan, especially once I tamped down the nagging little voice that tried to tell me how many calories were involved. What the heck. I called Elsa, who jumped right on board with the pajama party. Her posole was simmering already, she said. I told her to call me when it was ready and not to attempt to carry the heavy pot over by herself.

"We can do the big turkey dinner as soon as the boys get home," she said. "No reason it has to be on any certain day. And I baked two pecan pies. One of them can be for tonight."

With overnight guests now in the picture I bustled around, checking the twin beds in the guest room and hanging fresh towels in the bathroom. This might turn out all right after all. I'd just located two butane lighters and checked them so I would be ready for the dusk lighting of the luminarias when there was a tapping at my front door.

Freckles went into full guard-dog mode, sounding as if

she wanted to rip the head off of whoever would dare come around. I peered out the peephole and saw a flash of pink.

"Katie! Hi, come on in."

Once again dressed all in black she slipped in with a waft of cold air. She wore the same sweater she'd had on last night, which couldn't possibly be warm enough with the temperatures hovering in the low thirties.

"You're out early," I commented. "Want some more of that cocoa?"

She gave a nod and followed me to the kitchen. I watched her rub Freckles under the chin for a minute, wondering why she'd come. I could truly sympathize with the girl's home situation but wasn't sure I wanted a new best friend who might make a habit of dropping in daily.

I tore into a packet of the hot chocolate mix for her and poured another cup of coffee for myself, making small talk by asking if she was getting excited about Christmas. She shrugged halfheartedly.

"Is it what we were talking about last night?" I asked. Maybe I should have made more effort to talk to Jerry about his daughter's feelings.

"Adam's not feeling good today," she said. "My dad took the morning off work so he and Felina could take him to the doctor."

"How about you? Doing okay?" I poured hot water into the mix in her mug, gave it a stir and handed it to her.

She sank into one of the kitchen chairs. "I'm kind of worried about him too. But they didn't, like, ask if I wanted to go along. He's always getting sick. I don't like it."

I sipped at my coffee, privately glad that I didn't have kids to worry about. Except that this one kept showing up in my life, and wasn't I already concerned about her? I studied Katie's face while she drew circles on the table with her finger. Was she really that troubled over her brother's health, or was it more a case of jealousy over her father's attention?

"Could I tell you something, Charlie?" The circling motions stopped.

"Sure."

"I think Felina, you know, does things to Adam sometimes."

"What kinds of things?" I asked cautiously.

"I don't know . . . just . . . things."

"Like the day he broke his arm? Did she have something to do with that?"

Katie shrugged again and her mouth went into a little twist. "I didn't see anything, if that's what you mean."

I waited.

"When he was little, like still drinking from a bottle, he would puke a lot. Drink his bottle and then throw up."

"Well, I've heard that babies do that some."

"Yeah, maybe."

"Anything else? Things you saw Felina do?"

She went back to making the circles. "I don't know."

Conversations with teens could be so productive. I began to wonder if she really had anything to tell me or if she was stalling, wanting to spend time here rather than at home. I was thinking of ways to hint that I had other things to do when I caught sight of a white head coming toward my back door.

Elsa tapped at the glass, sending the dog into another barking frenzy, which caused Katie to slosh her hot chocolate over a placemat. I gave the dog a pat, the kid an it's-okay smile, and opened the door for my neighbor.

"Here's the cornbread," Elsa said, "for tonight."

She stopped short when she caught sight of the girl in black at the table. She comes from a generation where no real creature has pink hair or rings through its eyebrows.

"Oh, this is Katie Brewster," I said. "Katie, this is my neighbor Mrs. Higgins."

The two of them sized each other up, but Elsa soon broke the ice by asking where Katie got her hair done. I took the pan of cornbread while Katie described how she did the hair color herself and laughed over the way she'd shocked her stepmother by making her pink-haired debut at the dinner table one night. Elsa chuckled right along with her. She gave me a wink and let herself out the back door.

I watched her cross the swath of lawn between our houses and go through the break in the hedge. I turned to Katie, wondering if she would pick up the conversation where she'd left it but she was happily slurping at her cocoa. My mind wandered over the list of errands I'd planned this morning, things I wasn't getting done because of my unexpected company. Options went back and forth in my head; I could take Katie with me but didn't really want to do that without her parents' knowledge, I could drop her off at home but wasn't sure she should be there alone.

"Is Adam's nanny home now?" I asked.

"I don't think so. Dad gave her a few days off to have Christmas with her sister. It's okay, Charlie. I can be there by myself."

I fidgeted for a few more minutes, wiping down the countertops and rechecking my shopping list against the contents of the fridge. Katie finished her cocoa and left the cup on the table while she tussled with Freckles.

"I guess I better go," Katie said.

Relieved that she'd made the first move I offered to drive her home again. She insisted she could walk back but once we stepped out into the frigid air she changed her mind. I wove the maze of neighboring streets to avoid the city workers who were already setting out barriers in anticipation of the luminaria tour this evening. No cars were visible near the garages at the mansion and I insisted on walking Katie inside to see if anyone was home. They weren't. I gave her my cell number and told her to call me if she got worried or anything. Secretly hoped she wouldn't; surely she would first call her father.

Free of my little charge I consulted my scrawled shopping list and headed for the market. Cranberries (how could I have forgotten those?), stuffing mix (in case no one made the from-scratch kind), and whipped cream (everyone always thought someone else remembered that). I plunked items in my cart and stood behind three other people in the shortest line at the registers. *The Scoop*, one of those cheesy tabloids caught my eye with *They Got Away With It* in two-inch letters. Below the screaming red headline was a photo of O.J. Simpson and a couple of other, smaller pictures of faces not so readily identifiable. A secondary story promised details on some alien abduction. The woman ahead of me had a cart heaping to the brim so I picked up the newspaper and flipped it open.

Where Are They Now? Famous Criminals and What Happened to Them headed the two-page center spread. They hadn't even bothered to use a different picture of O.J. for the inside page. I skimmed that—everyone knew his story. Below that headliner, smaller versions of six mug shots with a short paragraph about each. There was the drunk driver who'd run a school bus off the road but the jury found some kind of reasonable doubt about his guilt. A teen who'd shot up his school had been sentenced to community service and, according to the article, was back living at home with mom and dad at the age of twenty-seven—unemployed and continuously enabled. A couple of the stories seemed vaguely familiar as I skimmed them.

A man with a loaded cart tapped my shoulder. "Move up," he said in a very non-merry tone.

I came out of my trance to see that the woman ahead was nearly done so I loaded my few items onto the conveyor, tossing the tabloid on top at the last minute. I pulled out money and wished the checker Merry Christmas.

Chapter 8

Before I forgot about it, I walked over to Elsa's and brought the posole home. I had just set it and the whipped cream into the fridge and was about to go back and reread the tabloid article when my phone rang.

Ron sounded like a man surviving on no sleep. I could picture that he hadn't shaved or brushed his teeth in more than a day. When I asked about the weather situation he actually growled.

"Ice. That's what they do here in place of snow," he grumbled. "The roads are closed, can't even get a cab to a hotel. *If* there was an empty hotel room anywhere nearby. They say the storm won't pass through until tomorrow night and then it could be almost another full day before they get all the planes off the ground."

I made sympathetic noises and assured him that things

were going fine at home.

"How's Rosa doing?"

"She's been on the phone with Mel and Ivana. I get the feeling her sister's condition is worse. Each call upsets Rosa but I can't blame her for wanting to hear their voices." An electronic beep cut in. "Look, my phone's dying. I didn't pack the charger because I was supposed to be in and out of this city in under twenty-four hours. I guess I've used up my charge talking to Victoria and to the boys. So, Merry Christmas. See you when I get home."

I wished him luck but the connection was gone. The darn phone had either died or he'd cut the call short to save battery. I felt for both of them, mainly Rosa because of the added worry over her sister. I set my phone down and reminded myself that it wouldn't be a bad idea to top off my own chargeable devices, just in case. I'd begun to rummage in the junk drawer for my charger when the phone's musical tone went off again.

"What's your weather like?" Drake asked.

I stepped out the kitchen door and stared at the sky. A chill wind sent the clouds eastward at a pretty good pace. I couldn't see the western horizon for all the trees but it didn't feel as if a clear spot would open up anywhere out there. I told him all this.

"It's still snowing like a bi—blizzard out here," he said. "I won't be able to get out today, hon. I'm sorry for messing up the Christmas Eve plans."

I assured him it would be okay and told him that the girls had come up with an alternate activity that would be fun in its own way.

"I'm saving the turkey dinner for whenever you do get home," I said. "Ron was stuck in the Dallas airport overnight, so there's no point in cooking a big dinner without two large man-appetites to help polish it off."

"At least I have a motel room. Something to be thankful for in that," he said.

I pictured him in some small town roadside place with wood paneling from the '70s and orange shag carpeting that didn't bear thinking about. The image wasn't a whole lot cheerier than Ron's description of his sleeping arrangement.

"I know one way we can spend Christmas Eve together," he said. "Watch *It's a Wonderful Life* on TV tonight. I will too, and I can pretend you're cuddled in beside me."

A romantic thought—what a guy—but I knew it wasn't going to be the same. However, I couldn't pout about the situation. We had to play the hand we were dealt. We exchanged a bunch of suggestive ideas, priming ourselves for a really good reunion in a day or two. Just as things were warming up I got another call. A glance at the readout told me it was Victoria. I didn't interrupt Drake's sexy voice but the mood was definitely broken. When we hung up, five minutes later, I called her back.

"Just checking to see if there are any last minute things you need from the store," she said. "I'm taking gifts by for Jason, Justin and Joey then I'm headed your way."

I wished her luck. Encountering Ron's ex, Bernadette The Witch, was never pleasant but Vic had refused to be drawn into the fray and managed to stay cool no matter what b.s. got flung her way.

"Come early," I reminded her. "Our street isn't on the tour route this year, which means they'll have us barricaded in by five. Plus, I'm going to be more than ready to break into the wine once it gets dark and I've finished lighting the hundred-plus luminarias at my house and Elsa's."

She laughed and agreed wholeheartedly with that plan, offering to help with the candles when she got here.

I set Elsa's pot of posole on the stove with a low flame. The house would cheer up once it smelled of the spicy pork, hominy and chile stew. I put the rest of the groceries away, dropped the tabloid paper onto a stack of mail that I hadn't opened yet, and began pulling out chips and crackers and dips so we could have a little appetizer before the meal. It took only the sound of crinkly cellophane bags to bring Freckles to my side. Well, that and the fact that I couldn't resist tossing her an occasional broken cracker.

Setting the dining table for three seemed kind of sad. Elsa, Victoria and myself—without our guys and the extended family it would be such a small group. On the other hand, it promised to be casual and congenial and a whole lot less work.

A tap at the back door interrupted my thoughts.

Elsa stood there with a covered basket. "Blueberry muffins for tomorrow morning," she said as she edged into the warm kitchen. "My, it smells good in here."

I laughed. "It's your recipe, warming on the stove."

"Well, I guess at home I get so used to it I don't notice anymore."

Or maybe it's such a rarity to walk into my house and catch the scent of a home-cooked pot of stew. I hugged her and put the basket of muffins on the counter. I'd just taken her coat and was hanging it on the hooks near the front door when I caught the flash of Victoria's blue Cruiser pulling into the driveway.

"Hey, everyone," she said with a big smile when I opened the door for her. "What a cheery Christmas Eve this is going to be. Oh boy, does it smell good in here!"

I waved a hand toward Elsa. "It's all Gram's doing. I wish I could take credit."

I also wished I could get past the fact that Drake wasn't here for Christmas Eve but the situation was what it was. My low-grade worry about my husband getting home safely would not change the circumstances. I vowed to stop being such a control freak—to settle in, enjoy the moment, and let all other extenuating circumstances work themselves out. Putting on a smile I offered beverages.

It didn't take us but about fifteen minutes to find ourselves laughing over the image of my brother trying to catch a few winks in the confines of airport lounge seating. It wasn't really funny, but Ron's slightly chunky physique is much more suited to a recliner chair and the three of us, stretched out across the comfy sofa and armchairs in my living room, weren't exactly a sympathetic crowd.

The light in the room began to fade and when I got up to plug in the lights on the tree I realized with a start that I still had other civic duties to perform.

"Vic, help. We need to get those luminarias lit."

Her eyes went wide and she stood up suddenly, nearly upsetting her wine glass. Elsa got up too, ready to pick up her coat. I thought of the chill, now that the sun was setting.

"Gram, why don't you take charge in the kitchen? Check the posole and get out some bowls for later? We can handle the outdoor stuff for now."

Victoria and I donned our coats and gloves and grabbed the butane candle lighters. Several neighbors were already out in front of their homes, checking the straightness of the paper sacks and lighting the candles. Down the way, I could see that a couple of places were already done. Even though the tour buses wouldn't come directly past our house this year, it was practically a mandatory tradition that every house in the area at least provide luminarias—other lights and decorations were optional. That way, as people gazed out the windows of their cozy transportation they would see a show no matter where they looked. Plus, those of us who live here love to stroll the back streets where the vehicles aren't allowed. It's a lovely and private little world we enjoy, in return for the work involved.

"I'll start in front of Elsa's," I said, "if you can begin down here by the driveway."

The air was calm, with a moist cold, and we made fairly short work of the job. I could remember windy evenings where the process was a near-impossible challenge and those nights of my childhood, before the invention of the long lighters, when we struggled with matches. See? This year was actually full of blessings.

By the time we met at the property line between my house and Elsa's, Victoria commented that she could hear the buildup of traffic. I took another look at the sky, which was now dark behind the low-hanging clouds. The kind of clouds that promise snow. I envisioned the possibility, how beautiful the neighborhood would be with a coating of white, but didn't get my hopes up. We rarely get snow on Christmas, and I spent a lot of childhood holidays being disappointed.

I have to admit that, as a group, the three of us are pretty light hitters. We ate Elsa's delicious posole, which tasted even better than it smelled, exchanged the little gifts we'd gotten for each other, put on our cozy p.j.s and sat in front of the fire with glasses of eggnog, and by eight o'clock Elsa was yawning through *It's A Wonderful Life*. I sneaked into the kitchen and called Drake; I had to ask if he was watching the movie, since he'd suggested it. We talked through the scene where Jimmy Stewart and Donna Reed are staring at the moon. Finally, I told him I better get back to my guests.

By nine, Elsa abandoned the slumber party and decided to walk back through the hedge to sleep in her own bed. I didn't blame her; there's something about being in different surroundings that never quite lends itself to sound sleep. I told her to come back for breakfast.

After I walked Elsa home, Victoria and I polished off the remains of the wine we'd opened earlier. She got a little emotional over the fact that she and Ron were missing out on the romance of their first Christmas together. And that brought back memories of Drake and me on our honeymoon in the mountains, which was our first Christmas together. So we were both getting a little maudlin by the time we decided to call it a night.

She settled into the guest room but I had a hard time falling asleep. My mind wouldn't slow down, missing Drake and having the holiday plans fall apart, and the fact that Ron was having to deal with Rosa Flores and her worries over her sister. I rolled over at least eight times before I finally gave up on sleep.

Restless, I slipped on my jeans and sweater that I'd worn earlier in the day and tiptoed into the living room. Freckles sat up in her crate and perked her ears at me. I didn't want to let her run around the house—she would most certainly wake Victoria.

"Let's go outside," I whispered. The bus tours were over so I put on my coat, scarf and gloves then reached into the crate to clip on the dog's leash.

She bounced with excitement and it was all I could do to get her out the front door quietly. Very first thing, she wanted to sniff at one of the luminarias but the thin stream of candle smoke must have gone up her nose. She quickly backed away.

I took a deep breath and looked around. Complete quiet blanketed the late-night streets. Tiny multicolored lights sparkled from rooflines, trees and shrubs, and the luminarias continued their all-night vigil in golden silence. My body soaked up the peaceful feeling and my earlier low-grade tension faded away. Even the dog relaxed and stopped tugging at her leash.

Without a word, we began walking. At the corner, I turned left and continued for two more blocks before I saw a car. It cruised slowly, the couple inside peering out and pointing toward the light displays. I gave them a small wave.

Freckles trotted along, more adult than I'd ever seen her, seemingly in awe of the beautiful frosty night. I lost track of time and distance, eventually figuring out that we'd wound our way back toward home and were only a block away from our warm beds. It was only when I stepped back into the house that I realized how icy my hands and feet had become. I turned up the gas logs in the fireplace and reheated water for a fresh cup of cocoa.

A paperback book I'd been trying to finish for a week lay on the end table. I picked it up, pulled a fuzzy blanket over my lap and began to read. My eyelids began to feel really heavy.

The mantle clock chimed, startling me into realizing it was one o'clock—Christmas morning. Freckles had fallen asleep at my feet, her spotted little nose resting on my fuzzy slippers. I gently set the book aside and leaned over to stroke her head. This time last year I'd been watching our dear old Lab as he spent his last aging days, deeply saddened that our time together was ending. Who knew that this little cutie would come along and heal the empty place for me.

She stretched in her sleep and I didn't have the heart to make her get up and go to her crate. I edged my feet free, stretched out on the sofa and pulled an afghan over myself. The dog's deep breathing lulled me and I drifted off.

When my eyes fluttered open I became aware of two things. The smell of coffee and the fact that the room was still cloaked in gray gloom. Little sounds began to register. Victoria's smooth alto came through, humming *White Christmas*. A little embarrassed at being caught sleeping on the couch I sat up and rubbed at my eyes.

"Hey, Sunshine," she said, walking up behind me with a mug of coffee. "I guess I crashed a little earlier than you did."

I took the coffee and slurped two generous sips. "Um. I couldn't sleep right away. Ended up taking a walk and then trying to read."

"Was it snowing when you went out?"

I shook my head.

"Well, it happened at some point."

"Really? Oh, yay!" Like a kid, I jumped up and ran to the front window. Sure enough, a coating of white blanketed the streets. It probably amounted to two inches, but it was enough to put me in the spirit.

Freckles caught my excitement and leaped around me until I nearly tripped over her. I scrambled to the bedroom for warm clothing and bundled into my coat and gloves.

"Aren't you joining us?" I asked Victoria as the dog

danced near the kitchen door.

"I'd better stay in here and mind the breakfast." She pointed toward the oven from where, now that I noticed, the heavenly scent of cinnamon and vanilla emanated. "Remember? Elsa said she would be over this morning?"

Truthfully, I had spaced out most of the plans we'd made, once I saw the new snow. I stepped outside. The sky was a clear, deep blue and the air was crisp with that dry cold that speaks of single-digit temperatures. Freckles tore across the yard, raced back, snuffled at the snowy lawn. I tried to make a snowball but found the white stuff too dry to cling very well. I tossed the handful of powder at the dog and she tried to nip at it in midair as it flew around her head in a misty cloud.

We kept this up until we'd pretty much worn the pretty snow down to the barren winter lawn beneath. I heard voices behind me and realized that Elsa had come from next door and was talking to Victoria at the back door. I beat my gloves together to get rid of the snow and brushed it from the dog's coat as well.

Inside, the kitchen table was set with some of my mother's pretty dishes and a teapot sat in the middle of the table, wrapped in its little cozy. Cinnamon rolls and Elsa's blueberry muffins waited in a basket, everything ready for me to get out of my snowy clothes and join the group. Before I could get to the table the phone rang.

"Sally wanted me to let you know," Ross said. "She's in labor. We're heading for the hospital now."

Unless I could actually be of help, which was certainly not a possibility, I told him I would come by the hospital once he let me know the baby had arrived. I passed the news to my little brunch group and we speculated whether they would give the baby a Christmas name.

"If it was a boy," Elsa said, "he could be Nick."

"Well, hopefully not Saint Nick," Victoria joked.

"And if it's a girl, maybe Saint Nicola?" I suggested.

The ideas became sillier all the time, with regular names like Noelle and Christiana taking a back seat to Rudolpha and Frostina." Soon we were laughing like crazy loons.

When the phone rang again, I picked it up in mid-laugh.

"Well, it sounds like you're having a good old time," Ron's voice said. He didn't sound very merry at all. No wonder. "Is Victoria there with you?"

I handed her the receiver and wandered into the living room while she chatted with Ron. Hearing their loving voices made me miss Drake all the more. Elsa came up beside me just in time to catch me dabbing at my eye.

"He'll be home soon, sweetie," she said.

I draped my arm around her narrow shoulders. "My life got so much better once he was in it. I can't imagine being without him now."

She smiled up at me. "I'm glad you two found each other."

"Ron's got a flight." Victoria bustled through the doorway, a little breathless. "He'll be here by early afternoon."

The portable phone rang in her hand and she answered it, then realized it would be for me.

"Charlie? Ross again. Just wanted to let you know not to come out. The roads are a mess. We were nearly in an accident."

"Are you both okay?"

"Yeah, we're fine. Sally's in a room, getting checked over I guess."

I sent them both a hug and good wishes. Then I turned to Victoria. "Ross advises against going out."

This was so typical. Albuquerque gets snow so seldom that no one here learns how to drive on it. Even a couple of inches throws the whole city into chaos. And I could imagine that it wouldn't be easy getting the necessary road crews to work on a holiday.

"I'm going to hold onto the thought that it will be better by noon."

"Turn on the TV and see what they're reporting," Elsa suggested. But that was like waiting for paint to dry. Most of the channels were running marathon Christmas movies or kid programming; one normally had a noon newscast but that wouldn't come on for two more hours.

I switched on my computer and found weather reports, but all I really learned was that the storm system had moved eastward and was now sending the Midwest into fits. The New Mexico ski areas seemed happy, but that was about all I got. We kept glancing out the kitchen window at the outdoor thermometer and watching it creep up one degree at a time.

Elsa decided to go on home around ten, and by noon Victoria was going crazy with the waiting. "I'm heading for the airport," she said. "It's warming up a little and the major streets are probably clearer than what we're seeing around here."

That much had to be true. Precisely two sets of tire tracks cut through the snow on the street in front of the house.

"Take my Jeep," I told her. I walked out and gave her a quick primer on what to expect from the four-wheel drive.

Then I watched her, a little nervously I admit, as she pulled away.

Back in the house my cell phone was blinking with a message. I'd missed Drake's call by only moments. He said he would be dropping a few final bales of hay, tidying up some loose ends and heading home by four. He should be here by dark.

I called him back to warn him about the streets. It could well be that the most dangerous part of his trip would be the drive from Double Eagle, the airport on the west side. At least he was getting closer with each passing hour.

Chapter 9

Time dragged. I called Victoria's cell to let her know that with the menfolk home again we could do the big holiday dinner tonight. Then I washed the dishes, tidied the house, changed the sheets, and put the turkey in the oven. That took all of thirty minutes so I set the table. I paced and watched the clock. Walked the dog down to the park and back, looked at the clock some more. This was ridiculous.

I flipped through that silly tabloid I'd bought at the supermarket, flipping past a blatantly ridiculous article on how aliens from the planet Zeroid had kidnapped three children and taken them to the North Pole where they claimed to have met Santa's elves. The center spread was the headline piece about the criminals who'd gotten away with murder and a mug shot of a woman caught my eye. This one had been in all the headlines a few years ago, a mother accused of killing her two children. I'd just read the first paragraph when I heard a vehicle in the driveway. The newspaper dropped to the floor and I raced to the front door, hoping Drake would be the first of the group to arrive.

My Jeep sat in its usual spot, with three doors opening simultaneously. Ron, Victoria and . . . a stranger? The man was close to my brother's size and build, a little portly in the middle, with thick gray hair and the kind of lines on his face that spoke of a no-nonsense life. He wore gray slacks and an all-weather jacket. I watched as they transferred Ron's carry-on bag and something else to the back of Vic's car, then the three of them walked up to the porch, stomping their feet to get rid of the snow which I probably should have swept away while they were gone. Freckles raced out the door the instant I opened it.

"Safe and sound," Victoria said, beaming.

"Hey, little sis," Ron said. He turned to the man. "Chet, this is my sister, Charlie. Charlie, Chester Flowers."

I took the hand he offered and ushered everyone indoors.

"Thanks for putting me in touch with Ron yesterday," Flowers said. "I worked on a case with your brother a few years ago, up in Seattle. I was with the Seattle PD. Retired now, taking on a few private cases." He had a careworn face with deeply etched lines, the kind of countenance that showed a life of worry and diligence.

"When Chet told me about the case he's working now, I suggested he come to Albuquerque," Ron said. He sniffed the air. "Something sure smells good."

By now they'd all shed their coats and I told them the good news that Drake would be here soon so we could have our big holiday dinner.

"Maybe we can find some drinks for everyone," Ron said to me, with a twitch of his head toward the kitchen.

I turned up the gas logs for a little additional ambiance and followed him.

"How's Rosa?" I asked. "I assume you got her on a flight before you left?"

"Her moods were up and down the whole time. Hard for her, getting the news about Ivana when there's so little time left."

"Sad situation," I said, locating some crackers to go with a smoky cheese spread that I had stashed in the fridge.

"Yeah, it is."

"So . . ." I tilted my head toward the living room. "Your old buddy?"

"He's working a cold case that intrigued me. It was very high profile a few years ago," Ron said as he reached into the cupboard above the fridge for his special bottle of Scotch. "He'll fill you in on the details, but basically it boils down to his wanting our help with it."

I could tell by the gleam in his eyes that he really wanted to do this.

"But, he comes from Seattle. Why would *we* be working the case?"

"Several of his most promising leads brought him here. He'll have to get back to the northwest in a couple days but he wants someone local to follow up here in New Mexico. What do you think?" He pulled two heavy crystal glasses from another cupboard.

"I think . . . sure, whatever you want."

Ron has so seldom heard those words come from me that he didn't realize he'd made his case. "It could bring us a real boost in business. This case was huge. That woman,

Tali Donovan, who was tried for killing her two kids and then acquitted. The bodies of the children were never found and that's a lot of what caused the 'reasonable doubt' in the verdict."

"Ron, I said yes."

"Chet's convinced she was guilty and he's putting together the evidence."

I waved my hand in front of his face. "Earth to Ron. I said yes. We should do it."

Aside from all of his reasons, I felt my pulse quicken a little. Wasn't this the case I'd just seen written up in *The Scoop*?

"Good. We'll go over it all. He can bring both of us up to speed on it." He poured Scotch into the two glasses and threw in a few ice cubes.

"But not right this minute. It's Christmas."

In answer to that statement, a small commotion erupted in the living room. The dog woofed a couple of times and voices came through. I hurried through the swinging door toward the sounds.

Drake was standing near the front door, trying to shrug off the jacket he wore over his flight suit, while Freckles danced around his legs. My heart thumped just a little harder and I rushed into his arms with a complete lack of self-consciousness.

"Hey you," he whispered. "Feels so good to be home."

I dittoed that.

Ron introduced Chet and offered to get Drake a glass of what they were having. He begged off for the moment, wanting to shower off the smell of work and get into more comfortable clothing. When he left the room, the other two men sank into the overstuffed chairs near the fire. Victoria offered to take over in the kitchen. I found myself standing near the sofa without any tasks for the moment.

"Ron told me about your request for us to work with you," I said to Flowers, as I took a seat on the couch. "Tell me more about it."

"Every retired detective has an unsolved case that bothers him. For me it was Tali Donovan's two missing kids. That verdict *still* eats me up." His vivid blue eyes met mine and I saw the old anguish. "We can go into the details later. I worked the case from day one, when the two children went missing. We always liked Tali Donovan for the crime, but it was hard to put together conclusive evidence. Most of what we had was circumstantial. The prosecutor's office got in a hurry because the media was all over it and everybody in the country wanted to see this lady hang. Frankly, they took it to trial too soon and couldn't make their case. Everyone seemed shocked when she was acquitted, but I had a feeling about it. My team members and I weren't surprised at all."

"But what can you do now?" I asked. "Can she be tried again? Double jeopardy and all that?"

"There's the possibility of a civil trial, kind of like the Simpson case. Plus, there are other charges that might be brought, even though they won't carry the severe penalties that a murder one conviction would have."

"Ron said you're retired. So . . . you're working this on your own?"

"There's an interested party. Boyd Donovan, Tali's now ex-husband. He's paying for this investigation." He sipped from his drink. "But we can get into all that when I give you the full briefing."

"Chet's going to stay with Vic and me tonight. Tomorrow we can all meet at the office and go over the files," Ron said.

From the kitchen I began to notice voices. Elsa must be back. "I better get in there and help with the chores," I said.

Drake emerged from the bedroom, looking extremely good in a soft green pullover sweater and chinos, his hair damp and his face freshly shaved. I sent a little flicker of longing his way.

In the kitchen, potatoes were bubbling away in a large pot and Victoria was stirring gravy in another. Elsa held up a bowl of cranberry sauce and asked whether I wanted it in the fridge or on the table. Things were moving into place nicely. I added another place setting to the table and basically let momentum take charge of the dinner.

To paraphrase—we came, we ate, we conquered that whole turkey. It took only twenty minutes to decimate the feast that had taken a half-day to prepare. That seemed about normal. Ron seemed beat after the sleepless night in Dallas, so the party broke up soon after the dishes were done.

I turned to my sweetheart and could tell we both had the same idea.

Next thing I knew, the clock struck eleven out in the living room. The guests had long gone and Drake and I had quickly found ourselves in the bedroom making up for the few nights apart. Then we'd opened our gifts and I tried on the lacy red teddy he'd bought for me, and that led us back to the bedroom. The clock barely intruded into my consciousness as I lay with my head against his chest and a sea of warm bedding around me.

"Good Christmas?" he murmured.

"Um, now it is."

* * *

The room was filled with half-light when I awakened. Beside me, Drake snored softly and peacefully. I slipped out of bed, thinking I would just go to the bathroom and come back. But I found myself mulling over work. Rosa Flores was home with her sister now. I hoped she would find a peaceful reconciliation there, whatever the real story was. Now the thing on my mind was the new case. Ever since Chet Flowers explained the basics of the situation I'd been intrigued. The anniversary of the children's disappearance and the coverage by *The Scoop* must be nagging like crazy at the devoted detective. I slipped on a pair of sweats and padded to the living room.

Freckles wasn't about to let me just tippy-toe past. In her mind it was time for breakfast. I let her out, came up with the obligatory nuggets, and started the coffee maker while I was at it. I had to rummage for the tabloid, which I'd tossed aside yesterday, somewhere in the living room, a space which still held the litter of wrapping paper and bows that we'd never cleaned up.

At the kitchen table I spread it open and poured my first cup of coffee.

Tali Donovan's eyes stared belligerently at the camera in her mug shot. The pudgy face was framed by stringy brown hair and she had dark circles under her eyes. No wonder; the jail-issue orange jumpsuit is no woman's friend, fashion-wise. I reread the story.

Her two children, a three-year-old girl and twenty-one-month-old boy were last seen playing in the family's back yard, a week before Christmas. Donovan claimed that she'd been with them but had gone in the house to answer the phone, leaving them to play in a pile of raked leaves. When she came back outside they were not there. She claimed she had run out to the yard and found a back gate that led to a wooded area standing open and she saw a man dressed in a black hooded sweatshirt running away. By the time she got to the path, he was gone.

No neighbors witnessed anything and Tali's story had become a bit muddled as to the timeframe and exactly where she'd seen the strange man. Eventually the jury acquitted her, mainly because the bodies of the children had never been found, despite extensive searches through the surrounding woods by Search and Rescue teams and cadaver dogs. Within two weeks after her acquittal, Tali Donovan left Seattle. Her husband divorced her, and her mother and siblings claimed that they rarely heard from her and didn't know where she was currently living.

The article quoted Chet Flowers as saying, "We feel certain she did it. You work homicide as long as I did, you have deep instincts about these things."

I studied the face of the woman again but, as with a word that you repeat over and over, the newness began to fade and I decided she only seemed familiar because I'd remembered her from all the television coverage years ago. I clipped the portion of the page that referred to Donovan and tossed the rest of the paper in the trash.

Drake wandered in, his hair tousled and eyes still looking sleepy. I doctored a mug of coffee according to his preferences and placed it in his hand. He slurped at it appreciatively and caught sight of the clipping on the table.

"What's that about?"

I quickly gave the rundown on the new case and the plan to spend the next couple of days in the office with Chet Flowers.

"And here I thought you'd be at the mall, snapping up all

those after-Christmas bargains," he teased. He knew better than that. "Well, I will be at the airport, doing a hundred-hour on the ship and making sure she's ready in case I get another call on a moment's notice."

"Breakfast?" I offered half-heartedly, since I still felt full from last night's big dinner.

He poked around in the packages that had become stacked up in one corner of the countertop and came up with one of Elsa's blueberry muffins.

"This'll do," he said as he bit into it. Crumbs scattered like snowflakes and Freckles went a little nuts, licking them from the floor.

"I'm going to leave you to it," I said.

I showered and dressed in my standard work attire of jeans and a sweater. Twenty minutes later I was at the office, letting my computer boot up while I started a pot of coffee down in the kitchen.

While it brewed, I keyed in a search for "tali donovan murder trial" and came up with a few thousand hits. I started with the most recent articles and read backward. The newest material basically reiterated what the tabloid had printed; that ill-regarded paper obviously had done no homework other than borrowing whole paragraphs from the Seattle newspapers. As Chet Flowers had told us, Donovan had been acquitted of the crime mainly because the bodies of the children were never found. The press must have given her no peace at all, and public sentiment generally went against her in every way. The fact that her husband didn't stick around afterward also added fuel to the fire of speculation. Shortly after the verdict she'd gone into hiding.

Before she vanished, though, there was the highly publicized trial, with pictures of the defendant walking with her lawyers into court. They'd made sure she was dressed conservatively in plain slacks and schoolmarm blouses, with her dark hair in a demure ponytail and minimal makeup. She cleaned up well and looked nothing like the disheveled version of herself in the mug shot. Guilty or innocent, they all usually manage to look respectable in court.

I found a long piece that pretty well summarized the history and read through that. It painted the picture of a model family—the good-looking husband a success with a giant tech company, wife who adored him, two beautiful children. Most of the photos showed the children in endearing poses. America fell in love with those kids and was disgusted with the mother, with her air of detachment during the whole affair. On the day they disappeared she had let them play alone in the back yard of their upscale suburban home. That in itself was practically portrayed as a crime, and I felt a stab of sorrow for the way society had become. I used to roam my entire neighborhood, climb the trees, ride bikes for miles with my friends. The restrictions on kids these days were a sad reflection on the times. I scrolled down the page.

On the day the children disappeared, Boyd Donovan came home from work around four o'clock, earlier than usual. It was a rare sunny Seattle day and he thought they could take the kids to the park. According to the police who questioned him later, Tali was a little flustered to see him. When he said he wanted to check on the kids, she grabbed his arm. That's when she admitted they weren't there.

She told him—and stayed with her story throughout— that the kids had been playing in the yard, she'd gone inside to answer the telephone, and when she came back they were gone. She swore she hadn't been inside more than ten minutes although she admitted that she couldn't see the entire yard from where she'd been standing as she talked. She became edgy and finally said that as she came out of the house she thought she saw a man, wearing dark clothing and a hooded sweatshirt, running through the forest behind the property.

Boyd immediately called the police and reported that the children had been kidnapped. Alerts went out all over the city and extensive searches were conducted but there was no sign of the little ones. No ransom calls ever came, as one might expect when it involved a highly successful family, and no bodies were ever found.

What led to the trial of Tali Donovan were her numerous suspicious behaviors. Why hadn't she called Boyd and the police the second she discovered the children missing? Why had she lied to him when he first got home? Why hadn't she brought the telephone outside so she could keep an eye on them? And why didn't she ever cry during all the ordeal?

I scrolled through the details of the trial. It appeared that Tali had gotten the best team of criminal defense attorneys the Donovans could afford. They pointed out the complete lack of real evidence that the children weren't alive and well somewhere. The kidnapper had probably acted on behalf of some childless couple who had admired the children and wanted them for their own. Naturally they would not make a ransom demand or come forward to admit what they'd done. For all anyone knew, the Donovan children were living in Switzerland or Croatia or somewhere, happily settling in with new parents. It was enough reasonable doubt to win Tali Donovan her freedom.

It wasn't enough to allay the suspicions of the public, though. According to the host of press stories after Tali walked out of the courtroom, a free woman, she began receiving death threats. More than once signs appeared on the front lawn of their home, with inflammatory words painted blood red.

Chapter 10

I heard voices downstairs, and went down to find Ron and Chet in the kitchen. Bless them, they'd stopped for bagels. I helped myself to one and we decided to convene in the conference room where we could spread papers out on the table.

Chet carried a large briefcase with him and from it he pulled a thick file. The ten-inch stack of paper was bound with brown board covers and metal brads, which held it all together by holes drilled in the top of all the sheets.

"That's just the homicide department's file," he said. "Transcripts of the interviews and such. The actual trial records fill boxes."

He pulled out a thick manila envelope. "These are the photos we took inside the house, all over the back yard and woods. I keep hoping some little clue will fall into place and give me the answers I need."

I took the envelope and pulled out the sheaf of pictures. I began sorting them by subject—the home, the surrounding outdoors, the trial and afterward. I got my first look at Tali in different settings and of her husband, Boyd Donovan.

Boyd was tall, with close-cropped dark hair. He looked somber throughout the trial. No camera ever caught him smiling, nor did they find an ounce of accusation in his demeanor when he interacted with his wife.

"Within two weeks after the verdict, the house in Seattle went up for sale and Boyd purchased another in California," Chet said. "He'd apparently courted another tech giant company that was more than willing to ignore a scandal two states away in order to bring Boyd's inventive genius into their corporate fold. When reporters pressed him on the subject, it was notable that Boyd only referred to the move in terms of himself. No mention that Tali would accompany him. The marriage was over."

Somehow, that wasn't surprising. But did it mean Boyd wasn't somehow involved?

"Tali Donovan went away and soon vanished from sight. The reporters tried hard but they couldn't seem to figure out where she'd gone. Some made the point that she'd been through a horrible ordeal and that the world should leave her alone."

Indeed, in the last known grainy photo of Tali, her face was puffy and she wore dark glasses and a scarf. Clearly, she was far more upset over losing her husband and home than she'd been at losing her children. I said as much to Flowers.

"You don't know the half of it." He shook his head. "That little lady was flat-out cold. I sat in that courtroom every day. Found myself a seat where I could watch her. If she noticed the judge or jurors watching she'd sniff into a handkerchief, but most of the time she fiddled with her fingernails, twisted her fingers around in knots, kicked at the legs of her chair. Sometimes, after her lawyers offered an objection to some testimony, she'd turn around in her chair and sneak a little smile toward her husband, sitting there in the front row. It was creepy."

"Were there cameras in the courtroom?" Ron asked.

"No. A few sketch artists were allowed in, but since Tali didn't testify and Boyd wasn't called either, there wasn't much for them to draw."

"I'm surprised the jurors didn't clue in to the smiles and her nonchalant attitude," I said.

"I think in a lot of ways they did," Chet said. "But in the end it came down to the actual evidence. And, like I told you yesterday, there wasn't enough."

"So, what was the most damning evidence?"

"The last time witnesses can swear to seeing the children alive was that morning. A few neighbors saw Tali drive away with them in the car around midday, both strapped into their car seats. One older woman thought she saw them come back home later, but no one could back that up even though it's a neighborhood where a lot of people are home during the day. Stay-at-home moms and retirees, mostly. Of course, the defense attorneys grilled the witness until she could no longer be sure what she saw."

"Not a peep from the kids after that?"

"Well, not quite. The woman who lived immediately to the east of their house said she thought she heard the children playing outdoors. She couldn't be a hundred percent sure it was the Donovan kids and she's a little unclear about the time. She was watching a talk show on TV and only heard the small voices when she muted her TV volume during a commercial. It was between two and three p.m. which agrees with Tali Donovan's story. The transcript of her interview is in there." Flowers indicated the brown-clad file.

"Tali said they were playing outside in the leaves and she went in to answer the telephone," I said.

"That's another thing that doesn't gel. We checked the phone records on their landline and on her cell phone. Neither company shows any calls going in or out after 11:37 that morning."

"So, wait. She didn't call anyone *after* she discovered the children were missing either?"

"Not until her husband got home in the late afternoon. She claimed that she'd only realized they were gone a few minutes earlier and was too shaken to think what to do."

"Wow," Ron said. "Doesn't that speak volumes, in itself?"

"You would think so. But when our detective testified about the phone records, the defense attorney twisted it around and got the jurors so confused that many of them came away with the idea that Tali's husband had left his phone at home that day, and that she'd probably gone inside to answer that. As I said, the prosecution wasn't very well prepared or they would have had his phone records too."

It sounded like a mess to me.

"Tell us just what you'd want us to do, Chet. What can we accomplish here in Albuquerque?"

The detective shifted in his chair. "We have reason to believe Tali Donovan might have chosen New Mexico when she ran from Washington state. She could very well be right here in the city."

My gaze dropped to the mug shot photo. It gave me a little chill to think of this woman living nearby.

"She had family here," Chet continued. "Her mother and a sister in Santa Fe. Her name is in the file. My interviews with them went absolutely nowhere. The women of that family pulled together during the trial and none of them would say a word against Tali. Two sisters and their mother. Apparently her father had passed away some years earlier. Mom went all moral on us, claiming to be a God-fearing Christian woman who'd raised her kids right. Tali would never do a thing like this and it was horrible of the police to even think such a thing."

The way he mimicked a fanatical sounding woman at the last part almost made me laugh.

"Between the three of them and the fact that at the time Boyd Donovan wouldn't talk either, we didn't have one single person who was close to her that might have given us something valuable."

I mulled all this over.

"So, what I'm hoping you can accomplish is to contact Babe Freizel, that's Tali's sister in Santa Fe, and see if you can somehow work your way in. Maybe time has worked its magic on some of them, just as it did with Boyd Donovan, and one of the sisters will have a change of heart about talking to us. As a woman, Charlie, I'm hoping you can bring out some kind of a need to confide."

It was a tall order. These women had their shared history to bind them. But if it's true that there is no honor among thieves, maybe there are no truly buried secrets among conspirators either. I'd certainly be willing to give it a try.

"I'm looking for two things as we search," Chet said. "One is to locate Tali. We can't apprehend her until we can firm up some charges and have the evidence to back it up. But we need to know where she is. Once I have my evidence I want to be able to swoop in."

"So, if we happen to catch her hanging out at her sister's house in Santa Fe we don't confront her or tip her that we're still working the case?"

"Right. Secondly, we need to find the remains of those kids. I'll be working that angle up in Seattle. With bodies, we can surely find a lot more evidence. How they died, who had access to the gravesite, that kind of thing."

"You're really sure they're dead, aren't you?"

"As sure as I'm sitting here. Those poor babies didn't live out the remainder of the day they vanished."

I brought up the question that had been nagging at me. "What about Boyd Donovan? Are you absolutely sure he didn't do it?"

Flowers started to take a sip from his coffee but discovered the mug was empty. "I never say never, Charlie. But I'm about as certain of this as a cop ever gets. For one thing, virtually everyone in Donovan's office says he was there all day. He did go out at lunch, but it was with another guy in his department. The alibi seems airtight. Plus, if you could see this guy now. He's wracked with guilt over standing by Tali at the time. He's spending pretty much his life savings to investigate this and bring her to justice. I watched him five years ago, and I've seen him as recently as last month. The man is a shell of his former self. He was on top of the world back there at Lightastic Chip in Seattle. He took a lesser job just to get out of the area, and I found out that he's been demoted in that. Drinks a lot more now. I think the only thing keeping him going is that he needs—I mean, *really needs*—to find those two children and give them a decent burial. The guy needs answers more than anyone I've ever met."

I nodded. I got nothing but honest vibes from Chet and his gut feeling was good enough for me. I offered to make more coffee but Chet said he had to get going.

"I'll leave these files with you. I've got duplicates at home. Plus, this way I don't have to lug this case onto another plane with all that weight in it." He gave a grin and stood up. "We'll stay in touch."

Ron left to drive the detective to the airport and I gathered the massive file and the envelope of photos. Seeing Sally's clear desk and her empty chair reminded me with a jolt that I'd never gotten out yesterday to see her in the hospital. Ross had never called to let me know that all was well. Oh, gosh, what if she was still in labor?

I looked up his number in my files and dialed it.

"Oh, Charlie," he said. "I am so sorry I never got back to you. It was a false alarm. We're home now, baby still inside."

I felt relieved that everything was okay, sorry for Sally that she was still walking around with her giant tummy. Ross handed the phone over to her and we talked for a few minutes. I could hear Chrissie fussing in the background. It must be lunch time.

Upstairs in my office I started a customer file for Chet Flowers and logged the hours we'd spent together this morning, as he'd instructed me to. All expenses would be passed along to Boyd Donovan, and I almost felt guilty billing the man who'd experienced such tragedy in his life. But then I usually feel sorry for all our clients in some way.

I considered the best way to start. Despite my assertions that Ron was really the investigator in the firm, sometimes clients needed a woman's touch—as Chet Flowers had just pointed out—and I often found myself more involved that I ever intended. And I must admit that sometimes pure curiosity grabs me.

Before simply barging in on Babe Freizel, Tali's sister in Santa Fe, I needed both a plan for my cover story and some additional background information. Boyd Donovan knew Tali's extended family personally, plus he was a key player in the whole scenario. I found his number among Chet's notes and picked up the phone.

A raspy voice answered, a guy who didn't sound quite as though he'd had his morning coffee yet. I calculated the time; it was after eleven a.m. in California. I tried to reconcile the voice with the photo I had in front of me of a tall clean-cut man in a business suit and striped tie.

Once I'd introduced myself and explained how RJP Investigations was connected with Chet Flowers, Donovan cleared his throat and perked up.

"I've been assigned to approach Babe Freizel and see what information I can get about her sister's whereabouts," I began. "I'm looking for any tips on working with her."

He made a scoffing sound. "Don't count on working *with* her, when it comes to getting at Tali. They stick together like glue."

Just as Chet had told us. "Can you tell me something about each of them?"

I could hear kitchen sounds in the background; he was probably getting a cup of that much-needed coffee and getting ready to settle in for a story.

"There's their mom, Roxanne Freizel. She was widowed

fairly young and raised the three girls on her own. To say they stick together is a little mild. Call it clannish, an exclusive little clique." He paused a moment and I heard a slurp. "The oldest daughter is Babe. She's ten years older than Scout who is two years older than Tali. Scout and Tali might as well have been twins—they're that close. They both had little birthmarks, light tan. Scout's was on her shoulder, Tali's in the middle of her back. She joked that it was the thumbprint of God."

"I understand Scout lives in Santa Fe now?"

"No, that's Babe," he said. "Well, I think so anyway. Since I moved to California I haven't heard boo from any of that family. Not that I wanted to. The whole thing was a nightmare for me. But you would think . . ."

I murmured something sympathetic.

"Scout married Dave Stiles at the same time Tali and I married. It was a double ceremony, at the girls' insistence. I thought it was a little strange but, you know, kind of romantic too. Tali was so devoted to me and I saw the same thing in Scout with her new husband. I don't know . . . I guess we were all just young and a little deluded about life."

"What do you mean?"

"I'd gone to school in California, UCSD, computer sciences and, since one of my projects had to do with a faster-than-light chip, I got recruited up in Seattle right away. It was the heyday of the dot coms and salaries were through the roof. Tali grew up in New Mexico and we met in college. She said she'd followed my rise among the science students. She seemed head over heels in love with me after our first few dates at UC and, well, I really fell for her too. Life was perfect for us once the kids came along. House in a nice neighborhood, I was making great money, Tali got to stay home with the kids and go for spa treatments and shopping whenever she wanted."

"But something changed."

"Apparently so. But I didn't have a clue about it until I came home that day when the kids went missing. Tali was so . . . I don't know how to describe it . . . so unconcerned. I asked about the children, and at first she told me they were napping. She poured us glasses of wine and we went to the living room to relax. But Tali didn't really relax. She seemed jittery and hyper-alert, I guess you would say—her eyes darting around, looking at the yard and the woods beyond."

He took a ragged breath. "I asked her what was wrong. You know, I half expected her to tell me she was having an affair or something. When she said the kids had been taken, I was in shock, numb. She convinced me that there would be a ransom call from that man in black. We had money. We could just pay the ransom and everything would go back to normal. I remember practically ripping my hair out for a few hours, waiting for that call. When it didn't come I knew we needed help and I called the police. When they arrested Tali it was my first clue that everything might not be as she'd presented it. But what could I do? I'd bought into the story all the way. She was so helpless in the face of all that drama. She needed me to support her." His voice broke a little.

"And I suppose her mother and sisters also came to her aid?"

"Immediately. Scout lived only a few blocks from us. She was so similar to Tali—they had nearly the same reactions to all the events that unfolded during that time. Roxanne and Babe flew up from Santa Fe as soon as it became apparent that Tali was being grilled by the police. Roxanne even hired the lawyer who defended her—on my dime, of course. I don't quite know how to describe the frenzy, the way I got caught up in the whole thing."

I jotted notes while he talked. "So you made it through the trial, stood by her side. But then you two split right away afterward."

"As the evidence came out in court I began to see Tali the way the police did, how obvious it was that she was guilty. She would turn around and smile at me once in awhile, and it was all I could do not to scream and call her names and demand to know where the kids were. That was the hardest part, never knowing what really happened to my children. I—" His words broke off and I realized he'd set the phone down for a minute.

When he came back I tried to make my voice as soothing as possible. "It must have been horrible, Boyd. I understand." The guilt he must feel had to be oppressive.

"It was bizarre. When we walked out of that courtroom, Tali a free woman, I felt like I was made of ice. Like I was dead inside. Like my limbs would barely move. She hung onto my arm and kept looking up at me with the same adoration she'd shown when we dated. She actually thought we would simply drive home and resume our lives. I knew if I ever had her alone I would probably kill her."

"What did you do?"

"I put her in a cab and gave the driver our address. While she'd been in custody I'd already moved my things out of the house. I'd listed the place with a real estate agent. When her cab drove away I went to the hotel where I'd been staying. I didn't give a damn what happened to her."

"And then?"

"She found me and started calling at all hours. Begging me to come back, swearing she was innocent. Part of me wanted to believe her, but I'd seen the look in her eyes. She was glad the kids were gone, plain and simple. I told her we would never go back to being the honeymooners we'd once been. Told her to get on with her life; I was filing for divorce. She started coming to my hotel, pounding on my door, causing scenes in the halls. I hired a couple of security guys to try to keep the place peaceful, and I guess they warned her off.

"In the meantime, I applied for jobs outside the area. With my record for inventing new technology, I had replies practically before my emails went out. I landed the job in California within a week. Took off, never saw Tali again. When the Seattle house sold, the Realtor sent me a check. Pretty soon the divorce lawyer sent me a copy of the decree. I was a little amazed that she signed it without a battle. Whatever my security guys told her must have sunk in. Next thing I heard was when some article appeared in a news story that said she'd skipped out of Washington and no one seemed to know where she was living."

"Chet Flowers seems to think it might be New Mexico," I said.

"I wouldn't be surprised. That's where her family came from, where her mother always lived."

"So, why do you want to find her now?"

"Chet might have told you. Closure. I'm a haunted man, Charlie. I can't sleep, I drink too much, I'm a loser at work. I need to give my kids a proper burial. I need to find them."

Chapter 11

Wow. I hung up the phone with Boyd Donovan's voice filling my head. The poor man. If we couldn't do this for him, I briefly wondered if he might even become suicidal.

Ron came back from his airport run, and he'd brought chicken for lunch. I filled him in with the newest information then checked in with Drake to see how his day was going. He said he was up to his elbows in the turbine engine and suggested that we might meet for dinner at Pedro's later. I put back that second piece of chicken and wiped my hands.

"I better go through some of Chet's gigantic file before I start to make contact with any of the Freizel family," I told Ron.

I carried the monster thing to the window seat at the front of my office, where the southern exposure made a cozy spot to stretch out. For a few minutes, I'll admit it, I dozed. Refreshed, I gave the case file a skimming, picking out the places where Tali and her family members were interviewed.

"So far, everything in these transcripts gels with what Boyd Donovan told me and what we learned from Chet," I told Ron when he peeked into my office to see why I was so quiet. "Boyd was right about Tali sticking to her story. No matter how the detectives asked their questions, she answers in nearly the identical way each time."

"That's usually suspicious in itself," he commented, poking through the candy dish I keep on the bookshelf, looking for his favorite butterscotch pieces.

"Wherever they ask something she doesn't want to answer, she asks for her attorney."

"What about the sister who lived nearby?" he asked. "How does she explain it?"

"The same way Tali did, in nearly identical terms. She makes it sound reasonable that Tali thought there would soon be a ransom call."

"Where was the sister the rest of the day?" he asked through a mouthful of hard candy.

"Scout's movements aren't really brought up very much, other than those parts you just mentioned."

"That might be something to find out when you talk to her."

I agreed. I just hadn't quite figured out what my approach would be. At least Chet Flowers had done a lot of the homework for us. He'd provided addresses and phone numbers for both Babe Freizel and Scout Stiles. Judging by their interviews with the police and what I'd heard about their court testimony, I couldn't very well expect a warm welcome from either of the sisters or their mother if I divulged that I was asking on behalf of Boyd Donovan.

I puzzled over this long enough to watch the shadows lengthen across the scant remains of yesterday's snow on the browned lawn. Which meant there was not time to make the drive to Santa Fe this afternoon. I needed to go in there rested and prepared. Plus, there are only a few things for which I'm willing to miss out on a Pedro's dinner with my husband. This wasn't one of them.

The answer came to me later that night, as I admittedly was struggling a bit with going to bed on a full stomach. To get answers about the events of five years ago from Tali Donovan's family, I needed to make it about them. Not about her.

I woke with a loosely woven plan, happy to see that our normal brilliant blue skies had returned. Any residual snow would soon be gone from the roads and even the icy spots wouldn't probably make it past noon. I set a gentle kiss on Drake's shoulder as I got out of bed.

A slice of leftover pecan pie counted as breakfast, consumed while standing over the kitchen sink with a cup of coffee nearby and one eye on Freckles as she roamed the back yard. The moment she seemed ready to head through the hedge to Elsa's I opened the back door and called her in. It was almost comical to see her abrupt turnaround when she heard the word breakfast.

While the dog wolfed down her kibble, I located a steno pad and small tape recorder. I held up my navy blazer for inspection, deciding it looked sharp enough and clean enough to work for my purposes. Using Drake's computer I designed a fake business card and printed a few copies. I was now Charlotte Langston, freelance writer. A map of Santa

Fe was also a must, so I printed one from a website and I was in the process of poring over it when Drake emerged from the bedroom.

"You're up and at 'em early this morning," he said, sending me that smile that had melted my heart from day one.

"A mission." I'd briefly explained the new case over dinner last night. "I'm going to try the 'fascinated reporter' ruse on the older of Tali Donovan's sisters. Wish me luck."

Freckles looked ready to roar out the door with me and was severely disappointed when I didn't let her come. Drake dropped the word 'cookie' and she immediately switched her loyalty.

I'd counted on finding the interstate less crowded than usual for an early morning weekday. Under normal circumstances there's a lot of commuter traffic heading toward Santa Fe on a work day. But this being Christmas week I'd hoped many offices would be closed or people taking extra days off, and I figured many post-holiday shoppers would wait until a little later in the day. That was my hope. I was only moderately disappointed.

There was another reason for my timing. According to Chet's notes, Roxanne Freizel worked at one of the big box retail stores, which pretty well guaranteed she would have to work today. Babe, the eldest daughter who lived with mom, was (still, I hoped) between jobs and would likely be at home if I arrived early enough. The trick was catching that magic timeframe—after mom left and before Babe went anywhere. I roared up La Bajada Hill on I-25 and took the 599 exit, which I'd plotted on my map as the most direct route.

I was creeping along Calle Encino in my Jeep, looking

at house numbers, when I spotted a woman in her sixties walking out the front door of a single-story flat-roofed house that was stuccoed in one of the obligatory brown tones allowed in Santa Fe. She gave me a brief stare and I cruised on past while she got into a Honda sedan. She put the little car in gear nearly the moment it started, and she backed out with hardly a glance. My dashboard clock said it was 8:53 so obviously she was running a little late.

I pulled to the curb two doors up from the place she'd just left. Sure enough, that house was number 1620 and the woman must have been Roxanne Freizel. I wished that I'd had a better opportunity to get some details about her. Oh well. For today, my quarry was Babe. I pressed the doorbell and the door immediately swung open.

"Oh!" The woman standing there was clearly startled. "I thought Mother— Never mind."

Babe was an older version of Tali's mug shot. Disheveled, wearing a baggy pair of sweats with a dribble of something over one boob, no makeup and dark brown hair that had clearly been slept on.

"Hi!" I said as brightly as I could. "Babe Freizel?"

She nodded and her eyes narrowed suspiciously. "What are you selling? We got this sign." She pointed downward to a little orange thing that said No Soliciting.

"Trust me, I'm not soliciting." I squared my shoulders. "I'm doing a freelance article for *Cosmo*."

Cosmo? *Really, Charlie, that's the best you could do?* I chided myself.

"And, um, we're going to run a story next month on the fifth anniversary of your sister's trial."

She started to close the door and I edged in closer.

"Wait! It's not the standard piece about the case or any

of that. My editor wants the focus to be on family members who stick by their loved ones through the very worst of times. We're looking for those unsung heroes . . ." I kept making it up as fast as I could. ". . . those brothers and sisters—well, it has to be sisters, since this is *Cosmo*—who gave up *so* much to help a family member."

The door relaxed inward a tad.

"I read through a bunch of the articles about the trial. Background, you know. And it just seemed to me that you and your sisters and your mom . . . well, you just fit our ideal family for the slant of the piece I want to do. Do you suppose I could come in and talk with you for a few minutes? I mean, it would be a real interview, and I even brought my little tape recorder to be sure I get the quotes right."

There were so many holes in my story, starting with the idea that a major magazine would hire *me*, or that they could possibly assign an article on a month's notice. But apparently Babe didn't know any better. She opened the door, surreptitiously running her fingers through her hair as I passed her.

"Look, if there's gonna be pictures—" she started to say.

I held up a hand. "Not to worry. The editor will send a photographer separately and you'll have plenty of notice."

I felt a moment's twinge of guilt for the lie as we took seats on a beaten down brown sofa. The rest of the room was furnished in similar bargain-store stuff that holds its shape until the six months of interest-free payments have been made. The color theme leaned toward dirt tones with a two-foot Christmas tree atop a TV tray and an oversized photograph of a mountain and lake above the couch, to add sparkle and fun.

Babe's excitement at being featured in a national magazine grew as I led with a few questions that I thought a journalist might ask—how had the trial impacted her personally, how had her life changed in the past five years. Not an easy acting job for someone whose only real training came in accounting and taxes.

I scribbled away at my notepad, feigning fascination each time Babe mentioned her own role. My only true goal here was to gain her trust so she might give me the information we needed, but I felt obligated to wade through a lot of other useless stuff before I could get there.

"You must be a very close family," I said after she'd mentioned her mother for the first time. A little catch came into my voice, just to let her know how special I thought that was.

Babe shifted in her seat. Was I starting to see cracks in the solidarity?

"Mother and I have done our best. Scout and Tali were always a little bit in their own little world, being so much younger and all. When I graduated high school they were still in elementary. My first marriage ended by the time they met their husbands."

"And you stayed here in New Mexico when they both moved to the Seattle area?"

"That's right."

"How did you feel when your youngest sister was arrested?" That stupid appeal to the emotions which reporters invariably ask right after a tragedy. How do they *think* people feel? But if I were to keep up this charade, it seemed the thing to say.

She came back with the usual—shocked, stunned, couldn't believe it. What had I expected? It was pretty much the same thing they'd all said publicly for years.

"I imagine it's a hard thing for everyone to get over, even after all these years."

"Mother has pushed it under the carpet. The strain was too much for her. She doesn't speak to Tali at all. In fact, we don't even know where she is now."

Interesting, if it was true.

"And Scout? Is she still close to Tali?"

"Scout lives in Albuquerque and I imagine they communicate. I talk to her a couple times a month but we stay away from that subject. You know, it's nothing major. We've just gone different directions in life."

"I see." I pursed my mouth for a few seconds then leaned toward her. "I'd like to talk to her—Scout. Even though I can see that the focus of my article is going to be about you . . . I'm thinking a little additional background, a brief other viewpoint. You understand."

The poor ugly-duckling sister chewed at her lip a moment, not really wanting to share the limelight with her younger sister. I almost felt bad about deceiving her this way.

"She lives on the west side. It's a little cul-de-sac street, I can't think of the name . . . I'll have to get my address book to give you the exact street number." She got up and went through an archway that led to a hall.

I already had this information, but since she'd offered . . . She might relent and give up Tali too, for all I knew. I fidgeted, ready to get going.

Babe came back with a small paper book, the kind of

thing they used to hand out for free in stationery stores. It had little tabs with the letters of the alphabet and she thumbed down and opened the book.

"Here's Scout," she said.

I jotted down the address she read off. I eyed the book when she set it on the coffee table and resumed her seat.

"Um, can you think of anything else you might add to the story?" I asked. "Take a moment, if you'd like."

Babe's eyes stared toward the ceiling, thinking. I started a fit of coughing.

"Sorry," I choked. "Could I trouble you for a glass of water?"

"Oh, sure." She got up and headed for the kitchen. The second she was out of my sight, I grabbed up the address book. The sound of glassware in a cupboard, followed by the gush of running water. I quickly open the book to the D's. No entry for Donovan. Nothing under T for Tali either. And no Tali listed under F, in case she'd taken back her maiden name. The tap stopped running and footsteps were coming closer. I didn't have the luxury of paging through the whole thing, so I coughed a couple more times for good measure and set the book back exactly as I'd found it, seconds before Babe walked back into the room.

"Thank you so much," I said after a few gulps of the water. "Gosh, don't you just hate when that happens."

She smiled at me and accepted the glass when I handed it back.

Since she seemed to have forgotten that I'd asked for her final thoughts for the article, I used the space of silence to thank her and get myself out of there.

Chapter 12

I pondered the information I'd gotten from Babe Freizel as I drove back to Albuquerque. Basically, nothing concrete about Tali, although I found it interesting that the mother and older sister apparently had broken ranks with the troubled younger one. I would have to pass that along to Chet Flowers. Under pressure, in the event that more charges were brought someday against Tali, these two might turn out to be the cracks in the foundation, the ones who could burst the family solidarity wide open.

On the other hand, most of Babe's story could be pure hokum. These people had dealt with the media in droves and they might be experts at pulling the chain of any reporter who showed up. She might be on the phone with Scout right now, warning her. I could only hope that she'd not realized that my story was pure hokum too.

As I approached Albuquerque I took the Bernalillo exit toward the little suburb town of Rio Rancho and made my way in the general direction Babe had described. At a mall, I pulled into the parking lot and consulted my map.

Scout's house should be about ten minutes away. Would she be home this time of day? Only one way to find out without tipping her off in advance.

I parked in front of the house, a modest ranch with white siding and black shutters that was surrounded by spiky, winter-bare deciduous trees. No car in the drive, no response to the bell. The cul-de-sac wasn't exactly a place to spy from and if her sister had indeed warned her about my arrival, Scout Stiles could easily outwait me. I made the loop and pulled to the curb on the connecting street where I could see her house and hope to go unnoticed when she came back. My dashboard clock reminded me that it was after eleven. Why hadn't I thought to grab lunch first? I could be sitting here eating a burger.

Even a yummy bag of potato chips would be better than nothing. I searched the glove box and the little compartment on the console. Two minutes had passed. In desperation I twisted around to the back seat and rummaged for anything that might have been left over. A foolish mission. The dog often rode back there and any edible scrap had long since been polished off by her sharp little incisors. Another minute had passed.

I debated leaving and coming back. Where had I seen the nearest food places? Back near the mall. I really didn't want to be gone a half hour, but what if Scout worked until five, or even later? A girl could starve to death.

I drummed my nails on the steering wheel. I hate surveillance and this is why I always weasel out and make

Ron do it. My mind began to play various scenarios. What if I left and Scout came home, got her car into the garage and I sat out here until the middle of the night, freezing to death and not realizing she was within arm's length?

Geez, Charlie, get a grip. I knew it was the hunger talking. My high-sugar breakfast this morning had long ago digested and now my head felt fuzzy.

"Just go get some food and come back, dummy," I said to myself in the empty Jeep.

My alter-self answered with a practical plan and I decided to follow it. There was some kind of flyer lying in the gutter a few feet ahead of me. I picked it up and walked up to the Stiles house again. Rolling the page as if it were fresh and new, I stuck it between the doorknob and jamb. If anyone came home while I was gone they would remove the flyer. When I got back I would know. Ta-da.

Just to be on the safe side, I didn't drive all the way back to the cluster of fast food places by the mall. A convenience store closer by provided me with a whole bag of trouble—three flavors of chips, two packets of cookies and a couple of those pastries that have so much fake stuff in them that they leave a waxy sheen on the roof of your mouth. And to feel virtuous about all of that, I picked up a ham sandwich with a current date on it and two bottles of juice. If this didn't get me through until my quarry came home, I would just have to repeat the whole scenario tomorrow. That thought alone renewed my determination.

Back in the neighborhood I parked in a somewhat different spot, in case someone had seen me before. Who was I kidding? It was suspicious behavior no matter how I did it, and if the police showed up I couldn't be terribly shocked.

Luckily, Scout came before the police did.

A red Honda driven by a female with short brown hair pulled into her driveway and the garage door rose. In went the Honda and down went the door. She must have entered the house through a connecting door. So much for my plan with the flyer. I set my half-eaten sandwich aside and rinsed my mouth with juice, then chewed up a breath mint while I pulled into the cul-de-sac and stopped smack in front of her house. At the door I wadded up the flyer and tossed it into her flowerbed.

"Yes?" she said when she answered the door.

"Scout Stiles?"

"What are you selling?"

Okay, all the Freizel women were suspicious of sales people, but at least Babe hadn't given her the heads-up about my visit. I went into the freelance journalist bit.

Scout gave me a sharp stare. She wasn't going to be as trusting or as easily flattered as her sister. I dug into the side pocket of my purse and handed her one of the cards I'd made up. Since it had nothing but my formal name, my cell number and "Freelance Writer" on it, I was amazed she asked no further questions.

"An article about Tali's case?" she asked.

"For the fifth anniversary of her being found innocent." That seemed to be better wording than what I was really after. "I've already interviewed your sister Babe, and just wanted to fill in a few details. May I come in?"

She wasn't a hundred percent keen on it, but did step aside for me to enter. Her taste in décor was considerably more refined than her sister's and I commented on how nice her home was. She warmed a tad.

I started with soft questions that weren't really phrased

as such. "I feel lucky that I caught you at home today. My deadline for the piece is day after tomorrow."

She let go with, "My boss gave us a long weekend. Real estate is slow around the holidays."

"You're a Realtor, then?"

"Administrative assistant. I fill out forms and keep the listing files organized."

I nodded, as if that meant something to me. Then I proceeded with the same basic questions I'd posed to Babe. In case they compared notes about my visits.

"So, for the article," I said as things began winding down. "Do you suppose there's any way Tali would speak with me? I know it's a big favor, but it would make the whole piece feel so much more complete."

She gave me a look that said she knew this was what I'd come for all along. "My younger sister doesn't grant interviews. She has a new life now and she wants nothing to do with all the painful business of that time."

"Has she remarried?" I asked.

No response.

"You know, I don't blame her a bit for hiding out. This whole thing must have been incredibly difficult. Losing her kids, then her husband, having to move from her home . . ."

With each thing I listed, I watched for some sign on Scout's face that I'd guessed the key ingredient, but she remained impassive.

"You do stay in touch with her, don't you? Babe seemed to think so."

"I can't tell you anything," she said, finally.

I had struck a chord with that part. She knew exactly where Tali was. She just wasn't going to tell me. I thanked her as graciously as I could and reminded her that she had my card. She could call me if she thought of anything to add. She walked me to the door, a little forcefully, I have to say.

"You should talk to Boyd Donovan," she said as we stood with the door between us. "He left us all where we are now. *He*'s the one who left Tali. *He* stopped paying her attorney fees and left Mother with a huge bill. It's why she and Babe live in that *shack*. She hasn't even paid off all the bills *yet*. His *goons* scared Tali off. She was so afraid after that, she moved away where she couldn't be found. Don't go blaming *any* of this on Tali or our family. Boyd's the one who set up this whole situation."

Her voice had risen with each statement.

"The *whole* situation?" I said quietly. "Do you mean to tell me that he had something to do with the children's disappearance?"

She backed down. "He abandoned my sister when she needed him most."

It seemed to me that he'd stuck with her extraordinarily well, considering. But I didn't say it. I might need more information from Scout at some point. I made a few sympathetic noises and walked out to my Jeep. I would have given anything to be a mouse in the corner of that house right now because I would take bets that she called Tali the second she closed the door behind me.

By the time I got down to my part of town I was feeling twitchy. I dropped off my notes and recorder at the office, sending a quick email out to Chet Flowers to let him know that I'd spoken with both sisters but had not yet located Tali, then I headed home.

Freckles whimpered in her crate and I felt a stab of guilt that she'd been in there so many hours. But once she had my attention she seemed perfectly happy to zip around the house a couple of times. When I picked up her leash and said "Park" she led me to the front door. We both restrained ourselves on the trip. She would have been thrilled to race all the way to the park and I could have used a good jog myself, but I knew we'd better start concentrating on some leash skills before we had a full-grown dog that we couldn't control. I tightened my grip and was pleased that she stayed by my side and responded to my commands. We would have to show off for Drake when he got home.

Inside the walled park I let Freckles off the leash and she roared back and forth, her ears flopping and tongue lolling. She seemed so happy it made me want to do the same. I heard a laugh and looked across the way to see that Katie Brewster had come from the other entrance. I waved at her and started walking toward her.

"Hey, where's the pink?" I asked when I got close enough to really get a look at her. The hair was now a much more sedate shade of burgundy.

She scuffed a toe against the brown grass. "My dad said I could come to work with him if I, you know, toned down the hair and stuff."

Now I saw that all the eyebrow rings were gone.

"Hey, I like the new look," I said.

"Yeah, well, I'm not sure he'll go for the red either. He hasn't seen it yet."

"I bet he'll be impressed." I held up the ball I'd brought along for Freckles. "You want to throw this for her?"

I watched Katie give it a pretty good throw and Freckles return it within a minute. Katie laughed and threw it again. The transformation from Goth to teen girl was amazing once you took away the shock-value getup. With any luck,

Jerry's little girl would settle down and become a young woman who would find her way just fine. She raced the dog to the end of the park and back, arriving at my side panting. Katie, not the dog.

"So, how's your little brother doing?" I asked while she sat on one of the swings and got her breath back.

"Oh, fine. He's, like, running all over the place again and doesn't act like it hurts him much."

"Good." She met my gaze. "And you? Christmas Eve was a little rough. You doing better now?"

"Yeah." One shoulder came up as she said it, faking a casualness that I sensed wasn't really there. Then she grinned. "Especially since my dad said he'd give me a job."

That was the whole thing, right there. She just needed that connection with her father, the thing she feared was missing with Felina and the new baby in the picture.

Freckles pawed at me and I glanced at my watch. "It's her dinner time," I told Katie. "I better get home and finish up some chores too. Glad to hear about the job."

She jumped off the swing to give Freckles a hug. Then she ran off in the direction from which she'd come.

Drake's pickup truck was in the driveway when I arrived home. He'd plugged in the Christmas lights and started the gas logs in the fireplace and was standing in front of the refrigerator contemplating the contents.

"Hey you," I said, snaking an arm around his waist.

"More turkey dinner okay with you?" he asked.

I envisioned little heaps of all the trimmings, dabbed onto dinner plates and reheated in the microwave, but he pulled out a skillet and some other things. By the time I'd hung up my jacket, fed the dog and taken a deep breath he had come up with something elegant involving puff pastry and a fabulous looking saucy mixture that smelled wonderful. How lucky can a girl get?

We ate at the dining table, enjoying the fire and the lights and the companionship. I tried to put the day's work behind me but the interviews with Scout and Babe kept running through my head. Tali Donovan was somewhere in New Mexico. I could feel it.

Chapter 13

Ron showed up at the office wearing a new sweater and a rueful grin. "No comments," he warned.

I actually thought it was kind of cute, a grown man wearing a snowman on his chest, and I said so.

He growled at me before turning to pour himself a cup of coffee. "Joey picked it out. Don't expect to see it a lot when the boys aren't staying at our house."

His ex still had the majority of time with the kids, but since Ron had moved into Victoria's house, which was a dream in comparison to the dumpy apartment he'd been in since the divorce, he found that the kids actually enjoyed staying with him. I suspected it was partly because Vic was willing to make them pancakes every day of the week. However, since their school was halfway across town from their dad's new digs, they would go back to mom when

Christmas break was over. He'd be reprieved from wearing the snowman sweater until next holiday season—probably.

He carried his coffee upstairs to his office and the next time I passed his door he said he was going back out to the Department of Labor to see what information he could wheedle out of someone, using Tali Donovan's social security number. The snowman lay neatly folded on the visitor chair across from his desk.

"Don't you need your little pal there to help woo your way into the hearts of those bureaucrats?" I grinned at him and then had to dodge a ball of paper he aimed my direction.

"Listen, Frosty, don't blame me!"

The whole thing threatened to disintegrate into the kind of battle we had back when I was six and he was twelve. I ducked into my office and locked the door until I heard him leave. After he'd driven away I took the bright red sweater and draped it over the back of his chair so the snowman faced anyone who walked in. It really was kind of cute.

Okay, back to business. I called Chet Flowers and gave him all the info I'd gotten from the interviews with the Freizel sisters yesterday. None of the facts were new to him but he was interested in my impressions of their lifestyles and demeanor. I told him about Scout's little rant there at the end.

"She was absolutely serious in placing blame on Boyd Donovan. I think she has repeated this stuff to herself so often over the years that she really believes it."

"If she's in touch with Tali it's probably the two of them, feeding off each other's anger and resentment."

That made a lot of sense.

"I'd like to talk to him again. It would be nice if it

could be in person. You understand that, being able to see a person's face when you're talking to him."

"Absolutely. We'll see what we can set up. Look, Charlie, I've got a list of the jurors from the trial. I understand one of them has since moved to New Mexico too, and I want to see if we can track down an address. If you can locate her for me I want to come out and conduct an interview."

"I could do the interview if you'd like." After all, Charlotte Langston, girl reporter for *Cosmo*, was having a pretty good run so far.

"Let me think about that part of it."

I felt a little testy for a minute but I understood. He'd worked the case for a very long time. He wanted and needed to be in on the hunt and to be there for the resolution of this thing.

Chet gave me the name of the female juror he wanted us to track down and I put the note on Ron's desk in a spot where I hoped it wouldn't become lost in the perpetual clutter.

Meanwhile, I still had my real job to do around here. People who haven't done accounting work don't ever realize there are at least a thousand things to be done at the end of the tax year. December thirty-first isn't just New Year's Eve to us. Ron calls me obsessive.

Lost in my little world of accounts receivable and payable, trying to extract money from clients who'd let their bills fall behind, I didn't realize that nearly three hours had passed when Ron showed up again. His heavy footfalls on the stairs were followed by an exclamation and sputter when he spotted his snowman sweater draped over his chair.

"Cute, Charlie. Real cute." But at least he didn't sound as if he was going to hit me.

He appeared in front of my desk a minute later.

"If Tali Donovan is working in this state, she's not doing it under her own name or social security number," he said. "I've searched it every which way, including her maiden name."

"So, either she's unemployed . . ."

"And has been since she got here."

"Or she has a new identity?"

"Which isn't all that easy to do secretly. A person can have her name legally changed, but it involves publicly posting the intention and having it approved by the court. I didn't find that. And even if she did, her social security number would follow her, only with the new name on it. Most people don't want to lose their accrued benefits so they make sure to keep that sort of paperwork in order."

I drummed my pen against the desk. "Maybe she did it back in Washington state?"

"Possible. I'll ask Chet if he's already checked. I would imagine he has, or one of those reporters who were after her so relentlessly would have come up with that and made it public."

"What if she did it in another state? Before she ever came here?"

He sighed. "We might be able to find out, but it'll take a lot more legwork. Let's try looking for the simplest answers first."

Since that fit precisely with my philosophy I concurred wholeheartedly and then shooed him out so I could finish my computer entries. Across the hall I could hear Ron's voice as he made a series of phone calls. Since this is the normal office routine ninety percent of the time, I usually tune out most of it. When my intercom buzzed I practically jumped out of my chair. Ron almost never uses it.

"Get on line one," he said. "It's Chet Flowers. He wants to see if we can go to California."

I picked up, really hoping he meant next week.

"Ron and I have been talking," Chet began as soon as I said hello. "I think meeting Boyd Donovan face to face would be good. Let him see the whole investigation team in action, pass along your findings to him. I can get you seats on the four o'clock, which puts you into San Diego before five. Times zones work in your favor. I'll be flying in from Seattle and meet you at the airport."

I so badly wanted to plead any excuse I could think of—I was busy, I didn't want to travel right now . . . Then Scout Stiles's words ran through my head. *Ask Boyd Donovan. The whole thing is his fault.* I needed to know. And the best way to read his answers would be face to face. I looked down at my stack of invoices, which really had shrunk. Plus, there was that teddy-bear quality in Chet's voice.

"Okay. We'll be there."

"I'll email you the flight confirmation."

It came through a few minutes later, while Ron and I discussed logistics. Chet had told him he would book a return flight the next morning, which meant hotel rooms and a little overnight gear.

"This last minute planning must be costing a fortune," I said.

He shrugged. "They're willing to pay it, I guess."

I couldn't figure out why this had suddenly become such a priority for Boyd Donovan, but maybe the interview would answer that. Meanwhile, Ron and I decided to head our separate ways, pack a little bag and meet up at the airport.

A toothbrush and clean undies don't take up a whole lot of space. I ended up with an oversized purse to manage my needs, while Ron seemed to have brought the chunkiest bag legally considered a carry-on. The flight was short and uneventful, the best kind, and we emerged from the jet way to see Chet Flowers waiting in the crowd. We joined the flow toward the exit and he said he had a rental car already reserved.

Chet drove the streets with familiarity and I actually enjoyed riding along in the back seat and letting him deal with the traffic.

"I called ahead to tell Boyd we were coming," he said. "I figured we chat a bit, grab some dinner, check into our hotel. If anyone thinks of any new questions we have a little time in the morning to meet with him again if we need to."

We pulled up in front of an apartment building that combined modern urban professional with a few touches of the Mexican influences so common in San Diego. Red tile mini-roofs over each balcony, Saltillo flooring in the lobby. Chet punched the elevator button to take us to the fourth floor.

The only images I had in my head of Boyd Donovan were from the era of the trial. When he answered the door in jeans and a faded rock-band T-shirt, I saw that time had not been kind to the man. There was a slump to his shoulders that had not been there before, and creases had begun to form along the sides of his mouth. A few strands of gray touched his brown hair. Mainly, his grief showed in his heavy-lidded eyes. I got the sense that he never fully brightened up anymore.

He ushered us into a bachelor apartment. He'd made a hasty effort to clean up before we came; blank circles showed in the dust on the coffee table where he must have picked up cups or cans and plates. The place had the odor of old pizza.

"Sorry, the maid comes on Monday," he said. I didn't think he meant it as a joke.

"It's okay," said Chet. The retired cop seemed to have a knack for setting the mood, making his subject comfortable when that was called for. I could well imagine that he could make an interviewee rather uncomfortable when that suited his purposes.

"We wanted to bring you up to speed, give you the chance to meet Ron and Charlie of RJP Investigations. As I mentioned on the phone they're handling the leads we've gotten in New Mexico."

"We talked on the phone," I said, stepping forward to shake his hand.

Boyd seemed a little at a loss for the social niceties of entertaining guests.

"Why don't we talk over an early dinner?" I suggested.

"Good idea," Boyd said, clearly relieved at not having to entertain us at home.

We all rode the elevator back down.

"There's a little place where the food is pretty good, a sports bar a few blocks away. Is everyone up for the walk?"

Ron looked a little glum but then he always looks that way whenever exercise is the subject. I sent him a visual warning and he fell into step.

Padres baseball insignia in blue and white plastered the innards of the little mission-style establishment. We'd hit the off-season, with spring training still more than a month away, so the fans were missing. At the moment the crowd consisted of a few tables of retirees who were clearly there for the happy hour specials on drinks and the free nibbles.

"The burgers are great," Boyd said. "Sandwiches are good and the Mexican food is real tasty."

One thing you learn, coming from New Mexico, is not to count too heavily on Mexican food anywhere else. Some of it isn't bad, some is downright awful. None of it is like home. I ordered a chicken sandwich and noticed that Ron got the Big-Padre Burger which featured bacon, cheese and grilled onions, in addition to everything I would normally think of to put on a burger. He would never do this if Victoria was with him. I mouthed "I'm telling" in my best little-sister sass. Before he could kick me under the table I turned toward the others.

Our drinks arrived but no one offered a toast. It didn't seem that happy an occasion.

"We've contacted Tali's family," Chet said, "in hopes that we can find out where she is." He explained his strategy.

"Scout, in particular, seems very bitter toward you," I told Boyd. "She feels that you left them stuck with a lot of the legal bills."

"Well, that would only be right, wouldn't it? Their statements helped clear her. They let her get away with murder. Shouldn't they pay?"

He downed his beer and signaled for another. "Funny, Scout used to be very friendly toward me. We socialized with them all the time. Maybe that was the problem. Tali grew closer to her sister and farther from *our* family."

The second beer arrived and he put about a third of it away. I caught Chet's glance.

"You know, when Tali and I first started dating she was so attentive, so happy. We used to go to this park. Thick woods all around, lots of private places and we'd take a blanket and well . . . things got hot. She used to joke that this one statue thing, kind of an obelisk, reminded her of me in a certain way."

I think I blushed a little, even though Boyd didn't.

"Even after we got married we were so happy. Deni was born and that little girl took our hearts away. We could hardly wait to have Ethan because the two kids made our family complete." His lip started to tremble and his eyes filled with moisture.

"I'm sorry," I said. "This is really difficult for you."

He swallowed hard and blinked. His face went rigid. "I never had a clue that she felt any differently. Those kids were my world. I believed they were her world too. I kept believing it until I saw her in court. That bitch deserved a whole lot worse than she got."

I felt the air go out of the room. His hatred was palpable and in that moment I wondered if Tali's sisters could be right. Maybe they really didn't know where she was because Boyd had done away with her.

Chapter 14

Our food arrived and I had an otherworldly sense that no one else was seeing the same things I was seeing. I rubbed at my temples.

Chet had checked this guy every which way and swore he was the wronged party. I *had* to go with that. And so what if Boyd or his security men *had* caused Tali to vanish? There was still the torture he felt over his kids—not knowing where they were. I nibbled at the edges of my sandwich while the guys talked sports.

"You okay, Charlie?" Ron had obviously forgiven my previous impudence. "It's not like you to leave half your dinner behind."

"Yeah. Fine. I guess I got a headache from the flight." I pushed my plate away. Ron was right—it was unlike me to lose my appetite.

We all walked back to Boyd's apartment building and decided to call it a night. Chet drove us to the hotel he'd chosen near the airport. In one way I didn't think we had learned a whole lot from Boyd Donovan during this trip. In other ways, perhaps we had learned too much.

* * *

In the hotel lobby, I waited while Ron headed for a soda machine in an alcove, but he came back empty-handed.

"I feel like we should touch base with the Flores family while we're in town," he said.

My brother, acquiring social niceties? Was it possible that Victoria was actually civilizing him? He began fiddling with something on his fancy phone and came up with a teensy map.

"We're only about ten minutes from the hospital. I'd bet that Mel and Rosa are there." Just to be sure, he scrolled through some numbers he'd programmed in and connected with one of them. A short conversation later he turned and asked if I wanted to go along.

My head wasn't pounding any less fiercely than before, so I begged off to go to my room and take a few aspirin. It probably really was the plane flight and the fact that I was here in another city, when I'd wakened with completely different plans this morning. After seeing Ron into a cab, I rode the elevator to the tenth floor where I called home and told Drake I was going to bed early.

But sleep was a long time coming.

Boyd's words about Tali kept circulating through my head but I couldn't decide how to process the information. Did he truly hate her—enough to harm her?—or had the booze given him a bit of extra macho swagger this evening? The only way to know would be to track down Tali herself. Meanwhile, our true mission was to locate the children and give Boyd the closure he said he needed so badly. Perhaps then he could put his hatred of Tali aside and get on with his life. And that thought led me right back to the beginning of the relentless circular pattern—how much did he truly hate her?

Eventually, I heard Ron fiddling with the door to his room so I peered around my door and called out to him.

"How did it go?"

He looked subdued. "They're holding together. Rosa can't take her eyes off poor Ivana. She won't last long, I'm afraid. Mel and Rosa have reconciled. It was good that we went to the trouble of finding her. Seeing the three of them together—it felt right."

"Good. I'm glad." Especially glad that he'd ignored my reservations and insisted on taking the case. I told Ron I would see him in the morning.

The TV in my room was on a station that ran old sitcoms, the kind with laugh tracks that won't let you concentrate on anything else. I tuned out my thoughts of Rosa's family and of Boyd Donovan and, after about an hour of being immersed in the corny humor of Mayberry, I was able to switch off the lamp and fall asleep.

Over ham and eggs the next morning Chet informed us that he'd booked himself on the same flight as ours to Albuquerque.

"Remember that I mentioned having a list of the jurors in Tali's case and that one of them has moved to New Mexico? I'd like to get down there and talk with this lady. She was one of the last to come around to the idea of acquitting Tali. You familiar with the town of Belen? That's where she lives."

Ron nodded. It's only about twenty minutes or so from us by freeway.

Chet swabbed up egg yolk with his toast. "Meanwhile, have either of you thought of any other questions for Boyd, while we're in town?"

In the clear light of day my previous concerns seemed perhaps overblown so I didn't mention them. Ron didn't bring up any questions of his own. It seemed that we'd made a rather expensive trip for very little substantial information, but I guess Chet had an unlimited budget on this case. It must be a real luxury for a retired cop, accustomed to working within constant budget constraints, to have someone with money authorizing billable hours. I had to admit that he was certainly being diligent about following up on leads and reporting regularly to his client.

In a way that reminded me of my father, Chet picked up the breakfast tab and walked up to the register to pay it as I gathered my jacket and purse. Within minutes we were back on the road, making our way to the airport.

By noon we were retrieving Ron's car from the parking garage in Albuquerque. Chet Flowers had decided to rent a car for himself so he wouldn't be dependent upon us for rides everywhere. He followed us to our gray and white Victorian headquarters.

My office felt chilly and abandoned even though I'd been away less than twenty-four hours. I checked in with Drake by phone and gave Sally a quick call to see if there was any news on the baby story. Nothing new.

"I'm going to run down to Belen, see if I can catch Mrs. Vine at home," Chet was saying to Ron as I walked into the hall. "Want to come along?"

The phone rang and Ron automatically reached for it. He even remembered to answer "RJP Investigations" rather than his customary "y'hello."

The call seemed as if it would take some time.

"Chet, I could come with you," I said. "There's something I wanted to talk about."

"Let's go." He tilted his head toward the stairs.

I picked up my purse and sent Ron some hand signals to let him know where I'd be. I gave Chet basic directions to get to I-25 southbound toward Belen. He handled the rental comfortably, a hand draped over the wheel, a casual ease to his posture.

"So, what's on your mind?" he said. So much like my father.

I let it out, giving my thoughts and theorizing about the ideas that had run through my head after Boyd Donovan's vehement statements about his ex-wife.

"Bottom line, could he be the reason we can't seem to find Tali now?"

His relaxed demeanor didn't change a bit. "Well, it doesn't seem too likely that he would hire me to bring up all this past history if he'd caused her disappearance, does it?"

When he put it that way . . .

"I mean, there are guys who would. I've run across criminals in my career who love daring the police to catch them. They invariably think they're so smart, that they've out-thought us at every turn, that they've committed the perfect crime and no dumb cop is going to ever see through them. I *love* taking down those guys." He glanced over at me. "But Boyd Donovan? Not the type. In my professional opinion."

He made a good point.

"But if you still think he's involved, present your case. I'm willing to hear all arguments, either way."

"Mainly, it was his vehemence about Tali and her family, how they all deserved to pay. And Boyd's profound disappointment and shock at discovering Tali didn't seem to love the children the way he did. But, you're right. It would be stupid of him to bring in the very officer who worked this case in the first place, to try to pull something over on you. What would be his reason?"

"To find out what I know. To see if there were leads on the whereabouts of the kids that we never released on the first go-round. To find out what the rest of Tali's family knows."

I stared at him. "So, are you telling me that you think he *might* be playing around with you?"

He chuckled. "I'm saying that anybody can have a motive. You can never entirely figure out how people's minds work. Even the best of the criminal profilers sometimes get that wrong. But Boyd Donovan? I think the man is too smart to screw around with me. I think his motive is exactly what he says it is. The fate of his kids has been a big unanswered question in his life for more than five years now. He wants peace of mind."

"That makes sense."

"Peace of mind before he really does go off the deep end."

He just had to throw in that little bit of doubt for me, didn't he? I gave him a rueful grin.

We exited the freeway and I read off the directions he'd written out from his study of the map. In ten minutes we were pulling up in front of a small house with cream-

colored stucco and a brown pitched roof. A fluffy wreath
of fake evergreens hung at the front door. Real evergreens
flanked the sidewalk, junipers that had been trimmed with
precision. Some brave pansies struggled to stay upright.
The snow a few days ago had pretty well tromped them
down. A tan Buick sat in the driveway and I could see lights
on inside.

Chet rang the doorbell and as quickly as the door
opened, I knew the tiny woman had been watching us. She
came about to my shoulder, had a head full of springy gray
curls, and wore red polyester slacks and a sweatshirt with a
big candy cane on the front.

"Mrs. Vine?" he asked. "I'm Ch—"

"I recognize you," she said with an impish grin. "Wait—
just give me a second. I'll remember."

His mouth started to open.

"I'll get it," she said. "You are . . . you . . . Seattle. I was
in a crowded place . . ."

She suddenly shivered. "Well, darn it, it's cold out here.
You better just tell me."

"Chester Flowers, Seattle PD, retired."

"That trial! Tali Donovan." Her whole face lit up. "I was
on the jury for that trial, you know."

He nodded. "Anna Vine."

The head of gray curls bobbed merrily. "Yes! That's me.
And I'll bet that's why you all are here. Well, come on in.
You're letting all the warm air out."

Chet introduced me and we stepped into a room that
could do with less warm air. No one had to ask me to take
off my coat. I draped it over a chair as she invited us into
a living room filled with tinsel and Styrofoam snowmen. It
was all they could do to keep from melting. It must have

been close to ninety in there.

"I was just having myself a little toddy," Anna Vine said. "Could I make one for you all?"

The steaming beverage beside her recliner didn't hold much appeal for me. When Chet asked for water I seconded the request. We exchanged a little smile while Mrs. Vine bustled away to an adjoining kitchen.

"It won't take me a minute," she called out. "You just make yourselves at home."

We accepted juice glasses with cartoon patterns on them that must have been older than I, each filled with tap water and a single ice cube.

"You're that policeman who got up on the stand in the trial," she said as she handed Chet his glass. "That's really something, that you would be here to see me now."

"I'm retired now," he said after his first sip. "Sometimes it's what we old cops do, go back and look up cases that we worked in the past."

"Well, with that one I'm not surprised. That was quite the hoopla afterward. A little scary. Some of the jurors got threatened I heard. I wasn't all that unhappy to move away. Although that wasn't the real reason I came here. You see, I'd gotten pneumonia twice and the doctors said I couldn't handle that humid climate up there any more. And then my daughter got a transfer with her company. She works for this—"

Chet cleared his throat.

"Oh. I guess none of that matters much to you folks, does it?" She took a long draw on her toddy and giggled a little.

We had to catch her somewhere between tales of her personal life and the point when the toddy would be gone.

I wondered if Chet could read those thoughts on my face.

"I'm glad to see that you've settled in here so well," he said. What a diplomat. "Of course, I am mainly curious about the outcome of the trial. You were one of the last holdouts who thought Tali Donovan was guilty, weren't you?"

She studied the ceiling for a few seconds. "The first vote was taken and it was about half and half—guilty or innocent. One man with long hair was very firm in saying we couldn't find her guilty unless we were absolutely sure. Everyone pretty much agreed with that, but the sticky part came in getting them to agree whether that prosecutor lawyer had really proved her guilty. They kept bringing up things that were said, then they'd take another vote. After that first day it was me and one other lady who still thought she'd done it."

"What was the main thing that made you feel that way?" I asked.

"Well. I guess it was her manner. She just had this way about her. I raised four kids—three girls and a boy. And I could always tell when those kids were hiding something. That Tali Donovan was hiding something. I would have bet the farm on it, and I still would today."

"But you couldn't convince the other jurors of that?"

"Every time they voted somebody else had gone over to the not-guilty side. Pretty soon it was only me saying guilty."

"Did you have any reason other than her manner? Was there some part of the evidence that convinced you?"

I could tell that Chet wanted to know what part of his case had broken down. What had been lacking.

"When the neighbors testified about the day it happened. Miz Donovan didn't much seem to care what any of them said, except one. Remember that neighbor who talked about how she heard Tali's little kids playing outside in the yard?"

Chet nodded. He knew it well.

"When that lady first started talking, I watched that Tali Donovan, more than I watched the lady. She—Miz Donovan—looked real nervous when the lady first came up to the stand and they started asking questions of her."

"Really? Can you think specifically what about the woman's testimony made Tali nervous?"

"No. See that's the thing that kept tripping me up. When those other jury folks started to get impatient about how long it was taking . . . I mean, all of us wanted to go home, you know. Well, they kept asking me what specific thing I didn't believe and I just couldn't put it into words. I knew, but I couldn't explain it. I finally got tired of being pestered about it and I knew I wasn't going to change *all* of their minds. So I just gave up and changed my vote." As she spoke she'd picked up the corner of a knitted coverlet and had unconsciously twisted it into a knot.

"That thing—the part you couldn't explain to them? That's been bothering you a long time, hasn't it?" I asked.

Her lip quivered a little. Finally she nodded.

"It's okay," Chet said in a gentle voice. "Tell me about it. Take your time."

"When that lady, the neighbor, started talking Tali Donovan looked pretty nervous. Like extra alert. But as soon as the lady told her story, about how she'd heard the kids playing in the yard, especially when she said what time she heard them, Tali Donovan got this little smile. I only know it because I happened to glance at her right then. This tiny smile. It's the same one kids get when their brother takes the punishment instead of them. You know what I mean?"

"You mean kind of smug?" I'd hung so many crimes on my two brothers when we were little, I knew exactly what she meant.

She nodded vigorously and the curls shook crazily. "Yes. Exactly. Like she'd gotten away with something. She had the very same look on her face when the verdict got announced."

She drained the toddy and her whole body relaxed. I doubt she realized how stiff she'd been in that chair while she was talking to us.

Chet thanked her for the information and she insisted on giving both of us hugs as we left.

"She was right, Charlie," he said once we were underway again. "About that superior look on Tali's face at the reading of the verdict. It was what crucified her in the media."

"But the earlier time, during the neighbor's testimony? No one else must have caught that one."

His jaw twitched. "I can't believe I missed it."

Were his terse words about the neighbor, or about Tali's smile?

Chapter 15

Chet pulled up in front of our office and I got out at the curb.

"I'm going to pull a surprise visit to that sister of Tali's who lives here in town," he said. "I agree with you, I don't think they've had a falling out at all. I'd bet money they are in contact all the time. And at some point, Scout Stiles is going to give away a vital clue. Who knows? I might even happen upon Tali herself, visiting sis at home."

I wished him luck and watched him drive away, a warm feeling settling over me. He was a sharp cop but he was also a kind man. I was glad we'd agreed to help him.

My own thoughts had trailed off in another direction during the ride back to town. Tired of turkey leftovers, I was ready for something entirely different for dinner tonight. I debated between grabbing a pizza or making something fresh at home. After days of potatoes and gravy, meat and sweets, a salad sounded like the right thing. And I knew we didn't have much in the way of fresh greens and veggies at the moment.

After a quick check of my desk I closed up and drove to the market a few blocks from home. Everyone else must have gotten to that same point in the week because the parking lot was pretty full. I snagged a plastic hand basket and headed to the produce aisle.

"Hey, Charlie," a young voice said.

"Well hey, Katie. How's it going?"

She was clutching a bag of candy that must have come from the mark-down basket near the front door. I had bravely resisted those myself. I turned toward the bundles of romaine.

"Katie, huh-uh, no way. Put those back." Felina Brewster came up beside me and she'd obviously spotted the candy immediately.

Katie glared at her stepmother and held her ground.

"Now. I mean it."

The girl slumped away.

"I swear," Felina said with a sigh. "It's a battle all the time. Do you and your husband have kids?"

I said that we didn't and she went on.

"You don't want them. Trust me. It's the hair, then it's those horrid piercings, and she's been threatening to go out and get more tattoos without our permission. I'd search her room for drugs but who knows what awful thing I would catch."

"Really? Last time I talked to her, Katie seemed eager to get her act together so she could work with her dad."

"Oh yeah, like a weekend job at the dealership is going

to be a long-term thing with her. She changes interests as often as I change Adam's diapers."

"How is Adam's arm, by the way?" If I could steer her off the subject of Katie it would probably be better all around.

Felina shrugged. "You know kids. They heal fast. The doctor sees him again next week."

I spotted Katie two aisles away, eyeing the bags of snack mix. I turned toward the tomatoes to divert Felina's line of sight.

"Jerry did invite you and Don to our New Year's Eve party, didn't he?" she asked.

"Drake. Yes, I think he mentioned it."

"Oh, excellent. It should be a good crowd. I love doing a real dress-up party at least once a year. So much fun to get out the bling, don't you think?"

I nodded but felt a little like a deer in the headlights. I could probably find one piece of bling in my entire wardrobe. And that was only if gold hoop earrings counted. Yikes, what was I going to wear to this thing?

Felina sent me a hasty "see ya" and headed toward Katie, apparently to head off the kid from picking up whatever she wanted. I grabbed a few tomatoes, the lettuce and some other things I could throw together for a salad and then searched out the shortest of the checkout lanes.

Drake was home when I got there and said he'd already walked Freckles around the block. I noticed he'd also picked up the dead luminaria sacks that I hadn't even thought about for several days. We stood in the kitchen, washing and chopping the new produce I'd brought home.

"I ran into Felina Brewster at the market. She reminded me that we're invited to their house for New Year's Eve.

Had Jerry told you it was a super-dress-up event?"

He rinsed a cucumber and started paring the skin off it. "He might have. I don't remember what he said about it."

"You are such a guy," I teased. "Don't you know that the first thing a woman needs to know about a party is what to wear?"

He sneaked a kiss onto my neck. "I'm sure whatever you choose will be perfect."

"That was diplomatic." I mentally ran past the contents of my closet, which included one simple black cocktail dress. Without something brilliant to jazz it up, I knew that wasn't going to make Felina's bling list. I would have to go shopping at some point. I felt my inner ogre growling as I attacked the grater with a carrot.

We ate our salads, feeling virtuous, and settled in front of the fire, happy to be home as a family without social commitments for a change. Drake switched on the TV and became engrossed in an aviation program while I continued to fidget over the need to buy a new dress. I was in no mood to go out shopping after the long couple of days I'd had, so I wandered to the desk and browsed online for possible sales. But clothes soon lost their appeal and I found myself rereading the articles about the Donovan case.

Within an hour I felt my eyelids getting heavy. I planted a kiss on top of Drake's head and told him I would see him whenever he came to bed. Fat chance. I was out cold, in minutes. The next time I became aware of anything it was the phone on the nightstand ringing insistently. The room was in complete darkness except for the red numerals on the clock, which said 12:47.

Drake picked up the receiver and sounded remarkably alert when he said hello. Years of practice, I supposed, being ready for a night flight on a moment's notice.

"Charlie?" he said in a half whisper. "You awake?"

I groaned something incoherent.

"It's Ron."

I came awake in a flash and switched on my lamp. Late night calls were not his norm.

"Sorry to wake you guys," Ron said. "I just got a call from the police."

A hundred thoughts flashed through my head, none of them good. One of Ron's kids, our brother Paul in Arizona, Elsa?

"Chet Flowers was in an accident near Santa Fe this evening," Ron said. "He was killed."

I made him repeat it.

"That doesn't make any sense. What happened?" People always ask that, even when it's just been stated. I mumbled something else and sat up.

". . . found our business card and the notes we made on the Donovan case. Ours was the only New Mexico number programmed into his phone so they called me."

I think he gave a few more details but my brain had shut down. Chet. That sweet guy who reminded me of my dad, who'd devoted his retirement years to finding a man's two lost children.

"Nothing we can really do tonight," Ron said. "We'll pick up in the morning. Looks like it's only you and me on the Donovan case now."

I clicked off the call and buried my fingers in my hair, scraping it back from my face. Drake took the phone and replaced it on the cradle on his nightstand. I had to repeat the scraps of information for him. Something about retelling it made it feel more real. Chet really was dead.

"I'll go in the kitchen," I told Drake. "You get your sleep."

"Come back soon."

I doubted I would sleep all night after this but told him I just needed a minute. He rolled over. I pulled on my thickest robe and wormed my feet into my slippers before turning out the light and feeling my way to the door. Freckles snored away in her crate as I edged through the living room. Enough light came through the window in the kitchen for me to find the light switch over the stove top and I used that to fill the kettle and set it on a burner.

Chet. I still couldn't believe it. How does a guy have a long career as a police detective and end up dying so suddenly? Had he hit an icy patch? I'd thought all the roads were clear now. I went through a whole set of possibilities and justifications as to why none of them were true. The kettle began a slow shriek and I pulled it off the stove.

Instant cocoa mix was my go-to comfort food at night. In automatic mode I dumped the contents of a packet into a mug and added the water, stirring absently and watching tiny, hard marshmallows bob on the surface.

The problem with getting four hours' sleep before the phone rang was that it was just enough to keep me going. My mind stayed in overdrive until gray light began to show at the windows. I wondered if Ron was having the same sleep problems.

I padded to the front door where I'd hung my purse on a hook with my coat, pulled out my cell phone and reached for the speed dial number for Ron's cell. When the readout lit up I noticed that I had missed a call the previous evening. I walked back to the kitchen while I listened to it.

"Charlie, Chet Flowers here. Sorry I missed you. Wanted to chat for a minute. I've got some new information and I'm driving up to Santa Fe now to see if I can talk with Roxanne Freizel. I'll be going to the airport early in the morning and I'll try to call you from there."

He sounded so normal, all business. He'd been on the road. On the way to his fate.

I held the phone against my chest. *What* new information? It would have helped us immensely to know. I looked again at the listing of messages and saw that he'd called around seven-thirty last night.

Freckles whimpered in her crate. Now that the room was getting light she expected attention and I let myself become distracted from the earlier problems by getting dressed and attending to her. By eight o'clock when I arrived at the office I'd cleared my head enough to start making plans.

Ron and I would keep working on Chet's leads in the Donovan case, but without the advantage of his knowledge and insights. This wasn't going to be easy.

Ron's car pulled into the parking area behind the building as I was filling the coffee maker at the kitchen sink. He looked more rested than I did, but there was a somber cloud around him.

"Hey," he said.

"Hey." I set the switch on the coffee. "Wow. Can't believe this."

He wagged his head back and forth. "I need to call Boyd Donovan. Make sure he wants us to stay with the case."

I hadn't even considered that, had only assumed we would. But Boyd *was* paying the bills. When I carried two mugs of coffee upstairs a few minutes later, Ron was hanging up the phone.

"We're still on it," he said. He accepted his cup and sipped noisily.

"I want to know what happened to Chet. Specifically." I told him about the message from Chet about his evening drive to Santa Fe.

"Yeah," he agreed. "We'll have to know. I don't like this."

I didn't like it either and was glad he agreed with me.

He picked up the phone and punched numbers from memory. He started the conversation with a request to talk with someone in traffic who might have information about an accident. That led from a dispatcher to someone in Santa Fe who apparently hadn't arrived at work this morning quite awake. A series of frustrating obstacles and I found myself losing patience. I penned a note on a sticky tab and held in it front of his face.

"Good idea," he mouthed quietly. He thanked whoever was on the phone, disconnected and dialed another.

"Taylor," he greeted. A little polite chit-chat but he got to the point quickly.

"I know this isn't your department, Kent, but I could use some help. There was an accident near Santa Fe last night, a guy we knew. We need some details and I need any files he had with him. We were working a case together."

I hadn't specifically thought about the files but it was a good point. My attention wandered but soon Ron had come up with a contact at the State Police.

"I want to see the car," Ron said to whoever was on the line, "and the accident report."

He'd tossed in Kent Taylor's name and it must have been the magical open-sesame because he hung up and turned to me. "We can go up to State Police headquarters this morning and get what we need."

Finally, it felt as though something was happening.

Ron's foot seemed a little heavy on the gas pedal of his Mustang this morning but I didn't mind. The Christmas morning snow had vanished except in small shaded spots and the road was clear and dry. We pulled into the parking lot at the State Police building an hour after we'd left our place.

After being issued Visitor badges we got escorted to the desk of a Sergeant Ramirez, the guy Ron had spoken to on the phone. A short explanation of our role in the current case Chet had been working, signatures on release forms, and Ramirez handed over the familiar battered briefcase and a plastic bag of personal items including Chet's wallet, keys and cellphone.

"We'd like to see the car," Ron reminded him.

"Sure. It's a bit of a walk. They put the impound lot at the far back corner of the property."

I zipped my jacket up a little higher and we set out, through a vast parking lot full of police cruisers and some other official vehicles, past a huge metal maintenance building, and out to a chain link-enclosed lot with barbed wire strands around the top. Beyond the wide gate sat an assortment of cars and trucks, some in perfect condition, others smashed beyond recognition.

"Do you know what the vehicle looks like?" Ramirez asked.

I'd ridden in it yesterday and I still couldn't recall exact details. A generic rental in some light color, maybe white or silver.

He consulted a page he'd brought with him and started down one of the long rows of vehicles. Apparently there was some kind of numbering system that wasn't obvious to the casual visitor. When his pace slowed I pointed to a cream-colored Ford sedan.

"I think that might be it."

He looked at the note again and nodded. "Yeah. It's got the Alamo rental sticker on it. Gotta be the one."

As we approached the passenger side, I noticed the car had a bashed quarter panel on the right rear. Minor. It hadn't even touched the tire. We circled the rear end of the car. Along the left side a long scrape dented both the back passenger's and driver's doors. The windows on that side were broken out. Otherwise, the car seemed undamaged.

"You sure this is the one?" Ron asked. "It doesn't look that bad."

My thought exactly. I'd really expected to see something that had rolled over and was completely mangled.

Ramirez looked at the report. "The officer on scene notes that it was a hit and run. Another driver observed a vehicle swerving out of control, going into the lane of Mr. Flowers's car and hitting the rear. Mr. Flowers held it fairly straight but the force pushed the Ford against the guard railing. That's what caused the damage to the entire left side."

"But—?"

"He notes that the victim's head must have swung outward through his broken window and come in contact with one of the upright metal posts of the guard rail."

I stared at the driver's missing window. There was blood on the door right below it.

"The victim's injuries were to the head, and the man was deceased at the scene. The medical investigator in Albuquerque has the body and will determine official cause of death. Their office can tell you more. All I have is what our officers on scene reported." He put on the sympathetic face he'd been trained to use with families.

As if he'd divined my next question, Ramirez spoke again. "We haven't located any next of kin for Mr. Flowers. That, and Kent Taylor's vouching for you guys, is why we're able to release his personal effects to you."

I circled the car once again. A smear of dark blue paint attested to the collision that had set the whole tragic thing in motion.

"Will you pursue the hit-and-run driver?" I asked Ramirez.

"Of course. But we don't have a lot to go on. The eyewitness's car was too far back to get a plate number. We've got word out to all the body shops, though. The owner lost a headlight so they'll have to get the work done soon. Unless they've got connections with a chop shop or someone's brother's garage operation, we'll get a report on it."

I got the feeling that Ramirez didn't at all discount the under-the-table operations he'd mentioned. A drunk driver who had caused a fatal crash would certainly look for a way to hide the evidence.

The drive home went pretty silently, Ron and I both lost in our thoughts. When we got back to the office he dropped me off, saying he would go down to the Office of the Medical Investigator and see what he could find out. Neither of us expected the results to be different from what we'd learned in Santa Fe, but it never hurt to dot the i's.

Upstairs in my office with a fresh cup of tea at hand, I opened Chet's briefcase and dumped the bag of personal items on my desk. A ring of keys, some coins, a couple of wrapped peppermints, a ballpoint pen and his little spiral notebook where I'd seen him write notes. His wallet held less than a hundred dollars in cash, three credit cards, his police ID with "Retired" imprinted on it, driver's license, an insurance card and a few business cards. None of these seemed related to our case.

Everything in the briefcase was about the Donovan case, from the notes on our conversation with Boyd—hard to believe it was only yesterday—to the visit with the juror Anna Vine. There was a list of all the jurors from the trial. I had a feeling that might come in handy at some point.

What we were missing—those huge gaps in our knowledge of the case—would be files and possible evidence Chet had gathered. And the only way I could think of to get them would be to go to Seattle.

I sighed and snapped the briefcase shut.

Chapter 16

I love the Pacific northwest. I really do. All the green is a palette of freshness for those of us from dry climates. But when that blast of humid December air shot straight through my clothing and flesh and went deeply into my bones I nearly ran right back into the terminal at Sea-Tac so I could beg for a return flight. We're used to clear blue sky and sunshine to go with our winter temps.

Ron caught my panicky look and shook his head. He flagged down a cab and before I knew it we were roaring toward the city, heading for the address on Chet's business card. It turned out that Suite 412 was really Apartment 412 and the building was located in a pleasant area near a park full of huge trees, a place that would have been appealing on a day when the frigid wind didn't threaten to rip your face off.

We used Chet's keys to let ourselves into the lobby and then into his apartment. It was tidy enough, for a bachelor pad. The TV screen was big, the recliner chair looked comfy. Beyond that, what do most guys need, really? Chet had the added comforts of books on shelves, a neatly made bed in the one bedroom, and a desk in the corner that appeared fairly well organized. The fridge held white take-out containers, a bottle of ketchup, a carton of milk. At least there weren't food wrappers or dirty dishes lying about.

I stood in the middle of the tiny kitchen, feeling a little tentative. It was strange being in the home of a man who'd become a friend, knowing that he would never come back there. I felt as if I should at least clean out the fridge and call someone to deal with the furniture and such. But we were here for a purpose—to find Chet's case files and retrieve the information we would need to continue working it. Period.

"I'll take the living room," Ron said, "if you want to get the desk back there in the bedroom."

We had each brought an empty suitcase. I wheeled mine into the adjoining room, sat in Chet's large swivel chair and pulled out the first file. It contained receipts for paid bills. After studying a few of them I realized it could take me days to determine what was personal and what was business. We would get one shot at this and I knew I better grab anything that could be remotely connected. If the personal stuff ended up being someone else's responsibility we could always forward it along. I ended up emptying the two drawers into my suitcase and discovered that the bag was probably going to be over the airline's weight limit.

"How is your search coming along?" I asked Ron. He sat on a stool he'd pulled up to the shelving that held an MP3 player docked to a tiny speaker system. He seemed to be thumbing through a stack of newspapers on one of the bookshelves.

"Just checking to see if any of these papers are relevant to the case," he mumbled.

I noticed that he'd only tossed a couple of small items into his bag. I suggested we divvy up the paperwork between the two suitcases and he nodded absently.

Back in the bedroom I rearranged things more equitably. With the drawers empty I scanned the rest of it. Taking the laptop computer was a no brainer so I unplugged it from the small printer and wound up the power cord. This thing could be a treasure trove.

Small cubbyholes lined one side of the desk and I prowled through them. A calendar caught my eye when I saw that Chet regularly made notes on the little page-a-day sheets. Of similar interest were an address book and two more of those pocket-sized spiral notebooks. There were two checkbooks. Got 'em. Most of this smaller stuff could probably fit into my purse. A photo fell to the floor when I pulled the notebooks from their cubby. Chet, looking much younger with dark hair and his police uniform, stood with his arm around a teenaged girl. From their identical smiles I knew they had to be related. On the back was written in a looping script: *Dad, remember this day? Love, Shayna.*

So there was someone, a next of kin to be found and notified. I left the photo on the desk, making a note to tell someone back at the New Mexico State Police, in case they hadn't located her yet. And I wrote a brief note to Shayna, letting her know where her father's files and computer had gone, promising we would return them as soon as we could.

I glanced at my watch. Our flight would leave in three hours. Just another minute, I decided, to take a peek at the most recent entries in Chet's calendar. I leaned back in the chair and opened it. On the date he'd met us in San Diego, Chet's calendar showed notations for the meetings he'd scheduled. He had the name of Anna Vine, the juror I'd met in Belen, written down. As meticulous as this was, I decided to look ahead.

The edge of a sticky note showed from the page for December 31 and I realized with a start that was tomorrow. *After the holidays*, the note said. Then there were a couple of names. I recognized one as the Donovan's next door neighbor, the one who had testified in court that she heard the children playing in the yard. I remembered Anna Vine's impression of that testimony.

Ron was still hunched over the stack of old newspapers when I went back into the living room. How can a man spend so much time on something so boring?

"I think we better change our flight," I said. "Today is going to be our best chance to see things firsthand and talk with people here." I told him about finding the list of jurors and the impressions Anna Vine had of the neighbor's testimony.

"This will be our one opportunity to visit the Donovan house and to talk with people."

He agreed. In a couple of minutes he'd done some little thing on his fancy phone and told me he'd switched our flight to another one in the morning.

"So, if we're going to make good use of our time here, we better get busy."

He found the number for a rental car agency that would deliver to the apartment. While he arranged that, I went back to the bedroom, organized the bags and zipped them shut. After a little discussion about getting a hotel room we decided we might as well stay in Chet's apartment. Ron offered, only semi-graciously, to take the sofa and leave me the bed, so I located some spare sheets and made it up. It was weird enough sleeping in the bed of a man who'd so recently died, but to be on the sheets he used just a few nights ago . . . no, I couldn't do it.

By the time the rental car arrived I'd found the addresses we needed. The new auto came with a GPS so I programmed our first stop while Ron played with the controls. Within thirty minutes we were cruising past the former Donovan house.

Most of the houses on the block in this upper middle class neighborhood were two-story, the kind with perfect lawns and full-grown trees. In summer I imagined colorful flowers bordering the walks and kids riding bicycles. Now, most of the places were buttoned up against the cold. Lights shone from occasional windows but not at Boyd and Tali Donovan's old place. Although it didn't appear abandoned, there was nothing welcoming about the house either. While other homes sported wreaths on the doors and lighted Christmas trees in windows, this one sat alone and dark.

Come on, Charlie, you're letting your imagination go wild. A house is a house. I consulted Chet's list and directed Ron to pull over at the next house to the east, the neighbor who had testified in court about the kids playing.

I wasn't sure if Chet had talked to this woman in recent times or whether their encounters were cordial or antagonistic. Had she been a friend of Tali's or merely a snoopy neighbor? I chewed my lip for a second, trying to decide my best approach. The freelance journalist ruse had worked pretty well with Tali's sisters, but the Seattle witnesses provided a bunch of unknown factors. By the time we stepped out of the car I'd decided to just go with the truth.

Nelda Richards must have been watching from behind her sheer curtains because she opened the door less than two seconds after we rang the bell. She was taller than I, closer to Ron's six feet if I had to guess, with gray hair pulled into a tight knot at the back of her neck. She wore gray sweats and a purple turtleneck that hung loosely on her thin frame. She greeted us with raised eyebrows, ready to reject whatever religion she was sure we were peddling.

Ron gave the quick explanation—that we were from Albuquerque and had recently begun working with a retired detective who was trying to help Boyd Donovan locate the children.

Nelda shifted her weight from one foot to the other before agreeing to let us come inside to talk. Her face gave away nothing.

"You have a beautiful home," I told her, looking for some common ground.

In truth, the place would never make it into a decorating magazine and Nelda Richards knew it. A television in another room sent bursts of female laughter and enthusiastic chatter our direction. We had interrupted a favorite show and Nelda was impatient to get back to it.

"We're just going over some of the facts in the case," I said. "We don't want to take up much of your time."

"Good. I said what I had to say in court." She didn't offer us seats.

"I know. We were just hoping that maybe something else has come to mind since then. Maybe some little thing you remembered after the trial was all over?"

She gave a slight shake of the head.

I pulled out Chet's little notebook and pretended to consult it. Since a visit to Nelda had been on his calendar for today, there were no notes yet.

"You testified that you heard the Donovan children playing in their back yard that day. It was December, and frankly I've noticed that it's pretty cold outside this time of year. Didn't it seem odd that they stayed out there so long?"

"I didn't think about it. I can't see over the fence between the two properties. Plus, there are tall shrubs between us. I assumed the children would be wearing warm clothing. But I couldn't actually see them."

"How long would you say they were out there?"

Her mouth pursed in an impatient little move. "I don't know. Fifteen minutes? Twenty? I heard them when I muted my TV during some commercials and went to the kitchen for a cup of tea. Then I went back to my show. When the next commercials came on I carried my empty cup to the sink. I heard the noises from the Donovan place both times I was in the kitchen."

"Even with your doors and windows closed?"

"You sound like a damn lawyer. They try to pin a person down that way. But I've already been through this. Yes. Even with my windows closed. I heard the sounds of the kids playing."

"Were you pretty good friends with the Donovans?"

"Not especially. I enjoy peace and quiet in my home and I don't care much for children. As long as they stayed in their own yard and didn't run through my flowers, they didn't bother me too much."

"Before Tali and Boyd had kids, did you socialize much with them then?"

"There's a neighborhood block party every year and we

all went to it. Tali asked for my apple pie recipe and I gave it to her. She was more interested in clothes and shopping and lunch out with friends her own age—things like that. I'm more of a homebody. It turned out we didn't have a lot in common."

"Was there ever any fight between you, an angry incident of any sort?" Ron asked.

Nelda stared him down. "Of course not. We are civilized people."

I came up with a couple more little questions about the comings and goings of the Donovans but she gave only one-word answers and clearly wanted to get back to whatever was happening so raucously on television in the other room.

That seemed our cue to leave.

Out front, I told Ron about the earlier conversation with Chet and what the juror Anna Vine had said about Nelda's testimony and Tali's reaction to it.

"Even though they weren't really chummy, I didn't sense any animosity. Did you?"

"Not between the neighbors," he said. "She didn't exactly warm to *us*."

"Understandable. She's been through this for more than five years and is probably sick of the questions."

As anyone would be. But I still groped with Tali's reaction, as Chet had when he'd heard about it. What unspoken message had passed between this witness and the defendant during that trial?

I watched the Donovan house for a few minutes. No lights inside, no sign of activity.

"I need to have a look," I told Ron. Before he could

stop me I walked up to the front door of the white house with its blue shutters. I gave one press of the doorbell and when no one answered I walked around to the side where I'd noticed a gate. Ron followed.

Knowing that Nelda Richards couldn't see us, we let ourselves into the back yard. The children's swing set and sandbox that had been described during the trial were gone. The new owners had done nothing to improve the property, other than removing those sad reminders. The lot was bordered on the sides by a wooden fence. Chain link crossed the back, affording a view into the woods beyond. The gate through which Tali claimed her children were taken was still there. I walked toward it.

The gate, like the back fence, was chain link and closed with a simple hasp. A rusted lock hung from it, non-functional. Could it be the same lock that was here five years ago? Beyond the fence, a path led along the backs of other neighboring properties. A few yards to the east of the Donovan's property line, another path headed into the thick woods that backed against the small neighborhood. The woods where Tali claimed the black-clad man had taken her kids.

I walked back toward the house and then turned to look at the gate once more, to see what Tali might have seen that day. While it was possible to see out the gate, the view was limited and the path into the woods wasn't visible until I edged my way to the right. I tried to imagine seeing a person running away. It would be possible if he was fairly tall. The better view of the path would actually be had from Nelda's back yard, assuming she had a similar gate on her property.

I debated going back to Nelda's to ask whether she'd

observed the man in dark clothing or the children going into the woods. But surely that question would have come up in the investigation and testimony and, even more surely, I would not get a welcome reception by interrupting her one more time. We headed back to the car.

"So, where to next?" Ron said as we pulled away from the curb. We had already discussed whether it would be worth waiting around for the new owners of the Donovan place but decided that the people who'd bought the house—if they would agree to speak with us—wouldn't be able to provide any information. And they might be even less receptive than Nelda. Curiosity seekers and reporters could have made their lives miserable. We discarded the idea of becoming just one more pain in their necks.

"I wonder if anyone has informed Chet's old colleagues about his accident," I said. "We could check in and see if there were other officers who worked the case with him."

I had come across other names in the file, the team of officers who worked the case at the time. But five years had passed. Men like Chet had retired, others were on to new cases. Still, we might get something. I remembered the precinct description and mentioned it to Ron. He queried it on the GPS and soon came up with precise directions.

The police station reminded me very much of the one in Albuquerque—a solid, utilitarian building decked out with a few garlands and bows to remind people of the holiday season. A public relations coordinator listened to our request and called a couple of detectives who had worked with Chet Flowers into the conference room where she'd parked us. Both men were in their forties, reasonably fit and dressed in standard plain-clothes business suits. Blondell was the short, dark-haired one and Cunningham had reddish hair and a black smudge on his white shirt. They greeted us and soberly received the news of Chet's death.

"Sorry to hear it," Blondell said.

"We understand both of you worked with Chet on the Tali Donovan case a few years ago," Ron said.

We spent a few minutes explaining our interest in it and the fact that we'd been working with Chet just prior to his death.

"I wish I'd had the time to help him with it recently," Cunningham said. "But our caseload is always out of control. We barely have time to work the current ones, let alone dig up an old one that's been tried."

It was pretty much the answer I expected.

"Had Chet been in touch with either of you?" Ron asked. "Since he started looking into it again?"

"He came into O'Sullivan's a couple weeks ago," Blondell said. "A cop hangout where we have a drink now and then. He had a beer with me and told me a little about it. The ex-husband wants to bring a civil suit, maybe?"

"Something like that," I said. "Mainly, he wants to find out what really happened to his kids. To find them if they are alive, to bury them properly if that's what it comes down to."

They both wagged their heads sadly. "That's the rough part about that kind of case," Cunningham said. "Hard to watch the families who just don't get any answers. I wish it was always tied up nice and neat like on TV."

I tossed out some names—Nelda Richards and a couple of her neighbors, some of the jurors, including Anna Vine—but neither man had spoken to any of the parties since the end of the trial. Ron asked a couple of specific questions but I could tell that the detectives were anxious to get back to their work.

We thanked them and left, empty-handed and more than a little discouraged.

Chapter 17

Street lights were coming on as we drove back downtown. I realized the sun was setting, although it was more a dimming and fading of the light than actually being able to observe the round globe of it hit the horizon. We found a good seafood restaurant and stopped there. I managed to go into a joyful overload of all the shrimp and scallops I could handle, since I never get the chance to do that at home. Sitting at a table where we watched ferries traverse the Sound, and basking in the warmth from the fireplace nearby, I thought of the dinner and ambiance as compensation for the bleak weather outside.

We got back to Chet's apartment and made coffee to go with the desserts we'd brought back, spent a few minutes reviewing what we were taking home with us, and set an alarm for six in the morning. Around eight, I left Ron to peruse the offerings on the big TV and I fell into the newly made-up bed and was asleep in minutes.

I knew I hadn't been asleep long when I wakened to the sounds of a squabble. It took me a few seconds to remember where I was and become alert enough to realize that a woman's voice was shrieking and it was Ron's voice responding. I pulled on my jeans and sweater and dashed out to the living room.

A woman about my age stood with her back to the door, facing Ron, pointing a two-foot long black nightstick at him. Her blond hair spilled out of the clip that was supposed to be holding it, and her blue eyes were wide with shock.

"Who *are* you people!" she gasped when she saw me.

"Shayna?" How I pulled the name out of the air at that moment, I'll never know. "We knew your dad."

She lowered the baton a tad.

I held my hands up. Ron wrapped his blanket around his waist and reached down to gather his clothes. I gave her our names.

"We're from Albuquerque. We were working with your father on an old case—the Tali Donovan case. He'd been out to New Mexico to see us when the accident happened."

"Accident?"

Oh boy. She didn't know. I took a deep breath and suggested she sit down. But she wasn't quite ready for that, seeing as how Ron was standing there wearing not much besides that blanket. She held her ground and repeated, "*What* accident?"

I told her as succinctly as possible and offered our sympathies.

"Don't move," she said, fishing a phone from her pocket and pressing buttons left-handed while keeping a steady hand on her weapon.

Whoever she called apparently didn't know anything and she tried another number. She asked for Detective Cunningham and he confirmed the news. All the spark went out of her. She clicked off the call with tears in her eyes.

"I'm really sorry you had to learn this way. The New Mexico state police were trying to locate you."

Shayna pressed a switch that caused the baton to collapse into itself, and she set the eight-inch rod of metal beside her leg as she sank into the recliner chair. Ron grabbed up his clothing with one arm and headed toward the bathroom.

"I can't believe it. Dad." She scrubbed at her face with hands that were a little on the grubby side and had broken nails. "I should have come sooner. I hadn't seen him in over a year."

The tears welled again.

"Can I get you something? We made some coffee earlier. Maybe some water?"

She shook her head. "You still didn't say exactly how you got in here."

I held out Chet's key ring. "His personal effects. I'm sorry we didn't know about you sooner. I only found your picture when I got the case files from his desk this afternoon."

"We weren't close," she said with genuine regret. "I grew up resenting police work because of the amount of time it took away from the family. My mother probably fostered that attitude in me. A lot. She left him when I was pretty little, and then she died. I went a little wild in my teens—my shrink said I was trying to get his attention by being arrested. I did that a few times and then I just split. I've been living in Portland."

I glanced over at the key she'd dropped near the door.

"The super gave it to me. Guess he didn't know you were in here."

"We'll go to a hotel," I said. "You should have the apartment to yourself tonight."

"No, it's all right. You're settled. I'm staying at a friend's house. We got to having a few glasses of wine this evening and she's the one who convinced me to come over and make things right with my dad. Man. This is the shits."

She stood up and picked up her baton and a purse that lay with the contents strewn near the door.

"Will you be okay?" I asked. "Ron can drive you back to your friend's place."

She gave a rueful chuff. "No, I think I'm pretty well sober *now*."

Ron came out of the bathroom, fully dressed, and reiterated the offer to drive her. Shayna just shook her head and walked out.

"Wow. Poor girl," he said after she'd gone.

I knew the feeling. When our parents died in a plane crash I hadn't exactly been on my best behavior either. There'd been no chance to make amends or say goodbye. It took years to work out some of those issues.

I retreated to the bedroom but with all hope of sleep gone I found myself sitting on the floor in front of my open suitcase. There was no sense hauling all this paperwork home with us, and now that we knew Chet had a daughter, by all rights she should get his personal stuff. I sorted until two a.m. and put a lot of it back in the file drawer. The folders related to the Donovan case would come with us. When the alarm went off at six, I was not at all ready to face a new day.

The rental car return guy was nearly as grumpy as I was, then the kiosk check-in refused my credit card and the TSA pulled me aside and scanned me every which way. By the time I found Starbucks and set the suitcase full of paper aside I was in a mood. Ron breezed through all of this with his usual imperturbable composure, which made me want to snap at him all the more. I sipped at my coffee and indulged in a big cinnamon roll; I gave myself a little pep talk and pretty soon I felt as if I could face the world again.

Then we got the announcement that our flight was delayed, weather in Salt Lake City had messed up a bunch of connecting flights. Ron gave me a look that said, *Don't start with me*. I didn't. It was just one more topper to an already messy day. Half the people in the gate area picked up phones to inform someone back home. We were no exception.

I got Drake right away and he wished me luck, reminding me that we'd told the Brewsters we would be at their party tonight. I groaned inwardly and told him I would keep him posted. I still hadn't resolved the question about what to wear to this deal but knew that I better figure out something quick.

Ron was getting a little gushy with Victoria and I jabbed him in the ribs.

"Let me talk to her," I said.

He apologized to her in advance for whatever I might say or do.

"Vic, help," I said. "I need ideas for something to wear to this fancy dress party at the Brewsters. You've seen their house. Well, it's even more elegant inside than out, and I just know the guest list will include every important person in Albuquerque and half the politicians from Santa Fe. Tell me what to do."

First, she told me to calm down. We could think of something.

"There are some shops here in the airport," I said.

"Charlie, you can't show up in something that says I Heart Seattle or has a picture of the Space Needle, no matter how much glitter they tacked on. I would venture to say that Felina Brewster's bling is going to be the real thing. What time will your flight get here?"

"They *say* the new arrival time is three o'clock. But what if we're delayed again?"

"Let's take it one thing at a time. The stores won't close until six. There's time."

She used a soothing voice, which is probably the only reason I didn't flip out. I hung up, actually feeling a little reassured. About what, I don't know.

"She's a peach," I told Ron. "You better be good to her."

I downed the last of my coffee and left Ron in charge of the bags while I went to walk off some energy by marching up and down the crowded corridors. I actually picked up a T-shirt with the F-word written in elegant script and lined with rhinestones. Well, it *is* bling, I told myself.

I put it back. Victoria was right about the occasion. I'd better behave myself.

The next four hours crawled but finally we were belted into seats and actually leaving the ground. A cheer went up throughout the cabin. The sun was low in the west by the time the jet lumbered at a record slow pace down the long taxiway and up to the gate in Albuquerque. I looked at my watch about every ten seconds. I was never going to make it before the stores closed.

My phone rang as I was waiting for twelve rows of incredibly slow people to gather up their thousand items of carry-on and get the hell moving.

"Charlie? It's Vic. I'm at the mall."

"What? I thought you were picking us up at the airport.

"Drake's doing that," Victoria said. "Look, I'm at Macy's. Your shoe size is seven and a half, right?"

"Uh, yeah. It is. What are you doing?"

"I just had this feeling about your flight getting in late . . . and well, there's this gorgeous dress and it's on sale."

Did I really want her choosing my clothes? At this moment in time, the answer to that question would be a big yes.

She gave a quick description of the dress. "I can check out now and be at your house in thirty minutes."

"Vic, you are saving my life, you know."

She laughed. "Probably nothing quite that dramatic. See you pretty soon."

Drake and I arrived home to be thoroughly greeted with doggy kisses from Freckles. I parked the bag full of Chet's paperwork in a corner. All work was coming to a halt in favor of a night out with my husband; I found that I was actually getting excited about the party. I left Drake and Ron to find themselves something to drink and to wait for Victoria. A nice hot shower was calling my name.

An hour later I stood in front of the mirror in my bedroom, staring at a stranger in a floor-length dress with a V-fitted bodice featuring softly draping pleats that tapered into the A-line skirt and a pair of strappy shoes that looked made-to-match.

"I just knew the copper sheen in the fabric would be absolutely perfect with the highlights in your hair," Victoria said. She stood behind me and pulled a handful of tresses up off my shoulders. "See? We could get this up off your neck, do a little fancy up-thing."

The shimmery fabric glinted in the lamplight and I, the girl who'd rarely put on a dress, felt like Cinderella.

"You look *gorgeous*," she said. "And the thing about this dress is that it doesn't just scream 'Christmas.' You could wear it for a lot of other occasions too."

I couldn't admit to her that I'd never once in my life had a need for anything remotely this glamorous. My eyes wouldn't leave the mirror.

Victoria was digging around in her bag. "I had these little clips . . ." she said, pulling out a handful of tiny objects. In about three minutes she'd gathered up strands of my hair and clipped them in some mysterious manner that made me look ready to walk the red carpet in Hollywood.

My eyes felt a little moist as I turned to her. "Thank you so much," I whispered as I reached out to give her a hug. "You are the best sister-in-law ever."

"Almost . . ." She said with a grin. "By this time next year . . ."

"What are you and Ron waiting for anyway?" I teased.

She brushed off the question and turned back to the bag of magic tricks, where she pulled out a tube of some kind of lotion. Rubbing it between her palms she smoothed it over my bare arms and my winter-dry skin shone with a hint of color. "Now. Slip on this robe while you do your makeup so there aren't any mishaps. I've got to get home. We're taking the boys out for pizza and then they are spending the night at my place."

Drake tapped at the bedroom door just then and Victoria edged out when he came in. While he showered I sat at my mother's antique dresser trying to figure out what to do with the array of bronze-toned eye shadows Vic had left for me. Sheesh. My normal makeup routine consists of rubbing on some sunscreen and applying a smear of lipstick on days when I'm looking a little wan.

I'd once stumbled across an infomercial on TV where some expert was doing the whole makeover routine to a rather plain woman, and since that situation seemed to apply to me now, I made a few swipes of the eye shadow and was wielding the mascara wand a little too close to my eye when Drake emerged from the bathroom. I shrieked and dropped it, leaving a nasty black smudge on my robe. Thank goodness for Vic's sound advice about putting it on over my new dress. I licked at a tissue and wiped away the little mark on my cheek and started over.

By the time Drake needed the mirror to get his tie just right, I decided to call the makeup finished so I moved out of his way. When I shed the robe and he caught sight of the finished 'me' his eyes widened.

"Wow."

"Thank you, sir." I gave him a flirty grin. "Mainly, thank Victoria. She found this amazing dress and I have no clue how she knew it would look this good on me."

He started to move in for a kiss, saw the lipstick and settled for a chaste peck on the cheek.

Freckles bounded into the room and headed toward me, but Drake grabbed her collar and steered her toward her crate, where she would be perfectly content with a chew bone while we were out for the evening. I shuffled hangers in my closet again, hoping a suitable coat would have appeared but it didn't, and my down parka certainly wasn't going to work for this outfit. A shawl would do, and

I found a brown cashmere in a drawer. It wasn't a great match with my glam outfit but at least it was brand new, a gift from some Christmas past, as I'm not normally much of a cashmere-shawl kind of girl.

I joined Drake in the living room where he was pointing to one of the living room chairs. Draped over the back of it was a black velveteen coat, and lying on top of that sat a tiny evening bag and an envelope. I opened the card.

"The dress is a gift," said the handwritten note. "Sorry, but the coat and bag have to be on loan. Love you, Vic."

I slipped into the coat and the princess effect was complete. My prince escorted me out to our awaiting carriage which was still, sadly, a Jeep.

Chapter 18

Drake followed two other cars that had pulled off the street and were winding their way along the drive to the porte-cochere at the north side of the mansion. Uniformed valets met each vehicle, assisted the passengers out and took the cars away into the night. When our turn came, I stepped out and took a deep breath. My only true goals for the evening were to check out the other women's bling, give Drake time to glad-hand some of the city's prosperous as potential clients, and be ready shortly after the stroke of midnight to get this gunk off my eyelids.

As soon as our Jeep moved away a friendly young woman in black slacks, white shirt, and cropped tuxedo jacket greeted us. We climbed three stone steps and a white-haired man in similar uniform met us just inside the door where he offered to take my wrap. That disappeared into a small anteroom and our attention was drawn to a cluster of people standing near the foot of the elaborate wooden staircase. A small fireplace opposite the front door gave a cheery glow to the richly paneled foyer and gold lights sparkled on a tall, thin fir tree that filled the corner by the stairs. I didn't remember the tree from our previous visit; Felina had toned up the decorations as well as the dress code. The sounds of big band music came from the second floor.

One of the tuxedoed men stepped forward and I recognized Jerry Brewster.

"Drake, Charlie," he greeted. "So glad you could make it. Charlie, you look beautiful. I'll bet you spent the day at the spa like my wife did."

If he only knew.

Felina appeared at his side, indeed looking as if she'd spent the day at a spa. Her floor-length strapless red dress perfectly accentuated her slender body and the strand of diamonds around her neck must have set Jerry back at least two Mercedes' worth. The matching bracelet could have easily purchased an ordinary SUV. I admired the jewelry in appropriately reverent tones until Drake gave my elbow a squeeze. I guess I was laying it on a little thick.

"How's Katie?" I asked, directing the question toward Jerry. "Did she start work at the dealership yet?"

"I gave her a little back-office job, doing some filing and learning a few basic accounting entries."

The same way Jerry himself had gotten into the business.

"How is she taking to that?" I asked.

Felina spoke up. "I'm sure it's doing no more than keeping her off the streets. But at least that's something. Meanwhile, there are bars both upstairs and down, and be sure to go up to the main salon where we've got a huge buffet. We're not waiting until midnight to break out the Perrier Jouet."

Someone distracted her and she turned away.

"Katie will do just fine," Jerry said quietly.

I smiled, getting the picture. I could certainly see why Katie favored her father.

"The kids are in my study, if you want to pop in and say hello." He indicated a closed door to the left of the stairs.

I found Katie and Adam seated on a heavy leather couch that dwarfed them. A Christmas movie was playing on a small television set on a walnut bookcase. Katie wore a party dress that was more suited for a seven-year-old than a young lady, and Adam had on a miniature version of his dad's tuxedo, the jacket concealing the small cast on his arm.

"Hey, Katie," I said, not commenting on her dress.

"Charlie! Hi." She got up and came to give me a hug. "We're supposed to wait in here until Julia comes to get us and then I guess we're, like, getting introduced to the crowd." She made a little face.

"Ah . . . very fancy."

"Adam has to go to bed after that but I get to stay up and have some food. *If* I act ladylike. Otherwise Felina threatened that I'll go to bed too. You don't want to mess around with Felina's threats, I'll tell you."

Something in her tone made me think she wasn't only talking about an early bedtime. The door opened. Julia, the au pair, stepped in quickly and closed the door.

"Oh, so sorry. I didn't realize there was a guest." She couldn't decide whether to stay or go.

"I won't interrupt your plans, just wanted to say hello. I'll see you at the buffet, Katie." I gave her a little wink.

Back in the foyer the crowd had cleared. Jerry must have decided that nearly everyone had arrived because he'd moved on from his duty as greeter. A few people mingled around the living room where the cocktail party had been, but most of the sounds came from above and I remembered that's where Felina said the buffet was set up. I started up, in search of my date.

The salon ran the entire width of the mansion and the wide doors were fully opened to create a huge room from three that had been merely big. I edged my way in, having one of those awkward cocktail party moments where you're standing there with no food or drink in hand and no one to talk to. I scanned the crowd for Drake. The only face I immediately recognized was Walt Frasier, an attorney with whom RJP had dealings from time to time. He caught my gaze and waved from across the room.

"Charlie?" said someone behind me.

I turned toward the voice to find that it was Sharon Ortega, an old friend who'd hired us a few years ago to look into the death of her business partner. We did a little oh-my-gosh exchange.

"How's the restaurant doing?" I asked, a little embarrassed that I hadn't been there in awhile.

"Great. Two locations now. And a catering sideline. It's what I'm doing here."

I hadn't noticed that she was dressed in the quasi-standard uniform of caterers everywhere, black slacks and a white tuxedo shirt with vest.

"Looks like they ordered up a huge spread," I commented under my breath.

"And at the perfect time," she whispered. "This job gave all my employees a decent Christmas bonus."

I sneaked her a little thumbs-up and she hurried off to check on the food table. Felina was right—there was enough food here to keep a huge crowd fed for a week. I spotted Drake heading my direction.

"You're going to love that egg dish with the green chile," Drake said, handing me a fork and a plate he'd loaded at the buffet. He pointed out something that looked like a slice of frittata.

I felt as if I hadn't eaten anything all day and I think I gave out a little moan when I tasted the heavenly mixture of eggs, potato, chile and cheese. I finished off the slice and then a blintz of some kind and three pieces of fresh fruit.

"I'll bring you some more," he said, watching me with an amused expression.

"No, really. I better pace myself. I just can't remember eating anything after a big cinnamon roll this morning."

He gave a little shake of his head. He's constantly reminding me that a junk food diet does not a healthy person make.

"I'll check out the buffet myself, a little later," I said.

He wanted to remind me about making good choices but knew I would do whatever I wanted to anyway. When Jerry Brewster walked over to introduce someone to Drake, I used the excuse of putting away our plates as a reason to meander toward that big, enticing table.

Katie was standing there, eyeing the dessert end of the table where everything from traditional flan to delicately decorated French pastries waited in a tempting array.

"That's my favorite too," I whispered.

She jumped, then grinned at me. "What, that one?" She pointed to a diamond shaped napoleon with chocolate shavings thinner than tissue paper on top.

I placed one on a plate and handed it to her. "That way, no one can accuse you of helping yourself. It's a gift."

Drake found me again and I introduced them.

"I love your dog," Katie said. "She likes to run in the park with me."

"She likes to run—anytime, anywhere. So you feel free to run to your heart's content with her," he said.

Katie turned to her dessert.

"I've met two businessmen who are talking about helicopter work," Drake said to me when we walked a short distance away. "And, guess who's here. The governor. I'm dropping a few little hints. More government contracts would be a huge boost to us."

It was fun seeing him enjoy the party. Normally he's pretty much all about piloting and safety and worrying about the logistics of a job. I watched him smile as someone walked up with a new introduction.

The room seemed more crowded by the minute and I edged my way to the hall, hoping to catch a few moments of relative quiet downstairs. The coat man must have taken a break. No one was likely to need their wraps until they began leaving, hours from now. Perhaps the guy did double duty by picking up used glassware or taking out the trash. A quieter group lingered around the bar in the ground floor living room, which was softly lit and still boasted the blue and green themed Christmas tree along with flickering logs in the fireplace. It seemed an oasis of calm in the noisy house. I stood in the doorway, noticing a tableful of nibbles but not especially wanting to get wrapped up in a conversation just yet.

A chime sounded somewhere near, bells that didn't quite fit with the jazzy tunes from the music system. I realized it was probably the doorbell, latecomers. Jerry and Felina were upstairs, engaged with other guests. No one had responded to the door chimes. I slipped out to the foyer and opened the carved door.

Two women in dark coats and a uniformed police officer stood on the porch. All three looked very official.

"Mrs. Brewster?" the officer said.

"Uh, no. I'm just a party guest. Um, she's . . . inside."

"We need to speak with Jerry and Felina Brewster," the woman said, her perma-scowl in place. "Child Protective Services." She held out a business card. A picture of little Adam Brewster with the cast on his arm popped into my head.

A gust of wind sent a frigid blast into the foyer and my instinct was to close the door, but it seemed rude to shut it in their faces and unwise to simply let them in. I had no idea of the protocol in these situations. I took the card and felt a presence behind me. Jerry Brewster to the rescue.

"What's this?" he asked. I handed him the card and edged away.

He invited the three officials to step inside.

"We need to speak with you and your wife," said the stern woman who'd given me the card.

Jerry looked at the card and back at the group. "What's this about?"

"Where is your wife, sir?" This time the police officer spoke.

Jerry turned around and I sensed that I could be useful, so I started up the stairs and waved Felina toward me when I caught her attention. She descended the staircase in her elegant red dress, coming to an abrupt halt when the saw the newcomers. Several people nearby stopped to watch the

Brewsters and the music became the prominent sound from the party as voices dimmed.

"Let's go into my study," Jerry said, ushering the black-clad bunch toward the door to the left of the stairs. He looked toward those hovering around the living room door. "Please, everyone, get another drink, have some food. This shouldn't take long."

He slipped an arm around Felina's waist and the five of them disappeared into the other room. Among the guests the word spread like a bad odor; wide eyes and slack jaws attested that having the police show up at a neighbor's holiday party was just not done around here. I watched with some amusement as everyone seemed at a loss. The notes of *Rudolph the Red-nosed Reindeer* seemed frivolous and tinny in the background.

Finally a man spread his arms and motioned them all back into the salon. "Come on, everyone. Let's do as Jerry suggested. I'm sure they'll be out in a minute or so."

Gucci-clad feet shuffled, Armani tuxedoes hung over hunched shoulders, but the group trailed obediently back.

Walt Frasier, the attorney I'd recognized earlier turned his sharp blue eyes on me. "Who are those people?"

I hedged, not wanting to be the catalyst that set the wildfire of gossip going.

"I'm Jerry's personal attorney, Charlie. Does he need me in there?"

I shrugged. "Child Protective Services. That's all they said to me."

He bit the edge of his lip, made a decision and tapped at the door to Jerry's study. I caught a glimpse of Jerry seated at his desk with Felina standing behind him drumming her fingers on his shoulders. Walt stepped inside and closed the door.

Hm. I glanced back toward the stairs, where a few folks stood around in small clusters speaking in muted voices. Well, I sure wasn't going to learn anything juicy standing out here in the foyer by myself. I picked up the wine glass that I'd set on a small table and carried it into the living room.

"I can't imagine . . ." "What do you think is going on?" "Well, I *heard*—" The comments were flying every which way.

Fifteen minutes must have passed, with the party operating in muted tones and the hosts still behind closed doors with the authorities and their attorney. No one wanted to laugh and drink, but no one was leaving either. Me included. Okay, I'm a snoop. At least I admit it. I helped myself from a tray of canapés.

When the door to the study opened, it was as if a party-bomb had gone off. Everyone suddenly began laughing and chatting, as if the earlier whispers and speculation never happened. Walt Frasier escorted the officials out of the house while Jerry and Felina rejoined their guests. Felina, I noticed, grabbed a champagne flute from the nearest passing server.

"Sorry about that," Jerry said to the group nearest me. "Purely a routine enquiry. Silly thing, really, but they're just doing their jobs."

Felina was handing out the same assurances to two couples who'd happened to be standing near the stairs. I nibbled at my plate of snacks and picked up conversational tidbits.

When Walt Frasier came back inside he seemed

completely relaxed and the mood caught on. Conversations resumed and guests began to flow back up the stairs, along with Jerry and Felina.

"Walt? Is that it?" I asked, catching the attorney on his way to the bathroom. "All's well that ends well?"

"Yes. Just routine. The little boy tumbled down three stairs and apparently his arm hit one of the balusters. Kids can be pretty flexible but they can break too. Doctors are under stringent rules anymore to report everything that happens. Then someone has to come around and check it out." He walked away.

I debated telling Walt some of the other things Katie had told me. But I didn't want to betray her confidence. Walt would surely have to take anything I told him straight to Jerry and Felina. I had to wonder . . . Linda Casper had told me she was the Brewster's family doctor. Was she the one who set Adam's broken arm? And was she the doctor who had reported the incident? I would have to devote some time to figuring out how to get the information out of my old friend.

Meanwhile, someone turned up the music and the party noises grew louder. I felt a headache begin to press at my temples. I discovered that the living room was empty now and I found a chair that faced the fireplace so I settled there for a few minutes. The clock said it was a little after eleven. I wished it would hurry up and be midnight.

Chapter 19

January first. I was probably the only person in the city who woke up without a bad case of overindulgence. I'd had one glass of wine and the few nibbles from the buffet at the Brewsters' party. At four minutes to midnight Drake had found me alone in the quiet of the living room and we laughed together at the thunder of feet above our heads when the crowd began shouting and cheering in the new year. For ourselves, we shared a long and romantic kiss, which led to the idea of getting out of there to continue the private celebration at home.

Now, out in the unnaturally silent city, I was following Freckles as she took me through our quiet neighborhood streets. I had awakened with thoughts of those two suitcases full of information from Chet Flowers's apartment. It had been a pretty busy end to the old year and I sent up a little wish to the universe that the coming weeks would settle down a bit for us. It was the closest thing to a new year's resolution that I could muster.

By the time the dog finished her business and we'd walked the three blocks back home I was more than ready to load up on coffee and start finding solutions to the case. Nothing would please me more than to call Boyd Donovan later today and say, "I've solved it!"

But things rarely go that well. I stacked the files on my dining table knowing they couldn't stay there. No doubt Ron would want all this at the office where we would both have access, but at the moment I just needed some sense of organization about the whole mess.

The kitchen phone rang before I could decide what to do next.

"Hi, Auntie Charlie!" Sally's voice sounded exuberant.

"The baby! When did you go to the hospital?"

"Yesterday afternoon. There was no time to call anyone. The little guy came very quickly. He missed being the first baby of the new year by about four hours."

"So, it's a boy." Sally and Ross were practically the only couple we'd known in years who wanted that part of it to be a surprise.

"Ross Bertrand, Junior," she said. She rattled off some data about his weight and length, but I couldn't remember them with any precision by the time we finished the conversation.

I hung up the phone, happy for them. Happy for the fact that they were happy. Sally and Ross were great parents and I wished them well.

Back at the dining table, I sorted Chet's folders by

subject matter: witness accounts, suspect interviews, court evidence, photographs, and some miscellaneous things like a ring of keys, a cassette tape, and some kind of hasty map that someone had inked on the back of a cocktail napkin. These last items had been lumped together in an envelope that Chet labeled Pending. I had no idea what that meant.

From our work together and the trip to Seattle I felt as if I already had a pretty good handle on the witness accounts and the results of the interviews conducted by the police when Tali became their chief suspect. I skimmed the pages in each of those folders, knowing that before this was all over I would probably have to go back and reread each of them carefully.

In the stack I'd called Evidence I came across the Search and Rescue reports. Teams had been called out within an hour of the call about the Donovan children's disappearance and, according to the incident commander's report, they had used both dogs and human tracking experts in the search for traces of the mysterious man or the children. In the SAR world you have to account for every possibility, and one that they had considered was that the two kids had simply opened the back gate and wandered away. Embarrassed that she hadn't been watching them more closely, their mother might have invented the story of the stranger and then hoped that the teams would find the kids, disoriented and cold, and bring them home. Things like that have happened.

But the teams found no evidence whatsoever. There had been rain the night before and on the day of the disappearance, but they found no footprints—adult or child size—and no whiff of the kids, which dogs would have picked up from samples of their clothing. After two days of searching—after all, there were a lot of fallen leaves in the woods and it was possible the strange man had been careful about where he stepped—the teams were called off and this report had been filed. That's when Tali Donovan became a real, viable suspect.

A notation on the cover letter suggested that the incident commander would be willing to assemble searchers for other areas, should the police decide that evidence pointed to some other part of the surrounding countryside. I saw what an impossible task that would be. Just about every scrap of land that didn't have something built on it was heavily wooded. How would they have a clue where to start? I set the report aside and moved on to the photographs.

Chet had said that he ordered photos of every room in the house, even though there was no sign of violence. He hoped that one day enough information would come together so that some item in that house would provide the final piece of the puzzle. Unfortunately, that had not happened in time for the trial and we all knew how that turned out.

I studied each eight-by-ten for minutes at a time. I knew Tali's china pattern and the colors of her bedspreads and the fact that she didn't wash her dishes right away in the morning. I knew the family hung their coats on a bentwood rack in the laundry room and a basket of clothing sat on the dryer, waiting to be folded. I knew that the kids' bedrooms were filled to capacity with every brightly colored plastic toy on earth, and I knew that Tali wasn't much of a housekeeper but that she loved high-end fashion and makeup despite the fact that she was nowhere near a size two. But I still didn't know what she had done with her children.

The photographers had been thorough. Cupboards

had been opened, with a separate photo showing the items behind each door. Drawers had been dumped and the contents spread out so everything—from utensils in the kitchen to lacy lingerie from the bedroom—was visible. I cringed a little. How completely un-private our lives become if we ever get wrapped up in a mess like this. Tali's life became an open book, and yet no one figured out what happened to those kids.

I sighed and went to the kitchen for a coffee refill. The sun was only beginning to cast long shadows across the yard. Drake came out of the bedroom and nuzzled my neck.

"I'm going to spend a thoroughly lazy day at home," he said. "Want to start it off with some eggs Benedict?"

Knowing good and well that I don't know how to make them, this was an offer for him to make breakfast for me and I quickly took him up on it. I did contribute by cutting up some fresh fruit. While we savored our special breakfast I ran a few things past him about the case.

"I flew a lot of SAR missions, hon, but it was years ago and my job was to get teams out there and to let the observers observe. I saw everything from hundreds of feet away and didn't have much to do with evidence. Sorry."

"Did you ever fly much in the northwest, around Seattle?"

"Yeah. Those forests are thicker than anything you can imagine around here. Miles and miles of nothing but treetops from the air. If you're looking for something among those trees, good luck. I can see why they wouldn't expend fuel and money to try to cover any amount of area. You have to have some idea where to start. Sometimes, even when you have a good idea where to search, you can't find a thing. Remember the stories of that guy who jumped out of the airliner with all that money, years ago?"

I pondered all that while he swabbed up the last of his Hollandaise and headed toward the sink.

"I'll take down the Christmas tree if you'd like," he said.

Well, I wasn't going to pass up that offer. By the time I'd put the dishes into the dishwasher and settled at the dining table with the files again he already had the ornament storage boxes out and the parade showing on TV to keep him company. For a guy who'd planned a lazy day, he was accomplishing a lot. I felt guilty poring over papers while he did the household chores, so after a little while I abandoned the table and got up to help him. Plus, I couldn't help staring at the television and all those floats made of flowers.

Ornament hooks looped over my fingers, I carried a handful to the storage box. It was always a little sad saying goodbye to the memories for another year. There were old glass ornaments from my childhood, a couple of which even went back to my mother's youth. Drake and I had collected a few from our travels—a tartan plaid wreath from Scotland, shells from Hawaii, and a replica of the Washington Monument from a quick trip we made there two years ago. I smiled, remembering that a comedian once said that the monument doesn't look at all like the man.

I set it into the box and a snippet of conversation came back to me, full force. Boyd Donovan. He'd mentioned a little obelisk, somewhere in the woods. A place he and Tali used to go. *Oh my god.*

Gingerly, I placed the other ornaments into their spots and dashed to the table. Scrambling through Chet's notes I came across the witness file and found Boyd Donovan's current phone number.

"Tell me exactly where that place is," I said with little preamble.

"Um, okay. Take Interstate 90 . . ."

I wrote it all down, precisely as he described it. Then I called Detective Cunningham in Seattle.

"I think I know where the Donovan children are buried."

* * *

The day dragged, as Elsa would say, slower than molasses in January. All Detective Cunningham told me was that he would work on getting the search launched again. I knew he wanted to reopen the case, but I could also hear in his voice that there wasn't a lot of urgency to it. If the bodies were, indeed, in that spot they'd been there for five years. A few days, even a few weeks, wouldn't change anything.

I paced for awhile until Drake pointed out that I might be helping him disassemble the artificial tree, since I had so much nervous energy to spare. It didn't help. I fumbled the branches and couldn't seem to stuff everything into the box—I swear, those things are never meant to go back into the box they came out of. Finally, he gave up and after carrying the ornament boxes out to the garage he finished doing the tree himself.

I called Ron to let him know about this new development but I could hear a football game in the background, and while he seemed genuinely excited that the case might break, he also gave out a cheer when his team scored a touchdown. I got him to put Victoria on the phone, and I thanked her again for my new party dress.

"I'm taking the boys shopping this afternoon," she said. "Want to come along? Justin and Jason both need new coats. I can't believe how fast they outgrow everything."

I passed on the trip, although it probably would have

helped fill the time. I called Boyd Donovan back to see if he'd heard anything from Seattle but he hadn't. After my second call to Detective Cunningham he basically gave me the "don't call us, we'll call you" response. He sounded busy.

Drake had found a show on how they make the blades for wind turbines and I flopped onto the couch to see if it could distract me. That lasted all of three minutes. But at least I could stare at the screen while my thoughts roiled, giving the appearance that we were actually having couple-time. I kept up that fakery through two more episodes on how things were manufactured and a movie that involved a lot of guys blowing stuff up. At some point I went to the kitchen and rustled up some greasy snack food; New Year's resolutions are always broken by the first week anyway.

When my phone rang at six that evening it startled me.

"Charlie?" It was Boyd Donovan. "Detective Cunningham just called me. He's at the scene of a grave. He said you helped provide the information that pinpointed the location."

Happiness and dread conflicted in my gut. "Were there—?"

Boyd took a deep breath. "A forensics team just got there. Cunningham said it'll be hours before they know for sure. I'm under orders not to speak with the media until a positive identification is made, but I had to tell someone. I need you to promise that you won't talk about this until we know."

"Of course."

"The detective said charges could be filed against me for talking about this too soon. Obstruction or something. If it's—" He cleared his throat. "If it turns out to be my kids, they'll intensify the hunt for Tali. This isn't over for her and they don't want to give her any advance warning."

"That makes sense. Ron and I will keep quiet."

He seemed a little uneasy that I would tell Ron, but after all we were on the case together.

"I'm flying up there, Charlie. I have to know. Sitting around San Diego is killing me."

"I understand. Stay in touch and let us know what they find. And, Boyd? Take care."

I dialed my brother after ending the call from Boyd, passing along what little I knew and swearing him to secrecy for the time being. I caught Drake watching me and I threatened no sex forever if he were to get me in trouble over this. It turned out that he really only wondered if we could order a pizza for dinner.

The night hours dragged. By the time I met Ron at the office the next morning I'd almost decided that we would never hear from them, that the case would be closed.

"After all, what Boyd Donovan paid us to do was to find his kids. This might be the end of the road for us," Ron pointed out.

"Yeah, but—"

"Charlie, leave it. We will learn what they want us to know, when they want us to know it."

I groused over that for a minute, jamming a filter into the coffee maker and spilling a scoopful of the grounds. When the machine finished brewing I poured cups for each of us and carried them upstairs.

I had gathered all the materials from Chet's place and brought them with me, so I spent a few minutes placing them in boxes that could be shipped to Seattle if the police requested them. It felt as if I was giving up; it seemed there were still so many unanswered questions. Besides, the police already had all these reports and photos; Chet's files were merely duplicates, other than his handwritten notes. I slipped the photos out of their brown envelope again and spread them on my desk.

Meanwhile, I reminded myself that the two children weren't the only victims. We still didn't know who'd run Chet off the highway. I couldn't let go of the feeling that it had something to do with the Donovan case.

I set the photos aside again and pulled out Chet's little spiral notebooks, intending to start with his most recent one and work my way backward to see what he might have learned in his final hours.

Since the New Mexico police were treating this as a simple hit-and-run car crash, they weren't likely looking into Chet's investigation or putting it together that the killer wasn't just a random stranger. I'd tried to tell them, but they'd given the notebooks to me anyway. I didn't feel a bit badly about checking this out on my own.

Chapter 20

Pacing sometimes helps one think. I was intently doing both—pacing and thinking—when I spotted Ron standing in my doorway.

"You didn't hear your intercom?" he asked.

I came to an abrupt stop and brought myself back to the present. "I guess not."

"Boyd Donovan is on the phone. He wants to talk to you." His face told me what the news would be.

I took a deep breath and picked up the receiver.

His voice sounded fairly steady. "Did Ron tell you?"

"Boyd, I'm so sorry."

"I'm—I'm almost glad. No, not really. But at least it's an answer. They tested the DNA. They're mine."

"Both were there?"

"Yeah. Deni and Ethan. Two sets of little bone—" A

huge sob escaped.

"Boyd, you don't have to go into this. It's too painful."

"No, I need to . . . I think it helps a little to talk about it."
He blew out a breath. "They won't let me see the . . . uh, the
remains. It's just skeletons. But there was a scrap of blanket
they were buried in. I recognized it."

"So that ties the burial to Tali. It would have to, unless
she claimed that the stranger somehow got hold of it."

"That's the thing. In the original testimony she said that
Deni had taken her favorite blanket outside when the kids
went out to play. Later, it was gone. So she covered her
bases on that." His voice got stronger as he talked about
specific facts.

"Do the police know how . . ."

"How it happened? Not yet. Or they aren't saying.
That's why I'm telling you all this. I told the police that you
were working with Chet. I want Tali found. I want them to
reopen the case."

My tiny nagging feeling that Boyd might have harmed
his ex-wife vanished.

"I don't know if they can do that." I explained a little
about what Chet told me about double jeopardy.

"I'll file a civil suit," he said. "In a New York minute I'd
do that."

"But you need evidence."

"Exactly."

"The police will work the case. I'm sure they'll find what
you need."

"To a degree. But it won't be the same because they
aren't taking it to a prosecutor. I'll need everything I can
get, Charlie. Maybe you can put together whatever Chet had
found, give it to them, tell them what you know."

His voice grew higher, tinged with desperation. Police departments weren't known for wanting to share case information with civilians, especially murder cases, but I would try. Cunningham seemed a reasonable man. At least he would take whatever evidence we could put together and give it a fair appraisal. I assured Boyd Donovan that I would do my best.

"Woo, rough, huh," Ron said when I walked into the kitchen to heat water for tea.

"I can't even imagine."

He plucked a donut from the days-old box and stuffed it into his mouth. I knew he was thinking about his own boys. As nasty as things had gotten between him and Bernadette when their marriage ended, at least the kids had been safe. Neither parent would ever neglect or harm them. I patted Ron on the shoulder and carried my tea upstairs.

Before I got back to the specifics of deciphering Chet's notes I decided to call Cunningham in Seattle. I figured Boyd Donovan would have told him the same thing he told me, that he still wanted our help in locating Tali, but it would be good PR to speak to the detective myself.

Cunningham sounded distracted when I got him on the line. I basically reiterated what Boyd had said to me, then told him about the final pages in Chet's notebook.

"Even though the accident is being treated by the police here as a hit-and-run," I said, "I can't help but think that it could be related to this case."

He asked a couple of sharp questions and then said, "I'll let you know. We're swamped here today. I've got forensics working on the remains of the two kids. There's visible evidence of trauma. The daughter had a broken neck, which is probably going to turn out to be her cause of death, and there's a broken arm and some ribs, older injuries. I trust that you won't say any of this to Mr. Donovan. We want a full report, not speculation, before we release any information."

"Are you saying he could be a suspect? That either he *or* Tali could have abused the kids?"

"Someone did. We take these things a step at a time."

"Boyd mentioned a blanket that was found in the grave."

"Yes. He identified it, along with some scraps of clothing. The little girl wore a pink top and jeans. Her brother had on a white sports-logo sweatshirt and dark pants over his diaper." He paused to listen to someone else in the room. "I've got a call. Like I said, I'll contact you if we need anything."

I reported to Ron. "It wasn't quite the brush-off, but near enough," I told him. "All he wanted from us at the moment was a copy of the pages from Chet's notebooks."

"About all we can do, I guess." He pointed at his computer screen. "I just got us a new client. Flagg Corporation. They won a big bid of some kind and now all their employees have to pass background checks. Forty-three to start with, eventually around three hundred once we get the files from all their other branches. That'll keep me busy for awhile."

I was so glad he phrased it that way. Background checks, to me, are deadly dull work. He could have them all. Truthfully, I'd rather do tax returns.

"I'll leave you to it," I said cheerfully.

I gathered the small spiral notebooks and took them downstairs to the copier, where I spent twenty minutes or more lining them up and getting images of the pages. Then I created a cover sheet and faxed the whole stack to the attention of Detective Cunningham.

Meandering back to my office I felt a little bit at loose ends. Clearly, the Seattle police didn't want us mucking about in their case; I understood that. But I had all this data on hand, everything Chet Flowers had left behind.

The one aspect I could check into was Chet's fatal crash. The Seattle police had bigger concerns right now and the New Mexico police were brushing it off as a drunk driver incident. If they could catch the driver who hit Chet's rental car, they would surely prosecute. But I'd gotten no indication from Ramirez that they would track this guy to the ends of the earth.

I did an online search for any news of the wreck. The Santa Fe paper had a two-paragraph story simply stating that a crash had resulted in one fatality south of the city. It didn't give Chet's name or even say that the victim was from out of state. If this was a simple case of DWI, as Ramirez believed, the driver himself wasn't going to come forward in a rush of conscience. As far as he knew he'd just lightly tapped another vehicle. He didn't know that the guy inside it had died, and even if he'd caught the miniscule article in the paper he would be full of justification as to why he didn't think it was the same car, or some such thing. I didn't hold much hope for Chet's killer ever being caught via the regular channels. Which was why I was determined to keep looking into it myself.

While Ron clicked away at his keyboard, digging up background information on folks who thought their jobs were secure, I went back to Chet's notes, from the first day he'd contacted us. As I read about the meetings with Boyd Donovan in San Diego, then on to our interview with Anna Vine in Belen, I began to get a glimpse into his shorthand system.

He always spelled out a person's name in full when he first met them; after that, references to that person usually used only their initials. So, my guess that SS and DS were Scout Stiles and her husband was correct. I found a place earlier in the investigation where their names had come up. BF and RF had to be Babe and Roxanne. Looked as if Tali's whole family were under Chet's microscope.

His final page contained: RF unfriendly, says nothing. BF sullen when ??

I took that to mean he'd gone to Santa Fe and tried talking to Roxanne and Babe Friezel. Since the accident had happened as Chet was southbound out of Santa Fe, it made sense that he'd driven up there that afternoon, maybe had to wait for Roxanne to get home from work, tried asking some questions but didn't get anywhere.

On the page before that one, he'd noted: SS screamed at me, DS says leave her alone. S will never give up Tali. In this city. Seems signif.

Okay, so right before going to Santa Fe to see Babe and Roxanne, he had talked to Scout and Dave Stiles? But I was completely at a loss for what the other notes about the city meant and some significant thing the Stiles's had said to him.

Oh, Chet, if only we could have had one more conversation.

A wild hair of an idea started to grow. This is not always a good thing. I've been known to get into trouble over such things. But I had to know.

Before I could talk myself out of it, I'd muttered to Ron that I was going out for awhile. I gassed up the Jeep at the nearest station and got on I-25 heading north.

The police do not have a suspect in the hit-and-run, I said to myself in justification. *The witness didn't get a plate number and they have nowhere to look. They're waiting for either a confession or the hope that some auto body shop will report to them if the damaged vehicle comes in. All the driver needs to do is keep the car hidden away for a few weeks until every shop forgets it's on the list. I, at least, have some idea where to look.* I was willing to bet pretty heavily that someone in either the Stiles or Freizel homes drove a dark blue car.

All of this rolled through my mind as I left Albuquerque behind and motored northward. The trick, I realized, would be to break in—something I've had a little experience with—and to get back out without being caught. If I found what I was looking for, the police could handle the rest of it.

The Freizel family were doing their best to cover for their little sister and to keep her out of sight. I didn't for one minute believe that none of them knew where Tali was at this moment. In fact, I wouldn't be surprised if it turned out that she'd moved in with one of them. Which got me thinking . . . I just might need to check out their homes as well as their garages.

I swatted at the little angel sitting on my shoulder who told me what Drake would say if he had any inkling about what I was considering. I already knew that my strictly law-abiding husband would tell me to phone my tip to the police and let them handle it.

I guess that could be one way to go.

But I was already halfway to Santa Fe and it would be a wasted trip if I didn't at least try to find out what else Roxanne might be hiding in order to protect her daughter. If one of this clan felt it necessary to get rid of Chet, then there surely was more evidence to be found. But why wouldn't they have destroyed said evidence years ago, I argued with myself.

I went back and forth this way for another twenty minutes until I had reached Roxanne and Babe's neighborhood. I cruised past the house, which appeared unoccupied. Even though I had discarded the idea of reactivating my freelance writer role—I didn't plan for this to be a face-to-face encounter—I thought it best not to give neighbors reason to report that I had returned.

I parked one street over and grabbed a notebook that might help me pass as a survey taker, a college student or maybe a charity volunteer. It really didn't matter as long as I appeared to be walking the residential street with some purpose other than breaking into a house.

Now that the holidays were behind us, it seemed that most people were required back at their jobs. Only two houses on this street had cars in the driveways. Gone were the lights at kitchen windows and sparkling Christmas trees in living rooms. For good measure, in case curious eyes were peering out, I stopped in front of a house, consulted the blank pages in my notebook then stepped up to the front door and rang the bell. When no one answered I walked around to the side and stood in front of their electric meter. While my pen was scratching notes on the page my eyes were scoping out the view past the back yard.

The Freizel place was visible directly behind this one. The houses on either side of where I stood had no windows facing me, so the only one where someone might catch me in the act was the place directly across the street. A momentary nervous flutter went through my stomach but I reminded myself that when you're doing something you shouldn't be, act confident. I squared my shoulders and let myself into the back yard through a side gate. Within a second I'd tucked myself neatly out of view of the street.

From behind a big blue spruce I watched the Freizel place for a good three minutes. Not a movement anywhere.

Come on, Charlie, just get on with it!

I used to listen to that little inner voice a lot more than I do now. Getting cautious with age, I suppose. But this time I listened. I tucked the useless notebook into my purse, slung the strap across my body, and made a dash for the block wall that separated the two properties. I hiked myself over it, and was standing behind the blank back wall of the Freizel's garage before any nosy neighbor could blink.

Loosely, the plan was to get into the garage, find the damaged vehicle and snap a photo of both the bashed front headlamp and the license plate. This could then be sent to the police and ta-da I would have Chet's killer cornered. The hitch in the plan was that when I peered through the window in the side door to that garage, it was empty. No vehicle at all—blue or otherwise.

Well, rats.

I chewed at my lip and drummed my fingers on the doorjamb for a minute.

Okay, so the car wasn't here. Maybe it had been Scout's car. I could check that out later. I glanced at the sliding door that led from the den to a wide back patio. Hmm.

The idea that Tali Donovan might very well be living with one of her sisters still hung out there, a nagging thought that wouldn't go away. Babe Freizel claimed that she'd not stayed in contact with Tali. But that didn't mean her mother hadn't. Or her other sister. Or that she wasn't a terrific liar. I really only had her word for it.

I gave a tug at the sliding door. It moved about a quarter

of an inch but the lock held firm. I could do the old rock through the window thing—petty drug dealers do it all the time. But I wanted to be more subtle than that. If I found something here, I didn't want Babe or Roxanne to know they'd been discovered, not just yet. And I didn't want them to have reason to call the police who would find my fingerprints all over the place. Nor did I want to risk an alarm system going off and alerting the police or the rest of the world.

Geez, Louise, Charlie—stop over-thinking everything. Just get in there!

The glass door was a cheap one and in the end I jostled it enough to get the latch to release. In a way it was the Freizel's fault anyhow; they should have put a dowel in the damn track. I slid inside, closed it behind me and let my eyes adjust to the dim interior.

The place was every bit as depressing with the Christmas decorations gone as it had been before. I gave the kitchen, dining and living rooms a quick scan. The juicy stuff would surely be in a bedroom.

It was pretty easy to tell which room went with each woman. Babe's reminded me of her—dumpy, frumpy, lacking color and all furnished in shades of brown—a feeling of temporary quarters, more like a hotel room than a home. Roxanne's digs gave off more of a permanent air. She used lavender—both the color and the scent. I choked slightly as I walked into the room.

Okay, no dawdling, I reminded myself. Tempting as it might be to poke into all the little family secrets, it would be foolish to push my luck. I was, after all, uninvited and there was always the possibility that someone might have seen my little over-the-wall leap awhile ago. With the stealth of a light-footed feline I crossed to the dresser and ran my hands through the contents of the drawers.

Touching Roxanne's undies was, frankly, somewhat creepy especially given the fact that I didn't come across a single letter, photo, or signed confession from her missing daughter. One drawer contained paperwork, but it all seemed to consist of Roxanne's bank statements and the receipts from her many entries into the Publisher's Clearing House contests. I took a quick peek at the bank statement on top. Her balance was under five hundred dollars and no tantalizingly large money had passed in or out of the account. I stuck all that aside and closed the drawer.

The closet was organized with an obsessive precision. Clothing favored the red and purple color palette and was arranged by item: slacks, blouses, jackets followed by dresses and robes. A pair of slippers, walking shoes, and a pair clearly for the garden rested on the carpeted floor. On the shelf above were clear plastic bins with dress shoes neatly stored, again organized by color. Two cardboard shoe boxes had been shoved to the far side; of course anything unidentified was the first thing to interest me. I pulled them down.

The first one contained photos, a batch of ruffle-edged black and whites. Way before Tali's time. The other box yielded keepsakes—of Tali. Along with photos that showed Roxanne with her youngest daughter in happier times, there were three Girl Scout badges that had never gotten sewn to the requisite sash—I had no idea what skills they represented—one of those second grade handprint mommy gifts, and a high school letter for choir. A cassette tape and some children's birthday cards rounded out the collection.

The cards appeared to be for Tali, from her kids. I opened one. The signatures had been written by an adult, most likely Boyd. I swallowed hard when I saw 'I Love You, Mommy" written there. The cassette being the only unknown, I stuck it in my pocket and closed the box, trying to put everything back in exactly the places I'd found them.

A quick scan of the room didn't show anything else of interest. I took a quick peek in Babe's room but nothing seemed promising. Plus I was getting the feeling that I'd overstayed my time here.

The sliding door presented two possibilities: go out that way and just leave it unlocked. They would notice but since nothing was disturbed in the house the two women would each accuse the other of being forgetful. But that put me leaving by the same way I'd come, which might be remembered by someone in a nearby house. I opted for another form of exit that has worked for me in the past. I locked the slider from the inside and went out the front door.

Immediately after closing it behind me (latch thingy turned to the locked position) I acted as if I'd just arrived and knocked at the door. Any neighbor or passerby who happened to see me there might do a double-take, but they would probably question their own eyesight before they would confront me.

After a long moment I simply walked down the steps to the sidewalk, my survey-taker notebook at the ready. I was about to cross the entrance to the Freizel's driveway when a blue car slowed and pulled in.

My heart pounded at the close call. One more minute inside that house and I would have been toast.

Then the thought hit me. Blue car. I pretended to tie my shoe, watching to see Roxanne Freizel get out of the small Honda sedan. As she walked away from me—quickly enough to avoid taking my survey—I checked out the car. The front headlight was intact.

Chapter 21

Roxanne lingered a few seconds too long on her front porch. She'd noticed me and that wasn't good. I dropped the shoelace and stood up, remembering her plate number without appearing to look at it. It's not easy. I got beyond her driveway before I heard her front door close. I kept my pace steady until I was three houses away and then went into a light jog until I reached my Jeep on the next street over.

By the time I settled into my seat my breath was coming hard and it wasn't only because I'm not used to jogging. I shakily wrote down the plate number of the blue car then started my engine and got the heck out of that neighborhood. In fact I made it completely out of Santa Fe before my pulse slowed down.

I came down La Bajada Hill and thought of Chet. It was

somewhere around here that his accident happened. A car following, a bump in the dark, Chet steering his rental to the breakdown lane but still hitting the center divider. I put those thoughts out of my mind. What I had to do now was to honor his memory by solving the case. Which reminded me of Tali; which reminded me of the tape in my pocket. I pulled it out and put it into the player in the Jeep.

The sounds of laughing and shrieking came through. Kids having a good time. Probably a birthday party. That would be the kind of thing a mom would keep. I listened for about ten minutes, wondering when they would get around to the singing and cake. Or a game of kick the can. Or something. I pushed the Eject button and looked at the plastic cassette. It was a sixty-minute tape, generic brand. No label on it. It might have been Tali's children, or it might have been Tali and her sisters at a young age. Hm. I wound it to the beginning, thinking someone would say what the occasion was. Maybe the Happy Birthday stuff came at the very beginning and someone had forgotten to turn the recorder off, so it had recorded until the tape ran its length. But I played it all the way through and it was the same. A very strange keepsake.

It was mid-afternoon when I got back to Albuquerque and instead of going back to the office or, better yet, going home to snuggle in with Drake and the dog, I decided to scope out the Stiles house and see if I could get a glimpse of their vehicles.

I parked a few doors down from the cul-de-sac entrance and leaned back in my seat to observe. The next thing I knew I was snapping awake to see the Stiles garage door closing. Was that a blue vehicle disappearing into the shadows?

Maybe it would still have its bashed headlight.

But the garage was fully enclosed—not a window or door for me to peer through. Then there was always the possibility that the car which caused the accident was Roxanne's and she'd somehow managed to get it repaired off the police radar.

I was second-guessing myself again and dozing off made me realize I was tired. This week had been too long, with too many cities and too many people coming in and out of my life. I wasn't thinking straight and knew this was no time to attempt sneaking around to look at cars or speaking with Scout to get information. I powered my window down and drove all the way home with the freezing air blasting me in the face.

The house smelled of meaty deliciousness when I walked in. Drake had put a roast in the oven earlier. I slid my arms around his neck, gave him a *very* grateful kiss, and promised him a suitable reward later on. We put together a salad and some veggies and the feast was complete. The result of a feast, as we all know, is that wonderfully lazy crash afterward. I fell victim to it on the sofa and next thing I knew Drake was giving my leg a gentle pat, suggesting that I call it a night. His reward for being the chef would have to wait until morning.

* * *

By the time I arrived at the office, nicely satiated, Ron was already at work with his duties as background checker. I told him that I hadn't really gotten anything valuable from my little jaunt to Santa Fe. I didn't go into the details about leaping the wall or nearly falling asleep in front of Scout's house.

"So, have you been at this computer all night?" I asked.

He barely looked up. "Nah. Vic and I took the boys to get new coats. Justin grows about six inches a day. His stuff could get handed down to Jason but he's so rough on everything. His clothes are worn out an hour after he puts them on."

"Fun stuff."

"Yeah, well, it's hard to say that when you're spending a hundred dollars per kid because they'll only wear a certain brand."

I wanted to tell him he could thank his ex for engendering that attitude but he'd already tuned me out as he typed away at the keyboard. I gave Freckles a doggie cookie and started down the stairs for coffee. Came to a dead stop when a thought hit me.

Coats.

You don't buy your kid more than one coat because they'll outgrow it too fast.

I spun around and dashed back up to my office. Pawing through the photos Chet had left with us, I found it. I dialed Boyd Donovan's number and got sent to voice mail. This wasn't something I could quickly or painlessly say in a recorded message. I told him to call me as soon as he could.

I walked to my bay window and looked down on the street. Frost clung to the grass in shaded areas while those in the sun glistened with dew. The seasons passed normally and life went on, no matter what grisly events happened in the world. It made me feel a little sad.

On my desk, my cell phone rang.

"Charlie? You called?" Boyd sounded all right. He'd had five years to prepare for this week's revelations. Apparently you really can absorb almost anything, eventually.

I picked up a photo that showed the Donovan's laundry room, with a bentwood coat rack next to the back door.

"Did Deni and Ethan have more than one coat each?"

"Huh?"

"Sorry. Detective Cunningham didn't say anything about there being winter coats along with the clothing they found at the, um, gravesite."

"No, he didn't. I don't think there were any."

"Do you see what this means?" I put it together as I talked. "One of the photographs shows two child-sized coats on the rack near the back door of your house. Yet Tali said they were playing outside when they were grabbed by the stranger. The kids wouldn't have been playing outside in December without coats on. So, they weren't snatched from the yard. However it was that they left that house, they were dressed for the indoors."

The phone was silent as he thought about that.

"They may have very well been unconscious or—or even worse," I said. "Tali wrapped them in that blanket."

"They were probably already dead." His words fell flat.

I caught myself nodding, even though there was no way he could know that.

"But does that fact really change anything?" he asked. "Could the prosecutor reopen the case with it?"

"I don't know. But be sure to tell your attorney about it. This little fact helps blow Tali's story to bits. She stuck by the 'dark hooded stranger' story and even got her family to buy into it. We've just proved that was impossible, and it proves premeditation."

He blew out a long breath. "Wow. I can't believe I didn't spot that, right from the beginning. I feel so—"

"You can't blame yourself. Even if you'd noticed the

coats the minute you walked into the house, the kids were already gone. Somehow, she had gotten them out to the woods and she'd come back home before you got there."

"I should have seen it, though. I could have testified. If I'd only known."

"I'm sure she manipulated you, Boyd. She misdirected your attention."

"And appealed to my stupid male ego to stick by her and protect her. I was so dumb."

For the next few minutes I tried to reassure him, say little things to lessen the pain. But it was something he would have to work through. I hung up feeling unsettled, as if there was still something I should be seeing. This wasn't the only piece of the puzzle yet to be set in place.

I meandered downstairs for that cup of coffee I'd never poured and doctored it with plenty of sugar. The fuel only served to keep me pacing my office until the phone rang. I growled under my breath. I missed having Sally here to field the calls.

"I just got off the phone with Boyd Donovan," Detective Cunningham said. "He told me how you'd spotted the kids' winter coats in one of the crime photos."

Oops. Maybe I should have told the police first.

"I seem to remember that we noticed the coats at the time. When we questioned her, Tali said each of the children had two coats. I don't recall if we got anyone to verify that—I would have to go back to the interrogation transcripts. I'm glad you thought to ask Boyd about it now. Good catch."

"I would have called you. Will it help? If you ever arrest Tali, I mean?"

"At this point, we're weighing a lot of options. We can't

retry her on murder charges. The DA jumped the gun on the original trial and lost it. But new evidence is coming out. The medical examiner has found evidence of long-term abuse of both kids. The older child had broken ribs at some point in her life. They had healed, imperfectly. According to all the medical records we've been able to get hold of so far, the child was never seen by a doctor for that."

"They don't do a lot for broken ribs anyway, do they?"

"It depends. But a responsible parent would at least have x-rays done and have the child under a doctor's care. The autopsy on the baby boy shows he had a broken arm at some point. The family doctor had a record of treating that, but he thought it remarkable that it happened at such a young age. Little boys don't usually get those types of injuries until they're old enough to ride bikes and climb trees. The autopsy results appear to be pointing toward circumstances that weren't addressed in the original case against Tali."

"So you might be able to prove charges of child abuse or something like that?"

"We're looking at that. Building a case slowly. I don't want to present any of this to the prosecutor until we have a lot more information. Too many variables. The mother might not have been the responsible party. The injuries could have been accidental. The father might have been culpable, or another family member or even a daycare worker. We've got a long way to go with this yet."

"And I'm to stay mum about this with Boyd Donovan, right?"

"Absolutely. I'm only telling you this much because, one, you were working with Chet Flowers and might come across something in his notes that backs up our case and, two, we'll obviously need to know where Tali Donovan is before we can question or arrest her."

"If you believe she really has come to New Mexico, won't you want the authorities here to work this case along with you?"

"Absolutely. At some point. Right now we still don't have the concrete evidence we need to show that she ever arrived in your state, much less that she's living there now. What I'm hoping you can contribute is to go back through Chet's material, weed out the unusable—the legwork every detective does to get to the goal—and report to me the bottom line: how close was he to finding Tali? And, if he got close, where is she?"

His voice got low and serious. "Do not attempt to confront her or apprehend her. That's for law enforcement to do."

"Do you think she'll be dangerous? To me?"

"I think anyone backed into a corner can get dangerous. She may have harmed only her children in the past, but faced with another trial she could very well strike out at anybody who is in her way. She's gone to a lot of trouble to disappear. More trouble, in my opinion, than an innocent person acquitted of a crime would normally do."

Good point. I had always assumed she went into hiding to avoid the press and the outpouring of public hatred toward her. But it could very well be that she was avoiding this very situation unfolding in front of us. I thanked Cunningham for sharing as much as he had, and I promised to stay in touch.

Two things kept bothering me about Tali Donovan.

Foremost was what my conversation with the police detective had just been about—where was Tali now? But also, I couldn't figure out how she had managed to kill and bury the two children and then cover up her actions that day, even to the point where her own husband hadn't figured out what she was up to.

Of course, I was still trusting Chet's assessment of Boyd Donovan, believing that the now ex-husband truly never understood what his wife was up to until it was too late. I reminded myself to keep an open mind to all possibilities. My eyes landed on the note I'd scribbled with Roxanne's plate number, sending my thoughts back to that angle of the case.

Ron buzzed me on the intercom just as I was picking up the phone to call Sergeant Ramirez. "Is it lunch time yet?"

I rolled my eyes. "Is that a hint for me to go out and get something?"

"It would be nice," he said with completely hokey politeness.

"I'll do it if you'll call Ramirez and see if he'll tell you about this DMV trace," I told him, slipping across the hall to his office and handing him the note.

Since his phone was already resting against his shoulder, he starting punching buttons to dial the policeman's number. When I got back from the deli three blocks away, he delivered his report.

"Ramirez says the plate can't be from the same car as the hit-and-run. The plate is registered to a Honda. The paint transfer from Chet's rental came from a Ford. Midnight Blue. They use it on several models, including SUVs manufactured in the last two years, the F150 pickup line, and a minivan. That's about all he could tell us right now."

Hmm . . . At least it explained why the Honda's front quarter panel was undamaged. So, if Roxanne Freizel's car didn't cause the accident someone else's did. It just opened up the possibilities, once again, to the rest of the world. Scout Stiles had been driving a red car the other day. But I still hadn't gotten a look at Dave's car and wasn't about to rule out anyone in that family.

I thanked Ron and handed him his ham-and-cheese on white bread. We each ate at our desks, Ron intent on getting through those background checks for Flagg as quickly as possible and me—I found my head whirling with the new information I'd picked up this morning. Information but not a lot of answers.

The telephone kept ringing with callbacks from Ron's inquiries, which really didn't help my state of mind. Each time I thought I was getting close to something, an interruption happened. I finally set the answering machine and told Ron he could deal with the calls he wanted to and ignore the rest. I packed up all the Donovan case information and decided I could get more done from my own kitchen table.

Chapter 22

I pulled into my driveway, a little dismayed to see that I had a visitor. Katie Brewster sat on our front porch, huddled against the wall with her arms wrapped around herself. I knew at a glance that she was crying.

She looked up at me with reddened eyes when I got out of the Jeep. Freckles jumped down and rushed to lick at Katie's face. She sobbed as she ruffled the wriggly puppy's fur.

"Katie? What's wrong?" I knelt so she would have to look at my face.

She shook her head back and forth.

"Katie . . ." All kinds of disaster scenarios went through my head.

"Me and my dad had a fight."

"Ah. You want something to drink? I was just about to make some tea."

"He called me a liar." She stood up and stomped her boots, as if there was snow on them.

I unlocked the door and she followed me inside. "You look kind of cold. How about some cocoa or apple cider?"

She trailed me into the kitchen as I put the kettle on. I heard a moist sniff so I handed her the tissue box.

"You want to talk about the fight?"

"I told him Felina keeps secrets from him. She had a nose job. Then he goes, 'hunh-uh' and I'm like '*yeah*.' And then he gets all bent cause he asked where I found that out and I said I found proof in one of her vanity drawers when I went to borrow some eye shadow. He gets mad at me and says I can't be going through Felina's stuff. 'Grownups have private things kids can't get into.' He means those disgusting thongs she wears. I've even found weirder stuff than that."

Whoa, too much information. I turned to the kettle, which was about to whistle.

"Cocoa? Cider?" I offered.

"You said you were having tea. Do you make it the same way the queen does? Cause I saw this TV show about England and they make their tea pretty fancy."

I had serious doubts about the queen preparing her own tea, but I offered to brew some in a pot and call it real English tea, and that idea seemed to interest her. Anything to keep her off the subject of her stepmother's underwear. I rummaged for a teapot and tossed in two bags, hoping she wouldn't point out that real English tea used loose leaves. I set out a pair of my mother's china cups and saucers and Katie settled at the table, while I put the final Christmas cookies on a plate.

"I just wanted some eye shadow that was a more adult color than my old black kind," she said, not yet finished with the earlier conversation. "I told my dad I'd, you know, buy my own once I get my paycheck.

"Plus, how insulting that he didn't even take this seriously." She pulled a couple of scraps from her pocket; one was a business card. "Look on the back. Isn't that word, rhinoplas— whatever. Doesn't that mean nose job?"

I poured the tea and sat down before picking up the card.

It was from a cosmetic surgeon in Scottsdale, Arizona. Written on the back was the word rhinoplasty and a dollar amount that would have fed a small African village for a year.

"That's her writing," Katie said. "Felina went to this doctor."

"Well . . . it could mean that she just asked for the price." The card looked a little beaten, as if it had been in the bottom of a makeup bag for awhile. "Maybe she consulted the doctor a long time ago and then forgot all about it." No way was I going to mention the tidbit of gossip I'd heard at the food bank to a twelve-year-old who was likely to go running straight to her dad with 'but Charlie said . . .'.

"So you don't believe me either." She leaned back in her chair and folded her arms across her chest.

"Sorry. I didn't say that. I'm just offering an alternate suggestion. It's called playing devil's advocate. It's not really an argument, it's just when you come up with other possibilities for a situation."

"Hm. Maybe." She held out the other scrap of paper. "So what's this, then? It's some kind of secret, I'll bet. I didn't even show this one to my dad after he accused me of being a snoop."

The folded square was an old newspaper clipping, even

more battered than the business card. The article was a short squib about a mugging. The victim was not named and the undated piece only said that the police were looking into it. An odd thing for anyone to hold onto as a keepsake. I handed it back and Katie jammed it into her pocket.

"So, what should I do?" Katie asked after a few noisy slurps at the hot tea. "About my dad being mad at me."

If a twelve-year-old girl didn't already know how to wrap her father around her little finger, I wasn't sure what information I could offer but she probably just wanted reassurance.

"All parents and kids have disagreements and parents are amazingly forgiving," I said, remembering a couple of my own grosser breaches of conduct. "I'd bet that if you just told him you were sorry and promised not to get into Felina's things anymore, that's all it would take. He won't stay mad at you for long."

"You think?"

"I'm pretty sure."

She gobbled down the last two cookies and looked a lot happier than when she'd arrived. I watched her walk down the block, then retrieved the files I'd brought home from the office. Clearing the tea things from the table I realized that Katie had left the surgeon's business card behind. Why would a person keep a card like that, from a doctor far from home?

Personally, I agreed with Katie. Felina probably did have some 'work' done and wanted, for whatever reason, to keep that fact from Jerry. The conversation between the two women at the food bank only added further fuel to the fire of my curiosity. On a whim I picked up the telephone.

Okay, I know this is really none of my business, and if

Jerry Brewster were my dad he'd be well within his rights to ground me for life . . . But I did it anyway.

A bubbly sounding receptionist answered the phone.

"Hello," I said. "This is Felina Brewster. I was a patient of Doctor Carter's a few years back. I need to have my medical records sent to me at my new address."

"Brewster? Hold a moment and let me pull your file. I'll need to verify some information with you."

This could get sticky. But before I'd made the decision whether to brave my way through it or hang up like a chicken, she came back on the line.

"Ms. Brewster? I don't find a record under your name." She verified the spelling. "That's what I looked for. Could you have used another last name when you came here?"

Eek. Felina probably had done exactly that. If she'd had surgery it was before she met Jerry Brewster, and I had no idea what her maiden name was.

"Um, no. Maybe there's another Doctor Carter in the area and I've just gotten the wrong number." I hung up before the woman could take the conversation any further.

I turned to the sink and washed the tea cups and teapot vigorously enough to cover my embarrassment over that stupid call. What had I hoped to accomplish anyway? Thinking I might find evidence to back up Katie's side of the argument? Or, really, just wanting to verify the dishy gossip. *Really, Charlie, you never go for that stuff.* I left the card on the table so I would remember to give it back to Katie. She could figure out how to deal with it at home.

I was standing in front of an open cupboard, staring at the packaged foods and trying to figure out what to make for dinner, when Drake got home.

"Hey you," I said. "Good day?"

"Pretty good. Got the hundred-hour inspection done, so I'm legal to fly again. How are you and Ron getting along at the office without Sally?"

I noticed that he glanced at the stack of files I still hadn't touched since I got home.

"The phones were going nuts and all the calls were for Ron. I couldn't get anything done."

"What part of the case are you stuck on?"

He always asks things like that, even though he has his hands full with his own business and doesn't get much into the details of the investigations.

"All of it," I admitted. "I've got some leads on finding the vehicle that ran Chet Flowers off the road. Just haven't had time to follow up on them. Macaroni and cheese okay for dinner?"

I reached for the box of that oh-so-easy dish that even kids can make. He pushed it back onto the shelf.

"I've got a better idea. I'll quick-thaw some steaks, throw together a salad . . . You can take your files into the dining room and work where it's quiet until I tell you dinner is ready."

How did I ever get so lucky? This man is priceless.

I spread the files out over the dining table where I would have more space. From that monster-sized police file that Chet had originally given me, I set out to create a time sequence of the day the Donovan children vanished. With a blank sheet of paper at hand, I started reading through the interviews. After an hour I had something like this (all times are approximate except for the police call, for which there is an official record):

8:00 a.m. – Boyd Donovan leaves for work. Says it's the last time he ever saw his children. (verified by Tali and by co-workers who say he arrived on time)

10:00 a.m. – Tali Donovan says she took the kids and went to do some shopping. (Two neighbors verify seeing the three leave the house, no one saw them come home)

12 noon – Tali says she came home, made lunch, put the kids down for naps. Her sister Scout says she phoned about noon and the kids were eating lunch. She heard Tali pause a couple of times to speak to them. (verified by Tali and Scout, phone records show a call at 11:37)

3:00 p.m. – Tali says the kids were playing in the back yard from about 2:00 onward. She was with them but went inside to take a phone call. (neighbor heard the children for a few minutes between 2:30 and 3:00 when she got up from her TV show)

3:10 p.m. – Tali comes back outside and the kids are missing but she sees a man running off through the woods. (no one can verify and searchers find no evidence of this)

4:15 p.m. – Boyd comes home for an early dinner with the family and Tali informs him the kids have been kidnapped. (Boyd and Tali agree on this)

4:29 p.m. – Boyd calls police. (a matter of official record)

Bite marks on the cap of my ballpoint pen attested to the fact that I'd been concentrating pretty intently when Drake called out that dinner was ready. How had I missed the fabulous smell of those steaks under the broiler? I carried my page of notes to the kitchen with me.

"Okay, help me spot the weaknesses in this story," I told Drake, laying the paper down where we could both see it as we ate.

He pointed to the early entries. "No one saw them come home from shopping. Tali took the kids somewhere and abandoned them."

"My first thought too. Except that Scout called around noon and Tali was talking to her kids."

"*If* you believe the sister."

"And I don't, necessarily. But she did testify to it in court."

He gave me a raised eyebrow that said, *People never lie on the witness stand? Get real.*

"Okay, okay. I know. The two of them were super close and none of that family's testimony may carry *any* weight." I forked up a chunk of baked potato. "But even more convincing is the neighbor's testimony that she heard the kids playing outside later in the afternoon. She wouldn't lie on the stand for Tali. I got the feeling that woman would take no nonsense from no one. She was pretty rigid."

"Tali says the kids went missing around three but didn't notify the police or even call her own husband. She just waited for him to come home. That's pretty weird."

"It's definitely weird. It's what put her on trial. No one could believe what she did, but they couldn't prove that she had time to take the kids away after three o'clock, dispose of them, and get home in time to be all cool and calm when Boyd got there. As it turns out, the spot where the kids were buried was nearly an hour away, depending on traffic."

"So, there's no way she could have made the round trip from their house to the grave and back—even if the grave was already dug and waiting—after the time the neighbor thought she heard them playing . . ."

My breath caught. "What did you say—?"

Oh my god, this was the answer. I dropped my fork and ran to the dining table, pushing papers aside as I looked for it.

The cassette tape.

Chapter 23

The phone nearly slipped out of my hands twice as I fumbled Detective Cunningham's number. By the time he answered, I was feeling a little breathless.

"Charlie. I didn't expect to hear from you so soon," he said when he came on the line.

I realized that he meant he didn't think I would locate Tali so quickly.

"I've got some new evidence. I hope it will help, but it isn't Tali herself yet. This is something she kept. Her mother had it in her possession."

I better not go into detail about how it had come into my hands. Hands. Fingerprints. I backed away from picking up the tape again. I would slip it into a plastic bag later.

"I know how Tali's kids could be gone all afternoon, even when Mrs. Richards testified that she heard them playing outside. It makes a lot of sense. Tali could have played the tape loudly, spoken up now and then to make it sound as if she was talking to them. Anyone who couldn't see through the thick bushes that separate their two properties wouldn't have reason to question that it was a mother and her kids spending some time outdoors."

"So the kids might have been gone from the house hours earlier than we believed," he said.

"It makes sense, I think."

"I do too. I'll need that tape."

"Will overnight shipping be good enough?"

He laughed. "It's been five years. We can wait a day."

I promised to package it up and send it first thing in the morning.

"Make a copy first. Even though we'll want the one she actually touched, it's good to have a backup. And, Charlie, I'm not asking how you got this tape but once someone realizes it's missing . . . well, things could get pretty desperate for Tali. She'll be like a cornered animal if she thinks the police will come after her again."

"Yeah, she might."

"Just be careful. I'm glad you are looking for her, but don't approach. Just call me and I'll alert the New Mexico authorities to actually bring her in."

"Okay. And if I can find out that she was somehow involved in Chet Flowers' death, I really want them to come down hard on her."

"Charlie . . ."

"Okay, I know. Just call. I will."

I used a plastic bag to pick up the tape gingerly by the edges and slip it into our recorder to make a copy. Then I slipped the bag around it and packaged it up for Fed Ex.

By this time Drake had cleared the table, made coffee and turned a slice of fruitcake into something fresh and delicious by topping it with some kind of warm sauce.

"How do you *do* this?" I said with a grin as he handed me a plate.

"Taste it first. It might not be all that great."

But it was and I ate way too much. Consequently, I had a heartburn-filled night and woke around five in the morning knowing that I had to get up and get moving.

Thoughts of how to catch Tali Donovan had filled my sporadic dreams. During a pre-dawn walk with Freckles, while I held a little brainstorming session with myself, verbalizing every possibility, I came to one conclusion. Scout Stiles was going to be my ticket to her sister. She *had* to be in contact. I merely had to ride her ass until she led me there.

That little question settled, I started to pick apart the details. Scout had seen my vehicle when I went to her house that time before Christmas. She might not remember it with one sighting, but she would certainly start to notice it parked outside her house and trailing her all over the city.

To do this right I should get a team together, but since Drake had flights every day this week, Sally had a new baby to nurse, and Ron was up to his neck with the Flagg contract, I wasn't sure who else I could ask. Too bad Katie Brewster wasn't old enough to drive; that kid was a pretty good little snoop. Right now it would be me, on my own.

At least I could switch vehicles now and then. Freckles and I got back to the house and she ate her breakfast. I felt itchy to be doing something toward the solution to this thing so I could be done with the whole case. I don't know how the police do it, stick with a case for weeks, months, years. I'm too much a child of the modern age; I want instant gratification and I want it now.

I gathered myself some granola bars and fruit, telling myself it was a healthy eating kick, but in truth it was the quickest thing to grab. Scribbling a note for Drake I told him I was taking his truck and leaving the Jeep for him. Freckles didn't especially want to go back in her crate so quickly but I could see real problems with having to feed and walk a dog while on surveillance. Thousands of icy-looking stars prickled the clear sky as I backed out of the drive and headed toward the west side. At a convenience store I got the largest coffee they sold and picked up a bag of Cheetos for later. Just in case healthy eating became too boring.

The Stiles house sat in darkness when I cruised past, no real surprise there. It was still not quite six. I gave it a pretty good stare on the first pass, circled the cul-de-sac and parked a few houses away in a spot that gave me a clear view of their front door and driveway.

Within minutes a small window at the side lit up. Bathroom. Somebody was starting the day. I sipped at my coffee and pretended this was my ideal way to start a glorious new day. When my legs started to feel like popsicles I started the engine and ran the heat for a few minutes. Sitting in a vehicle early on a January morning was noticeable enough; sitting there with the exhaust pipe puffing away would surely bring someone's attention.

I shut the heater down, ate two granola bars, finished the coffee, fidgeted in my seat. Another light came on at the front of the Stiles house, probably the kitchen, but the shade remained down and I really couldn't pick out movement at this distance. Two neighbors got into their frosty cars and drove away. I found myself starting a little mental checklist of which residents had left and which were still home.

At a quarter of eight, with sunshine beginning to brighten the rooftops, the Stiles garage door started to rise. At my angle I couldn't see exactly what was happening but it appeared that only one vehicle was parked in there. As the red Civic backed out I could see that Scout was driving and Dave rode shotgun. From their hand gestures and the intensity of their facial expressions as they passed it sure looked to me as if they were arguing. *Hey guys, that's not really a good way to start your day.*

I had to pull into another driveway and turn around in order to follow, but as they were so busy with each other they didn't appear to notice. I managed to get onto Coors Road before I lost sight of them, and then it was a matter of hitting all the lights green since I had no idea where they were going. If one of them had to be at work by eight, they hadn't allowed much time for the brutal amount of traffic that makes the commute across the river into the city every morning. I really hoped we weren't in for a NASCAR style attempt to beat the clock.

But Scout stuck to the surface streets and on the dot at 7:59 dropped Dave off in front of an office building. I didn't have time to study the listing of tenants, but the place seemed mostly to house small businesses; I spotted a graphic arts firm and an ad agency before I had to start paying attention to Scout again.

The little red car wasn't too difficult to keep in sight, despite the heavy traffic. She stayed on Coors for a mile or more before making the sudden decision to whip off the road at the entrance to a self-storage unit. Ah, now this could get interesting. I've watched enough of those reality shows to know there's always great stuff in these places.

She went through a high chain-link gate and made a left, clearly knowing exactly where she was going. I watched until she'd turned right at the third row in the little community of garage-sized buildings. Staying unnoticed in these tight quarters would be a trick. I needed to see exactly where Scout went but couldn't let her spot me. I wheeled Drake's small pickup into the facility and took the 'street' before the one where Scout had gone. Running parallel, I sped up, turned left, and peeked.

Sure enough, she had parked the Civic in front of a unit where she was in the process of raising the door. I grabbed a ball cap that Drake always seems to be leaving somewhere, gathered my hair into a ponytail and pulled the cap low over my eyes. Sunglasses added to my minimal disguise, and I worked my jaw as if I had a big wad of gum in my mouth. Hopefully, I'd not made enough of an impression on Scout at our first meeting that she would figure me out now.

Chewing like crazy, I cruised slowly past the units as if I were having a hard time finding a certain one. As I approached the Civic my eyes were squarely on the contents of Scout's garage space. Inside, was parked a big Ford SUV. Scout had the passenger door open and appeared to be rummaging in the glove compartment. She briefly glanced up at me. I turned my head back and forth, still looking for some unit I couldn't seem to find, until she went back to her business. I memorized the plate number from the SUV, then cruised to the end of the row and pulled the truck up to a unit about ten spaces down from Scout's.

I jotted down that prized number, then ever so slowly

got out of the truck, pulled my coat around me, and pretended to work at the padlock on someone's storage place. Scout came out of the unit carrying a large brown envelope, hopped into her Civic and drove past me way too fast for the tight space. The moment she went out of sight I got moving. By the time I spotted her she was already past the manager's office, out the gate and making a right-hand turn onto Coors.

The first traffic light caught me and I tapped my fingers impatiently as I lost sight of the red car in the rush hour traffic. The best I could do at this point was to make an educated guess. Two lights later, Scout's car sat at a red light and I waited six cars back. She continued to head for home and I hung back as we entered her neighborhood. All the other cars were going the other direction, people heading toward the business areas, not away.

I pulled to the curb three streets away from Scout's and looked through my phone calls to find Sergeant Ramirez's number in Santa Fe. Not surprisingly, my call went to voice mail so I left the plate number I'd gotten from the Stiles SUV and told him the name and unit number of the place where it was stored.

A break from surveillance was in order. I had to pee. Plus, I justified to myself, I'd reached one important goal and it wasn't even nine o'clock yet. With a little pat on the back I headed for a McDonald's I'd passed where I used the bathroom and ordered myself the big breakfast. Granola can only hold a girl so long.

Fortified, I cruised back through Scout's neighborhood. Her red Civic sat in the driveway where, as it turned out, it would sit until almost three o'clock. I slumped low in my seat, trying for invisibility but that didn't seem to matter in this working class neighborhood where it seemed that everyone except Scout Stiles was away all day.

The sun continued to warm the air and to keep from drifting off I made phone calls, checking in at the office (Ron had finished one batch of employee checks for Flagg and assured me that he had impressed them so well that another set was on the way) and with Drake (not so happy with me for taking his truck, but as he was currently in the air over a herd of elk he really couldn't say much). I called Sally and got a glowing report of how well mommy and baby were doing. Tried to think of other friends to call, but frankly couldn't think of anyone who would welcome a call in the middle of their work day. No one I knew had this much free time on their hands.

I felt myself getting dozy in the warm truck and was about to allow myself the luxury of a little break to rest my eyes when I became aware of movement in the distance. Scout was in the Honda and the car was in motion. I dipped down out of sight until I heard it go by then tried to adopt a casual pace as I kept her in sight.

Out on Coors the traffic was far lighter than it had been this morning but there were still plenty of vehicles to lose mine in the crowd and manage to stick with her through the four hundred traffic lights before we got to I-40 and aimed eastbound over the river. She exited almost immediately at Rio Grande Boulevard and started toward Old Town. Call me slow, but it took a full five minutes after she bypassed that popular shopping locale to realize she was heading straight for my house.

Chapter 24

Every thought in the world went through my head. Scout had somehow identified me; she'd gotten my address; she planned a showdown or maybe just a flashy little firebomb through my living room window. As we entered my neighborhood I held back, trying to come up with a strategy except that I had no idea what she was up to.

She continued on what was my normal route home but then . . . she made a wrong turn. I slowed and watched from a block away, then caught up as she made another turn. She turned into the long drive of the Talavera Mansion. I did a whole mental double-take. The Brewsters?

I parked around a bend in the road and pocketed my keys.

When I walked up to the edge of the property Scout was nowhere in sight. Her car was parked near the garages rather than in front of the portico. It seemed she knew the layout pretty well. I crept from spruce to spruce, shrub to shrub, trying to stay out of sight, which is a trick when a home has about a hundred windows on every side.

Laughter from the south side of the place attracted my attention. I edged to the corner of the house and took a peek through a tall arbor vitae. Scout Stiles and Felina Brewster greeted each other with a big hug; they were laughing over the beautiful weather.

"Let's sit outside for awhile," Felina said. "It's so nice not to be cooped up inside with the kids."

I moved a branch aside that was jabbing me in the ribs and positioned myself so I could watch as they arranged a pair of deck chairs to face the sun. Scout glanced up toward the third floor.

"Julia's taken him for a walk. They'll be gone for awhile. Katie's in school. God, finally. I just wish Jerry had taken some time off to be with me."

"You and I are just alike in that," Scout said. "Could easily do without kids in our lives."

"Kids are fine. As long as they belong to somebody else. I pictured this life with Jerry . . . we would travel in the lifestyle the dealerships provide . . . shopping in Milan, dining in Paris . . . Nobody else in the picture . . ."

Scout gave a little sigh. "You do seem to pick the right guys for that. Dave is never going to make it up the corporate ladder."

"I don't know about this time. Jerry is so into the whole kid thing. My idea of sending Katie off to boarding school—somewhere exclusive, mind you—he blew that off altogether. And what was I thinking with Adam?"

"You were thinking you would get the wedding done a lot quicker and then have a little procedure, call it a miscarriage . . . Jerry would have never figured it out."

"I should have done it anyway. I could have found some doctor."

"You made that mistake with the first one but you're lucky," Scout said. "You got the chance to start all over."

Felina laughed. "Had to completely reinvent myself. Thanks to you, sis."

I stared hard at Felina, a sickening feeling forming in my gut.

Scout Stiles had said in one of the police interviews that Tali only wanted a successful husband, one who could show her the good life.

Felina? Tali? Visions of the photos of Tali Donovan flashed back at me. She was a lot heavier than Felina. She had dark hair and an uneven complexion. Her features were different. And yet . . .

A breeze ruffled the shrubs and both women exclaimed over it.

"Ooh, chilly," Felina said. "Let's go inside."

They were out of their chairs before I had a chance to think.

"I've got Dave's car hid—" Scout's words got cut off as they closed the door behind them.

Okay, I had a lot to process and more to learn. I crouched below the level of the windows and worked my way around to the front of the house. The front door was locked but I found another, a plain one with a path leading toward the detached garages. I twisted the knob carefully and it opened, with only a small creak, into a laundry room.

I stepped in and closed it, my eyes adjusting to operating in the dim light from a triplet of small windows at the top of the door.

Aside from a washing machine and dryer, the room contained cabinets for supplies, a sorting bin with divided sections, and an ironing board. I realized with a start that I'd nearly run into it. I slowed my breathing.

I ran through the confusing data. Felina looked nothing like Tali Donovan but she had to be. She'd called Scout *sis*.

Boyd Donovan had talked about Tali's obsessive need to have him to herself, how she'd become more needy when the children came along and he'd failed to notice the little tortures she put them through. I thought of little Adam Brewster with his tiny arm in a cast. Ethan Donovan had also suffered a broken arm at a young age.

Their voices came closer, then faded. They probably wouldn't come in here, I reasoned, but hiding out wasn't gaining me any new information either. I needed to report this to Detective Cunningham, but I might as well use the opportunity to learn as much as I could. I opened the inner door a crack, trying to figure out where I was in the gigantic house.

The visible sliver of room appeared to be the kitchen. A wine bottle stood on the end of a granite countertop, with a corkscrew beside it. I edged the door a little wider and stuck my head out. I couldn't hear the women from here. A clock chimed four times in the foyer.

Sticking to the edges of the rooms, where I could quickly duck behind something, I worked my way from the kitchen, through the dining room and foyer. Finally, I began to hear the hum of conversation from the living room. I stood just outside the door and heard them perfectly.

"You know where? Hawaii," Scout said, giggling a little. "A girls' trip away. We get one of those big hotels where the desk won't let any calls through that you don't want. That way, Dave will leave me alone about the stupid Expedition and that little bashed place. I told him we shouldn't have it fixed right away but he doesn't get why."

"Not Hawaii," Felina said. "That's where Jerry and I went for—"

"Ah, yes, your neat little plan to snag him by getting pregnant."

Felina growled at her sister. "I don't want to go away right now. I almost have Jerry ready to take a romantic trip with me to Europe this spring. I just need to take care of a few lit-tle details."

The way she said 'little' sent a chill right through me.

I rubbed at my arms. The chill wasn't only coming from Felina's words. The front door had opened and Jerry Brewster stood in the center of the foyer.

Chapter 25

Jerry stared right at me.

"How much did you hear?" I asked.

"Enough."

Felina and Scout had gone quiet. I peered around the edge of the doorjamb just in time to dodge a flying lamp. It shattered against the heavy wood frame and shards stabbed at my face and arms.

"Felina! Stop it," Jerry demanded. But it was too late.

Scout had taken up the battle and each time I showed my face they threw something else, seemingly intent on ridding the elegant room of every breakable object.

Felina's eyes were wild, her hair flying like a mane around her shoulders.

"Jerry, call the police," I said as I dodged yet another missile.

"I can't believe it, you bitch!" Felina screamed. "You

had to interfere. Things were going just *fine*. I had a *plan*."

"I know about that," I said, as calmly as one can when a crystal rabbit is flying across the room. "Your plan to get rid of the kids."

Jerry had dialed 911 but he forgot to speak when he heard that part.

"Just like your plan five years ago when you succeeded at it. When you killed two innocents."

Jerry's face had gone white and I seriously worried that he might faint dead away. I felt sure that the 911 recording would contain only a babble of incomprehensible nonsense, punctuated by shattering glass.

"The Talavera Mansion!" I screamed, not daring to turn my back on the living room. "Jerry, tell them your address— we need help here!"

For the moment we had them cornered but I didn't have a weapon of any sort and Jerry, I could tell, was so stunned he would be useless in a physical fight. I could only think to keep them talking long enough for the police to get here.

"You killed Chet Flowers, Scout. You'll be up for murder once the police find where you have that Ford hidden."

"*If* they find it," she smirked. "And even then, it was an accident. I'll say I had a little too much to drink and didn't even realize I hit him. No one can prove otherwise."

"Maybe not, but what about when they prove that you helped your sister get rid of the bodies of her own children? You never went to trial for that. Double jeopardy doesn't apply to you."

Both women paused and looked at each other, and I knew I'd struck a nerve with my guess. That's the thing that had been nagging at me as I read through all the interviews in the Donovan case. Tali, the dependent one, needed someone more cunning than herself to pull off that crime. So she'd taken the bodies of the kids, stopped by her sister's house and begged for help. Scout had probably worked out the timeline and the cover story. She might have even helped dig the grave.

Chapter 26

Sitting in a police interrogation room for hours isn't exactly fun, no matter how comfortable they attempt to make it for you. Tali Donovan aka Felina Brewster and her sister Scout had been cuffed and taken from the house in squad cars. Jerry Brewster and I followed in our own vehicles, at the request of the two officers who had arrived at the mansion about the time the supply of glass projectiles was about to run out.

After thirty minutes or so of trying to explain that this was not simply a little domestic dispute, I placed a call to my brother and requested that Kent Taylor from homicide join us. Kent, fortunately, believed my assertion that this was a case of murder and child endangerment and probably a whole lot more, and he was happy to tell the detective who was grilling me that I had a history of getting mixed up in such things.

"At least she's trying to stay on the right side of the law as she does this stuff," he said to the officer. He sent me a wink as he left the room.

Ron showed up, presented his license and gave the background on how we'd been hired by Chet Flowers to assist on his investigation. Finally, nearly two hours into the mess, they began to believe me and we got on with the business of piecing together the events. Hours later I signed a statement and drove home, tired beyond even caring that I'd never eaten any dinner.

Drake patiently cleaned the scratches on my face and arms. "One of these could probably use a couple of stitches," he said. "I'm putting a little butterfly thing on it now, but you might want to see the doc in the morning."

I thanked him for the nursing care and the fact that he was not lecturing me for taking his truck without asking. We fell into bed and snuggled into a cozy little nest of comfort.

The phone began ringing before daybreak.

"What's this in the *Journal*?" Linda Casper demanded. "How badly were you hurt?"

I didn't remember being hurt at all until I scraped one of my tiny cuts against the receiver. I assured her I was fine.

"Tell her about the one that needs stitches," Drake mumbled from his side of the bed.

"It's nothing." He kicked me under the covers. "Okay, Drake says one of these stupid little things needs a stitch or two."

"Get into my office this morning," Linda said. "I'll take care of it *and* I want to hear the rest of this story."

"Did our newspaper come?" I asked as I stepped out of the shower awhile later to find Drake up and dressed, looking as if he'd already been out to walk the dog.

"It's on the kitchen table." He leered at me and pulled my towel off and we both kind of forgot about everything else for awhile.

A second shower, together, and then I felt ready to face whatever the day would bring. During the night my mind had run through all the loose ends of the case. I would need to talk with Boyd Donovan and fill him in, just in case the Albuquerque police hadn't quite gotten that far yet. Chet's daughter Shayna was another call I should make, but first a final wrap-up with Cunningham in Seattle. It promised to be a long day.

Before I'd tied my shoes I got another call. Ramirez in Santa Fe, letting me know that the paint and the damage on the dark blue Ford in Scout's storage unit matched. Although I knew it already, it was good to know that she was, at the very least, up for manslaughter in her hit-and-run accident. Once the connections with Chet's investigation were established, I had little doubt that the police could prove premeditation and make the charges a whole lot more serious. A tiny part of me gloated.

The front page story in the newspaper had gotten the essence of the story, with a few jumbled facts. But then, that's usually the case with most 'breaking news' stories anymore. I spread it out on the table while Drake made us some toast.

The mystery of Tali Donovan, the missing Seattle mom acquitted of the killings of her two young children, is at least partially solved. Donovan had changed her name and appearance and has been living here in Albuquerque for the past four years as Felina Brewster, wife of prominent auto dealer Jerry Brewster.

The piece went on to rehash nearly the whole Donovan case which the nation had heard *ad nauseam* five years ago. Then a whole section was devoted to the history of the Brewster's successful business endeavors in the city and how their home was a featured showplace on the annual Christmas luminaria tour.

Donovan was arrested yesterday at her home after a prolonged confrontation with local private investigator, Charlotte "Charlie" Parker. Parker sustained several injuries in the assault. Jerry Brewster was also present at the scene and he phoned the police. After her arrest, Mrs. Brewster was positively identified as Tali Donovan by a small birthmark on her back.

Jerry phoned the police after I screamed at him. And I hate how they always get that part wrong about me being the licensed PI in our firm. I sighed and read on.

Felina had said she had to reinvent herself and that's exactly what happened. The *Journal* had tracked down that clinic in Scottsdale and found a chatty former employee who agreed to speak only under conditions of anonymity—of course. Doctor Carter had done a lot more than a nose job for Tali. Cheek implants, silicone breasts and lip enhancement were among the procedures. I studied the before and after pictures the newspaper had dug up. Once a woman goes through all that, I decided, how hard can it be to shed thirty pounds and bleach your hair?

When the first calls began coming in from reporters—both local and national—who wanted my version of the events, we decided to unplug the phone and escape. I gathered up the case files and drove to the office. But a Channel 4 news van was parked outside and I just kept on driving. I called Ron on my cell and warned him. Drake, at least, could take to the air. I decided to head for Linda Casper's office. I could think about this while she went at my face with a needle.

"I don't often get to treat a celebrity here in my little family practice," Linda joked as she gathered her implements.

I growled. Getting my name in the paper had been the very last thought on my mind.

"Psychology never seemed the right field for me," Linda said as she spread something on my forehead to numb the area. "But I always found it fascinating. I read a paper once on these types of women. One writer referred to this as the Cinderella Complex—women who believe that prince charming will come along to take care of them and make their lives perfect. It really stems from an insecurity about being independent."

"When Tali, or Felina, was talking to her sister she went on about how she had envisioned having Jerry all to herself, how the kids always got in the way."

"Of her dream scenario. It's an attitude she might have gotten from her mother." She did something with the needle that tugged at my skin.

I closed my eyes and refused to think about it.

"I'll admit it, I read the whole story this morning and then went online to find out more of Tali's background," Linda said. "Her father was gone from an early age. Her mother had three kids to raise and no man around. Tali probably had idealistic memories of her dad since she was too young to remember any of his possible negative traits. If her mother groused about the displeasing aspects of single motherhood, Tali quite likely concluded that having a prince-charming husband and no children was the ideal life. He would accept her emotional dependence and provide complete financial security.

"On the face of it, this is the way we're hard-wired. Men have a desire to protect and defend their women. Women, being physically weaker and having the offspring to care for, need a man to fill that defender role."

"It's just that some women take it way too far."

"As do some men. Witness the guy who can't accept that his woman wants to leave him so he stalks her and will even harm her to keep her belonging to him."

People can be so messed up. I let Linda do whatever she was doing to my little cuts, reflecting how lucky Drake and I were. Having balance in the relationship—each of us equally dependent and equally independent—was ideal.

And keeping it fair, I really should cook a little more often.

Chapter 27

The end of January came around, a time when I was thankful to have a quiet spell—no murders, no drama. We were getting along by having Sally and little Ross Junior working at the office a couple hours a day. It helped that she could handle the filing and most of Ron's correspondence while the baby slept at her side. I was spending some of that time with Drake, logging flight time so I could qualify to go along with him this summer to Alaska.

It was a Tuesday afternoon, near closing time, when I looked up from Sally's desk to see a dark-haired young woman come in the front door.

"You must be Charlie," she said. "I'm Rosa Flores."

We did quick little acknowledgements and I buzzed Ron to come downstairs.

"I just wanted to stop by and thank both of you," Rosa

said. "I don't know what I would have done if Ivana had—had passed . . . without seeing her first."

"I'm sorry the circumstances were so sad," I said.

Ron inquired about Mel.

"He's doing okay, I guess. We've talked. I can't see myself ever going back to live in California. I've got a promotion at work and a great bunch of friends here. But he and I will stay in touch." Her face held the sadness of her recent loss, and I knew it would be awhile before it began to fade.

Ron and I both gave her hugs and told her to call if she needed anything, but I doubted we would hear from her. She seemed content and independent.

Almost four months went by before I saw Jerry Brewster again. I spotted him with his children at the playground equipment in the park one afternoon in late April. Katie called out to Freckles and the dog went dashing toward her.

"She's grown *so* much!" Katie exclaimed.

Funny how you never see that when you and your little one are together all the time. Sally was already noticing that about her infant son, cherishing both of her children all the more as the horrific story of Tali Donovan's crimes re-emerged in the media.

Adam Brewster's eyes had lost some of the haunted look. He ran through the sand now, shrieking and begging for Katie to push him on the swings. When the two had lost themselves in the rhythm of the swing set, I turned to Jerry.

"I'm so sorry about your business," I said. I'd read in the news that one of the dealerships was facing bankruptcy—a dramatic loss of sales after all the publicity of Felina's arrest and extradition to Washington as Tali Donovan.

He shrugged. "It's hard to see it happen, but I've got more time to spend with the kids as the business downsizes.

I can't believe I didn't see what was going on. Both of them had nightmares for the longest time and I just didn't see why."

He sounded so much like Boyd Donovan when he talked about his kids. I'd spoken with Boyd a few times as we wrapped up our work for him. He'd buried his children and felt better now that he had granite markers to visit, a place to sit with them and leave little toys on their graves. Boyd seemed happy that the prosecutor in Washington had found other charges to bring against Tali and Scout—child endangerment and burying human remains on public land, to start with. Scout, in a misguided attempt to lessen her own sentence, had admitted to helping Tali on the day of the killings, although she swore that Tali murdered them. Ethan had been smothered with a plastic bag and when Deni came to check on him Tali panicked and pushed her daughter down the stairs.

Scout helped Tali come up with a plan to bury the bodies, then concoct the story about how they were taken by a stranger. She frankly seemed surprised when Tali was acquitted. When the tide of public opinion turned so strongly against Tali, Scout had convinced Dave to move back to New Mexico, and then she'd accompanied Tali to Scottsdale for her surgery and had helped her come up with new identity documents. She swore Dave to secrecy about her sister's identity change.

"They did DNA tests," Jerry was saying. "She really was that Tali Donovan person."

He paused a moment, staring toward the trees in the distance. "I can't believe how she fooled me. I feel so stupid."

"Jerry, don't. You were in a happy marriage before. You

didn't have any reason to think that the new woman in your life wouldn't be every bit as wonderful a person as Kathie Jo. Focus on her and believe that most of us are not rotten."

"Thanks, Charlie. Thanks for everything."

Katie shouted out to her dad and Jerry walked toward the swings. I gave in to Freckles's whimpers and began tossing a ball for her. When she finally tired of chasing it, I turned to see that the Brewsters had left the park.

I clipped the puppy to her leash and reflected on the situation as we headed home. Both women would get a number of years in prison. Part of the payback for Tali/Felina would surely be the lack of pretty clothes, the awful food and the fact that there were no men on whom she could focus her attentions.

I hoped that Tali would get psychological help for her dependency and, if not, that another good-hearted guy like Boyd Donovan or Jerry Brewster wouldn't fall into her clutches if she ever got out.

Too bad we can't wear tags listing our psychological hang-ups, warning those who come in contact that we all have secrets, some of them buried very deeply indeed.

I gave Freckles a good, long hug then headed home to light the grill and make Drake's favorite dinner.

Connie Shelton is the author of nearly thirty best-selling mysteries, including her Charlie Parker series and her new Samantha Sweet mystery series. She has also written several award winning non-fiction pieces and was a contributor to *Chicken Soup for the Writer's Soul*.

Sign up for Connie's free email mystery newsletter and get announcements of new books, contests, discount coupons, and the chance for some 'sweet' deals.

www.connieshelton.com

Follow Connie on Facebook, Twitter and Pinterest

Books by Connie Shelton
THE CHARLIE PARKER SERIES
Deadly Gamble
Vacations Can Be Murder
Partnerships Can Be Murder
Small Towns Can Be Murder
Memories Can Be Murder
Honeymoons Can Be Murder
Reunions Can Be Murder
Competition Can Be Murder
Balloons Can Be Murder
Obsessions Can Be Murder
Gossip Can Be Murder
Stardom Can Be Murder
Phantoms Can Be Murder
Buried Secrets Can Be Murder
Legends Can Be Murder
Weddings Can Be Murder
Holidays Can Be Murder - a Christmas novella

THE SAMANTHA SWEET SERIES
Sweet Masterpiece
Sweet's Sweets
Sweet Holidays
Sweet Hearts
Bitter Sweet
Sweets Galore
Sweets, Begorra
Sweet Payback
Sweet Somethings
Sweets Fogotten
The Woodcarver's Secret

NON-FICTION
Show, Don't Tell
Novel In A Weekend (writing course)

CHILDREN'S BOOKS
Daisy and Maisie and the Great Lizard Hunt
Daisy and Maisie and the Lost Kitten